A Butterfly for Zhuangzi

Jon Wesick

This is a work of fiction. Names, characters, places, and incidents either are the product of the author's imagination or are used fictitiously. Any resemblance to actual persons, living or dead, events, or locales is entirely coincidental.

Copyright © 2016 Jon Wesick

All rights reserved

ISBN: 1523413484

ISBN-13: 978-1523413485

Cover Image: Butterfly on Flower by David Wagner

Available in Public Domain

http://all-free-download.com/free-photos/download/butterfly_on_flower_196981.html

ACKNOWLEDGMENTS

I wish to thank my writing teachers Sam Hamod and Glory Foster, all those who commented on my work through many years of read and critique sessions, as well as the book's editor Lauren Wellman.

CHAPTER 1

"You're late again!" Thisbe Anderton's supervisor clicked her long crimson nails on the desk. "It's the third time this month." Ms. Friedman wore gaudy rings on her fingers, a navy blue skirt and matching jacket, and enough perfume to choke a vulture at thirty paces.

"I'm sorry, Ms. Friedman. Andy has a fever, and his day care wouldn't take him. It took me forty-five minutes to find a baby sitter." Thisbe rested a hand on the door frame to Ms. Friedman's office. Rain dripped from her coat onto the industrial carpet.

"In the future sort out your personal problems outside business hours." Ms. Friedman clacked on her keyboard and pulled up Thisbe's performance record on the monitor. "I see you haven't been making quota."

"But the foreign customers take longer."

"Nonsense! Ninety seconds is plenty of time to finalize an order. I'll listen in on your calls today and see what you're doing wrong."

Thisbe's mouth fell open.

"What are you waiting for? Get to work." Ms. Friedman waved a gaudy ring in front of Thisbe's face to send her away.

Thisbe trudged to her colorless cubicle. The only decoration management allowed was a Splendid Resorts calendar, which spotlighted one of their hotels each month. Thisbe powered up her workstation and fitted the headset over her ear. The phone light blinked.

"Mahamuni save me." Thisbe pushed the answer button. "Splendid Resorts reservations. May I help you?"

"Yes, ah, I'd like to reserve a room in Las Vegas for March 17," an Asian man said.

"For how many?"

"Yes, March 17. The name is Kimura, Fumio Kimura."

By the time Thisbe had entered Mr. Kimura's credit card number, a red flashing rectangle showed in the upper right hand corner of her monitor to indicate she was behind schedule. Thisbe pushed enter and counted thirteen flashes of the red square before the system responded with an error.

"I'm sorry, Mr. Kimura, but the system will not approve your credit card."

"*Eh to*, let me use my Visa."

Thisbe entered the new information. When the system updated her screen with Mr. Kimura's confirmation number, she was already a minute behind.

"Mr. Kimura, your reservation is confirmed at the Splendid Resort Las Vegas for March 17."

"Did I say March?" Mr. Kimura said. "I meant April."

Thisbe started again. By the time she'd corrected Mr. Kimura's reservation, the call had taken three and a half minutes. The next customer, Mr. Amadou from Ethiopia, torpedoed any hopes of making up the lost time. The morning rush lulled at 10:30. Donna peeked around the divider.

"So what was the Iron Tampon complaining about this time?" The headphone Donna wore creased the red hair on top of her scalp.

"The usual." Thisbe rolled her chair away from her desk. "She says I should decide in advance when my son will have a fever so I don't disrupt her schedule."

"She's been sucking up to Mr. Hairless, ever since they announced that vacancy upstairs. What do you say we work some free overtime to get her promoted and out of our lives forever?"

"There's no point," Thisbe sighed. "They'd just replace her with someone worse."

Donna's computer beeped to indicate there'd been no keyboard activity for over a minute.

"All right! I hear you!" Donna turned back to Thisbe. "How about lunch today?"

"I can't. I need to save money to pay the sitter."

"Come on! I'll treat. George gave me fifty credits for my birthday."

At noon they took Donna's Mazda Sparcstor to a nearby Chinese restaurant. Donna ordered "sweat and sour pork," and Thisbe asked for a tofu dish. Over tea Donna confided her plans to escape Splendid Resorts' embrace by taking night classes and getting George to marry her. Only George didn't know about it yet. The talk darkened Thisbe's mood. Caring for Andy made night school impossible, but she didn't think it was right to marry a man to escape a dead-end job. It looked like Thisbe was stuck. The waitress placed two platters on the table.

"You can have some of mine if you want." Donna spooned steaming pork onto her plate and took a generous helping of Thisbe's tofu as well.

Thisbe looked at the remains of her lunch. This kind of thing always happened to her. Mahamuni had forbidden his followers to eat meat. Raising livestock consumed too many resources. Pork wasn't too bad, but beef was a definite no-no. She wanted to say something, but Pastor Nakagawa had instructed the members of his congregation to keep their beliefs to themselves.

"That's okay. I'm trying to lose weight." Thisbe made up for the missing tofu with extra rice.

After lunch Donna paid the check. Thisbe insisted on leaving the tip. The drizzle had stopped by the time they left the restaurant and returned to the parking lot. Late model Ferraris and BMWs flanked Donna's eight-year-old vehicle.

"Would you look at those whores?" Donna hissed.

Thisbe followed her gaze to two women exiting the athletic club. They wore the latest cyberskin leotards. The thin cloth displayed moving images on their supple, well-toned bodies. Thisbe had seen the style in stores, but the sleek outfits cost over a thousand credits. On her salary she could only dream. Both women wore their honey-colored hair swept on top of their heads, as if they were proud of the intercranial sockets embedded in the temporal bones behind their right ears. The sockets were unobtrusive blue plastic disks with an adapter for inserting an optical fiber virtual reality feed. So that was how they could afford the flashy clothes. The women loaded their gym bags into a Mercedes 1050 SL.

Thisbe nodded as if in agreement with her friend, but her eyes remained locked on the coveted leotards. She'd worked hard all her life. Why couldn't she have a pair?

"Come on." Donna touched Thisbe's shoulder. "We'd better get back."

That afternoon Thisbe slipped further behind quota but managed to escape another confrontation with her supervisor. Her Toyota Duster's windshield wipers quit on the drive home, forcing her to crane her head around rivulets of rainwater to view the road ahead. How would she afford the latest repair? She'd already replaced the car's torque converter last month. It took over an hour to get home.

Thisbe got the mail, trudged up the stairs, and shrugged out of her raincoat. Andy and the babysitter, Mandy, looked up from the chess game spread on the living room floor. Captured white pieces stood beside the board in mute witness to Mandy's impending defeat.

"He taught me how to play chess," Mandy said. "I wasn't much of a challenge."

Thisbe crossed the room and held her hand to Andy's forehead. "How are you feeling, honey?"

"Okay." He squirmed away from his mother's touch and moved his knight. "Check!"

"Time to stop, Andy. Mandy needs to go home and study."

"Couldn't she finish the game?" Andy pointed to Mandy's four remaining pieces. "It won't take long."

Thisbe sorted through the mail and tore open an envelope embossed with a gold logo. She read:

Dear Ms. Anderson:
Thank you for your interest in employment with Consolidated Retirement Systems. Your skills do not meet our current staffing profile. We will keep your resume on file for six months and contact you if a suitable opening becomes available.

Thisbe crumpled the rejection letter and tossed it in the trash just like she had a thousand others. The bastards hadn't even bothered to spell her name correctly!

"Checkmate!"

"You win." Mandy tussled Andy's sandy hair and packed up the game. "I think he needs some stiffer competition."

"Yeah," Andy said, "like a Deep Blue 2100 chess computer."

"I'll get you one of those, honey," Thisbe said. She'd be damned if she wasted her child's genius like her parents had wasted hers. Thisbe walked Mandy to the door and handed over two twenty-credit notes from her billfold. "Thanks for helping out today. You really saved my life."

"He's such a sweet kid. I could come tomorrow if you want."

"Thanks. I'll take his temperature before bed and let you know."

"Mom, can we get a pizza?"

"No, Andy. We need to finish the leftover nut loaf."

After Thisbe put Andy to bed, she sat under a lamp and opened her dog-eared paperback copy of Mahamuni's *Robe of Purity*. A few of the yellowed pages in the chapter on acceptance had come loose from the binding. Why was everything so difficult? Surely God had some kind of plan for her. The long day had drained her, and the sage's words became nothing more than black ants crawling on the page. The phone rang. Thisbe let the machine answer.

"Thisbe, it's Alf."

Thisbe set the book down and picked up the phone. "What do you want, now?"

"Listen, I'm going to be a little late with next month's child support. The contractor says I need to replace my wiring."

"Jesus, Alf! If I'm late with the rent again, they're going to throw Andy and me out of here. Do you want your son on the street?"

"The wiring's a fire hazard," her ex-husband droned. "It could burn the house down. Then you wouldn't have me as your meal ticket."

Thisbe set the phone into its cradle.

"Mom," Andy called from the other room. "Is everything all right?"

"It's fine, honey. Go back to sleep."

The bastard! The court order said he had to pay. Maybe she should take him back to court, but how would she pay the lawyer? Too agitated to sleep she made a cup of herbal tea and turned on the television to a sappy romance. For every minute of programming there seemed to be two minutes of commercials for products she couldn't afford. Thisbe reached for the remote. A scene made her pause. A woman was typing at a keyboard, when her boss dumped a foot-thick stack of papers on her desk.

"Why earn a living like this," the announcer asked, "when you can get paid for this?"

The screen showed the same woman in a bathing suit lying on white sand next to a turquoise sea. The camera cut to a waiting room filled with well-dressed businessmen.

"At Maya Escorts you can experience the dream of your choice while entertaining our exclusive gentlemen clients. We offer comprehensive monthly health exams and financial assistance for your cranial I/O surgery. So what are you waiting for? Call Maya Escorts today."

Thisbe scribbled the number on the back of a grocery receipt. She stared at the digits on the slip of paper. What was she thinking? Her mother didn't raise her to earn money like that. Thisbe crumpled the paper, turned off the TV, and went to bed.

CHAPTER 2

The next morning after getting Andy out of bed, Thisbe dressed in a knee-length khaki skirt and plain white blouse while her son watched reruns of *Walter and Willie* cartoons. As the animated, masked cat and mouse slugged it out in a Mexican wrestling ring she scrambled an egg in the skillet and popped an English muffin in the toaster. By force of habit she dug a plastic measuring spoon into a can of coffee and moved toward the percolator. She froze holding the spoon in midair. The English muffin popped out of the toaster. Thisbe put the coffee back and placed Andy's breakfast on the table. She took a slice of bread for herself and opened a plastic packet of generic protein spread for its topping.

"Why aren't you having any eggs, mom?" Andy set down his fork and reached for his orange juice.

"It's Renunciation Day, Andy."

"What's that?"

"You remember. We did it last year. It's the day we live simply and give the money we would have spent to help the poor people." Thisbe bit into her bread. Although the protein spread provided the nutrients to keep her healthy, it had a flavor halfway between wet sawdust and overcooked broccoli. Thisbe washed it down with tap water. "You'll see how much we help at the temple tonight."

A curtain of suspicion descended over Andy's features. He rested his hands on the table as if protecting his plate from being confiscated. Thisbe put a few slices of bread and protein packets in her purse before getting Andy into his yellow raincoat and driving him to day care.

It was a typical fall day. The drizzle and mist cloaked Seattle in otherworldliness. With its tall trees and mountains softening the harsh horizon, the Pacific Northwest's landscape had always seemed distinctly feminine to Thisbe. When she dropped Andy off at day care, Thisbe paid the fee with a check that overdrew her bank account. She prayed they wouldn't cash it before Friday's paycheck.

The day at work went as well as could be expected. Ms. Friedman chose remaining in her office over walking the floor to harass her subordinates. Dressed in the clothing of purity, Thisbe marveled at the skirts, perfumes, and jewelry the other women wore to work. No matter how hard she tried to visualize the Ethiopian families fed by the price of Donna's Pierre Couteau designer handbag, Thisbe could not quench her smoldering envy. By eating bread with protein spread at her desk, Thisbe managed to work through lunch and end the day only two calls behind quota.

Thisbe picked up Andy after work. Since there was no time for dinner before the Renunciation Day service, she paid seven credits to buy him a greasy bag of chicken strips so he wouldn't get cranky. Like all Divine Embrace temples, the Lynnwood temple was an octagonal structure. The sides represented the Eight Virtues of compassion, restraint, thrift, industry, generosity, resourcefulness, modesty, and wisdom.

Thisbe took off her parka, helped Andy out of his, and hung both in the closet by the temple's entrance. They found seats among the fifty worshippers on pews arranged in concentric octagons around the altar. Stained glass windows depicted scenes from Mahamuni's ministry, such as holding up the *Robe of Purity* to inspire pilgrims in the mountains and surviving a knife-wielding lunatic's attack. Like Thisbe, the worshippers dressed in simple, sturdy clothing approved by the church, the clothing of purity. With no flashy watches or expensive gowns to inspire envy, the environment created an island of sanity in a berserk consumer culture. Well, it created an island mostly of sanity, except for the occasional clean-cut, well-muscled visitor. It seemed one joined the congregation every year, stayed for a few weeks, and then disappeared. Thisbe had never felt threatened by these men. They were always exceedingly polite. She wondered what they were looking for. There had been rumors, of course. How could there not be, the way Mahamuni was cremated hours after his death? Ichiro Tanaka was supposed to have burned several of Mahamuni's papers afterward, a charge Tanaka denied. Whenever anyone asked about these mysteries, Pastor Nakagawa dodged the question. "How you live your life now is more important than anything that might have happened in the past," he would say.

Andy looked around to see if there were any children his age present. Unlike many other boys his age, he was well behaved in public as long as he didn't have to wait too long. He didn't. In a few minutes the service began with a chant.

"What need do I have for furs and silk,
When the love of Supreme Consciousness enfolds and
    protects me?
Why covet gold and diamonds,
When the Creator bestowed a jewel mind?
Why steal bread from the mouths of the hungry,
When God's love fills me with peace?"

Wearing a white surplice and purple ecclesiastical stole, Pastor Nakagawa walked down an aisle to the altar at the building's center. He was a tall man for a Japanese, but most of his height came from a well-muscled upper body supported by squat legs. Pastor Nakagawa opened his arms wide.

"The Divine in me embraces the Divine in you," he said.

As Thisbe echoed the greeting with the assembly, she glanced at a middle-aged woman to her right who, face in bliss, closed her blazing blue eyes and opened her arms as far as the seating allowed.

"You know, I don't like the term Renunciation Day." Pastor Nakagawa's English could pass for that of a native speaker if not for his tendency to elongate his Os. "The purpose is not to deprive yourself, but only to take what you need. In Japan there's an old story about the difference between heaven and hell. The inhabitants of hell sit at a banquet. Roasts, noodles, fresh fruit, and scrumptious desserts fill the table. Unfortunately, the inhabitants' hands have been replaced with chopsticks that reach past their ears. No matter how they twist and bend, they can't reach their mouths. Frustration builds. The inhabitants quarrel and fight.

"Heaven is exactly the same, except the inhabitants have learned to cooperate and feed one another. Friends, our world is like this. We can either help those with bellies swollen by hunger or fight off their desperation. That's what Mahamuni was trying to teach, when he thought up Renunciation Day. If the ushers could pass the collection plates, please."

A half-dozen volunteers fanned out with plastic food containers. The church prided itself on its lack of ostentation. Thisbe opened her billfold. It contained one ten-credit banknote, more than she'd saved that day. The collection plate came by. Thisbe eyed a five-credit note with the thought of exchanging it for the ten, but Andy was staring with his large brown eyes. She dropped in the ten and passed the container. It looked like she'd be eating lunches of bread and protein spread for the rest of the week.

While the ushers were collecting money, a four-sided video display descended from the ceiling. The picture focused on an overweight woman with doughy skin. The camera zoomed out to show her son, a six-year-old with a groove in his upper lip, sitting beside her on a ripped plaid couch. A church spokesman was also in the picture. He spoke into a microphone, but there was no sound. The speakers made a loud pop, and the man's voice blared. Andy made a face and covered his ears, until a technician turned down the volume.

"Members from all over North America are donating to fix Jason's cleft palate. There's 832 credits from Toronto and 627 from Seattle." North American headquarters insisted on calling Thisbe's temple Seattle, even though it was in Lynnwood. A display on the screen kept a running total of the donations.

Andy tugged Thisbe's sleeve. "I'm bored. Can we go soon?"

"It'll be over in a few minutes, Andy," Thisbe whispered. "Then you can have cake."

The program didn't last long. Within fifteen minutes they tallied twenty-seven thousand credits, enough to pay for Jason's surgery, since a plastic surgeon had donated his services at Children's Hospital in Phoenix. After a brief update on last year's recipient, an orphan who received a college scholarship, Andy joined the other children in the basement for games and goodies.

Once the children left and the video monitors had been stowed, Pastor Nakagawa said, "From time to time members of the congregation need to make public atonement for past sins. We have two volunteers, tonight. Could Walter Nelson and Amy Desmond come forward?"

Amy, a sweet-looking blonde in an oversized sweater, came down the aisle with her husband, Brad. Brad had a beefy, flushed face that wore a perpetual look of innocence. They took a seat close to the altar and held hands. Walter, a barrel-chested, middle-aged man with a short salt-and-pepper beard, took longer to reach the center due to his limp.

"Why don't we start with you, Walter?" Pastor Nakagawa stepped away from the podium. "Tell us why you want to share your story with the congregation."

"It's the war." Walter spoke with a gravelly voice. "I did some things that are hard to live with."

"And what would you like to gain from your confession?"

"I'd like to stop feeling dirty inside."

"Why don't you tell us about it?" Pastor Nakagawa said.

"As most of you know, I served in the War of Economic Secession," Walter said. "I was just eighteen, right out of high school, when I signed up. Got posted to the Chase Manhattan 103rd and took part in Operation Underbelly as part of General Nyquist's Third Army. After Buenos Aires and Montevideo fell, we pushed west toward the Chavez Line with the objective of cutting off the tip of South America from the rest of the continent.

"I was attached to a platoon assigned to mop up the rear after our front lines had passed through. We were ordered to occupy a town called Plata de la Vaca. Since it was supposed to be peaceful, SOUTHCOM didn't assign us any helicopters or armor. We sent in some Dragonflies to check things out. It looked okay, so we went in.

"At first things went well. Dressed in only light battle armor, we rolled into town in our Millipedes with recorded messages in Spanish playing from the speakers. The population seemed friendly. Women and children smiled and waved. It wasn't until we got to the center of town that the shit hit the fan. An RPG hit the lead vehicle and automatic weapons opened up on us. We threw our Millipedes into reverse, but another rocket hit the rear vehicle. We were trapped.

"We bailed out and provided cover, while others tried to push the wrecked Millipedes out of the way. When we called for air support, SOUTHCOM said all assets were tied down and wouldn't be there for hours. The rebel fire was murder. They had a fifty-caliber minigun that shredded the Millipedes and went through our body armor like it was tinfoil. We had a dozen men down and four Millipedes out of commission. Then another minigun opened up on us. That's when the lieutenant said to break out the VX.

"Technically, we weren't supposed to use nerve gas, but it's an open secret that our side did to solve its 'pest control problems.' We struggled into our chemsuits and retrieved the canisters from the command vehicle. I remember praying for the gunfire to just stop, and how after I opened the valve everything got quiet. It was peaceful, and I was happy until I saw the corpses when we drove out – women and children, their bodies twisted in agony, lined the roads. Blood came out of their noses and mouths. I told myself I'd never use this stuff again, but of course I did. It became easier and easier. By the end of my tour we were gassing whole cities at the least sign of a problem. Now the dead haunt me. When I look at my own boy, I can't help seeing the children I'd helped kill. Sometimes I think I should have died back then. I'd gladly trade my life for those kids' lives." Walter wiped his eyes. "I'm sorry," he squeaked, "I can't go on."

Pastor Nakagawa touched Walter on the shoulder.

"Are you ready, Amy?" the pastor asked.

Amy looked at her husband. He nodded. She walked to the podium.

"I, uh …" She looked back at her husband, who nodded once more. "I, uh was raped." Her words came faster. "When Brad was out of town, I went to this party and," Amy's eyes filled with tears, "and I don't know. I had a few drinks. The next thing I knew I'm waking up naked with this strange guy in a hotel room. I don't remember ever meeting him." She swallowed. "The police say he could have drugged me, but there was no evidence. They say if it went to trial, the guy would get off saying the sex was consensual. The worst thing was how that creep bragged to all his friends about how eager I was. I want to kill him."

"Mahamuni made it very clear," Pastor Nakagawa said while approaching the podium, "that you are only responsible for conscious actions. Know that whatever happened that night, your soul remains pure.

"Now if the congregation can focus their thoughts to help our friends. God's most wonderful gift, the mind, is bigger than the universe. In a mind so big even guilt the size of a thousand Holocausts would be as small as a caraway seed. But you must atone to access this great mind.

"Walter, Amy, and Brad, I'd like you to imagine you're walking in a huge field covered with snow to the horizon. Everything around you is pure and white except for a speck of guilt up ahead. You approach your guilt and examine it. Are you there yet?"

The three nodded.

"Good," Pastor Nakagawa said. "Your guilt and shame is nothing but a caraway seed sitting on top of the snow. Mahamuni's there behind you. He hands you a child's pail and shovel that you use to scoop up the seed of guilt. You place this in the pail and hand it to

Mahamuni. When you look up, the guilt, Mahamuni, and even your footprints have vanished. All that's left is purity."

On his way out after the service, Walter approached Thisbe. "Some of us organized our own unofficial Renunciation Day." He handed her an envelope. "The Divine in me embraces the Divine in you." He wrapped his arms around her.

After Thisbe got home and put Andy to bed, she opened it and found 150 credits.

CHAPTER 3

```
Memorandum
From: Alice Friedman, Customer Fulfillment
Manager
To: All Customer Reservation Staff
Re: Change in Call Quota Policy
Beginning with the next pay period your
hourly wage will be tied to the number of
customer calls you process. Thus if you meet
your daily quota, you will be paid your
current wage for that day. If you fall
behind, you will be paid the minimum wage
plus a remainder prorated for the percentage
of your quota that you met. Performing over
quota will not increase your hourly wage.
However, you may use over performance to
compensate for days you fall below quota.
```

"They can't do that!" Thisbe crumpled the memo and tossed it at the garbage can. "Can they?"

"They can do anything they want," Donna said. "It's called freedom of contract. They can offer us any terms they like, and we're free to accept, find another job, or starve." The phone rang. "Oh well, guess I'd better get to work on the day's quota."

Thisbe suffered through the morning. By lunchtime, thanks to a few quick calls, she was close to making quota. If she only took fifteen minutes for lunch, she might get back on track.

That afternoon Ms. Friedman stopped by Thisbe's cubicle.

"Mr. Harris wants to see you."

Thisbe logged off and took the elevator to the big office on the third floor. Fletcher Harris, the district manager, was a bald man in his mid-fifties. He motioned Thisbe to a chair across from his desk, while he wrapped up a phone call.

"Okay, Marty. I'll get right on it. Say hi to Susan and the kids." Mr. Harris hung up and turned his reptilian eyes to Thisbe. "Ms.

Anderton, you mind if I call you Thisbe?"

"No, Sir."

"Thisbe, then. Doesn't your name come from a Greek myth? The basis for *Romeo and Juliet*, I believe."

"My parents just liked the way it sounded, Sir."

"However you came by your name, you are a beautiful woman," He scanned her body.

Thisbe blushed.

"You know, some people say it's inappropriate to praise an employee's looks. I don't agree. If a woman makes an effort to look nice, I think she deserves some recognition. Don't you? I mean, you're not one of those prudes, who are offended by a little compliment, are you?"

"No, Sir."

"Good!" Mr. Harris began typing at his workstation. "Thisbe Anderton, I see you're having trouble meeting your quota. Oh yeah, Ms. Friedman told me about you." He sat back, folded his hands into a steeple, and regarded Thisbe. "Don't worry. I'm not one of those managers, who fires an employee for the least little problem. I'm going to help you. There are some tricks we can go over that will make you more efficient." He looked at his watch. "Unfortunately, I'm pretty busy this afternoon. Can you come back at 5:30? We can go over them then, and maybe get a few drinks afterwards."

Thisbe struggled to keep her expression neutral. How dare he! Thisbe ran over her options. She could file a complaint, but with Ms. Friedman chairing the sexual harassment committee, it wouldn't go far. The best she could do was stall. "I'm sorry, Sir. I promised my son, I'd take him to *Sammy the Woodchuck*, tonight. He's been looking forward to it for over a week."

"All right, Thisbe, but don't put it off too long. Even I can't keep you on the payroll forever, if you won't help yourself."

"Yes, sir."

"And call me Fletch. No need to stand on ceremony. After all, we'll be spending a lot of time together."

"All right, Fletch." Thisbe forced a smile and left. On the way back to her cubicle she grabbed the telephone book by the receptionist's desk and jotted down Maya Escort's number.

Thisbe fit her car between the white lines on the pavement, killed the engine, and unbuckled Andy from his booster seat in the back. He'd smeared chocolate on his face and hands. Thisbe fumbled in her purse for a tissue to clean him up. She took his hand, and they walked toward the entrance. Thisbe automatically matched her pace to the speed of Andy's tiny legs.

"Wow!" Andy pointed to an orange, wedge-shaped Ferrari. "Can we get one of those, mom?"

"Maybe you'll have one, when you grow up, Andy."

They reached the bottom of the steps, as a woman wearing matching powder-blue terry cloth shorts and top under an open knee-length sweater emerged from inside. She had ice-gray eyes and hair so black it seemed blue, but her skin caught Thisbe's interest. From its pink glow Thisbe could almost feel its soft warmth.

"Mom," Andy tugged Thisbe's hand. "That lady has a plug behind her ear. What's it for?"

"It helps her work, Andy."

They entered and approached the man behind the front desk. His wide shoulders and massive biceps stuffed the well-tailored suit jacket he wore.

"I'm here to see Anne Simmons," Thisbe said.

"Just a minute, please." The man picked up a phone. "Ms. Simmons, your appointment's here."

Moments later a slim woman came to the desk. Her gray skirt and jacket would have fit in any corporate boardroom. She had tiny blue eyes and her auburn hair hung to her prominent cheekbones.

"Ms. Anderton." She thrust out her hand. "I'm Anne Simmons. Thanks for coming in. Who's this?" She bent over toward Andy.

"My son, Andy. I couldn't find a babysitter."

"Tell you what, Andy." Anne put a hand on his shoulder. "You can play with the other kids while your mom and I talk. Okay?"

They took Andy to a room with cartoon animals, clouds, and a rainbow painted on the walls. He immediately sank to his knees on the rubberized floor and began rolling a toy bulldozer around with another boy. The caretaker smiled and nodded to Thisbe, who then followed Anne to her office.

"Coffee?"

Thisbe shook her head. Her knees trembled. Would they want her to take off her clothes?

"That's a cute boy you have there," Anne said from behind a

mahogany desk. "How old is he?"

"He'll be five in June. He wants a Deep Blue 2100 chess computer for his birthday."

"Isn't he a little young for that?"

"No, he picks up games almost instantly. My ex-husband showed him chess a few months ago. Now Andy beats him every time they play."

"Hmm, why don't I tell you a little about Maya Escorts?" Anne swiveled her leather chair. "Wim DeVries founded our first house in Amsterdam fourteen years ago. He was a graduate student working on a doctoral degree in neurology and computer science, when he thought of applying virtual reality to sex work. At the time one of the periodic British sex scandals had brought down their prime minister. Wim realized that having the woman in her own virtual world would guarantee the client's anonymity and prevent these scandals in the future."

"But why would men want to make love to a woman who's unconscious?"

"Honey," Anne's eyes focused on Thisbe's. "Men will screw anything. Besides, the implanted microprocessor causes the woman's body to make the appropriate motions. Maya Escorts became a big success in Amsterdam. With decriminalization five years ago, we decided to expand into the North American market. Business is good and our dream girls like it too. We've had some employees with us for over ten years. Would you like a tour?"

"All right."

"Let's start with one of the intimacy rooms." Anne led Thisbe up a flight of stairs and stopped by a cleaning cart to address a maid in a pastel orange uniform. "Is there a free room, Brenda?"

"Yes, miss. Number twelve. I just finished changing the sheets." The maid had long shiny black hair, an olive complexion, and a stocky body that resembled a badger's. She exuded an air of sensuality.

A man exited from one of the doors, gave a sheepish grin, and scuttled down the stairs. Thisbe was sure she'd seen his flushed, boyish face somewhere before, maybe on a TV show. She followed Anne into the free room. It was clean and simply furnished. A comforter covered a queen-size bed.

"This is the virtual reality or VR feed." Anne picked the cable off the pillow and offered it to Thisbe.

"It's so thin." Thisbe held the one-sixteenth-inch cable between her fingertips and examined the socket at its end.

"Fiber optic," Anne said. "Transmits the volume of data needed to create a virtual world. Gallium arsenide CCDs on the intercranial socket convert the optical signals to electric for interface with the brain."

Thisbe touched the mattress and poked her head into the bathroom.

"Let's go see the control room." Anne led Thisbe down the hall and knocked on a door marked "Employees Only." A man with terminally messy hair and thick, plastic-rimmed glasses answered.

"Hi, Lester. I wanted to show a potential employee the control room." Anne breezed past dragging Thisbe in her wake.

The dozen flat-panel displays on the wall showed couples in various forms of sexual congress. The low resolution made them appear as groups of flesh-toned squares, but the gross details were obvious. Thisbe blushed and covered her mouth with her hand.

"We monitor our dream girls on closed-circuit TV for their safety. We've never had a problem, but if there were we could respond in less than a minute." Anne pointed to racks of electronics that held what looked like DVD players. "These are our dream feeds. We have over five thousand selections and get more every day."

"Are they like movies that you watch from beginning to end?" Thisbe asked.

"The early ones were scripted," Anne said, "but recent research shows how to supply the brain with cues so it fills in the gaps. You could watch a disk over and over without having the same dream twice. For example, you could ski in the Rockies and go down a different run each time."

"Do you have anything," Thisbe stuttered, "more spiritual?"

"Heavens, yes!" Anne smiled. "You'd be surprised how many of our dream girls want religious themes."

"Do you have anything about Mahamuni?" Thisbe guarded her growing enthusiasm against disappointment. The job would certainly solve her money problems, but was it moral? Technically not, but wouldn't she have to sleep with that creep Mr. Harris to keep her current job, anyway? At least here she'd earn a decent living. She'd leave her choice to a higher power. Like Reverend Nakagawa always said, when the path ahead braches the Creator will always show you the way.

"Oh, you're a Hugger." Anne turned to the technician. "Isn't Stephanie interested in something like that?"

"Yeah, she has all kinds of disks." Lester dug into a drawer and began removing jewel cases. "*The Awakening, Sermon in Kamakura, Mahamuni Casts Out the Nafs, Mission to Africa, Nakasendo Pilgrimage.*"

A wave of relief washed over Thisbe. Maybe this could work. It wouldn't be like she was doing it for the sex after all. Hadn't Reverend Nakagawa said that Amy had committed no sin, because she'd been unconscious? And Thisbe would get to be with Mahamuni. Hadn't he always told his followers to abandon everything worldly to find their way to God?

Anne led Thisbe back to her office and handed her a folder.

"We have a pretty good benefits package – health insurance, two weeks' paid vacation, retirement plan. You've already seen the onsite day care. A lot of our dream girls are single mothers. We offer financial assistance for your neural implant surgery. Basically, if you work for us for over a year, you only pay 50 percent. You can also bill up to three hours a week for going to the gym. We have an account at Strong and Beautiful on Nordhall, but you can choose whatever gym you like and we'll pay your membership."

"That sounds great," Thisbe said. "Can I think it over?"

The cabin lights dimmed. Air rushed over the lowered flaps. Thisbe looked out the airplane's window at Shanghai's glittering lights. She'd never been overseas before. It would be nice to look around the city, but they'd keep her at the clinic until she recovered from the surgery enough to fly home. Thisbe looked at her watch and tried to estimate the time back home. It was probably too late to call Andy. He had put up such a fuss when he'd learned his mother would be gone for a week.

The plane banked and centered between the parallel lines of blinking lights that marked the runway. Thisbe felt a bump when the landing gear locked in place. Moments later the wheels touched the ground with a jolt. The pilot throttled the engines to maximum reverse thrust, slowing the plane and pressing Thisbe against her seat belt. The pilot let up and taxied to the gate.

Thisbe collected her belongings and joined the people exiting the plane through a ramp that smelled of kerosene and exhaust. Once inside the terminal she scanned the crowd of unfamiliar faces and felt panic grow in her chest. What was she doing here? Should she turn around and take the plane back home? It was too late for that. She'd chosen her course, once she'd signed the contract with Maya Escorts. The dark-haired people surrounding her spoke in odd, alien lisping tones. She spotted a thin longhaired woman holding a sign that said "Miss Thisbe Anderson." Though clean and not faded, the woman's clothing seemed somehow stale and lifeless, like dead flowers or the old blouses Thisbe had found in the bottom of her mother's drawers. Thisbe waved and made her way to her escort.

"Miss Anderson, I am Miss Wang, and this is Mr. Yu." The woman pointed to a short man with crooked teeth and a bad haircut. "How was your flight?"

"It's Anderton, with a T. The flight was good. I've never flown business class before."

"Do you have any other bags?" Miss Wang pointed to the wheeled sixty-nine credit green suitcase Thisbe pulled by its extended handle.

Thisbe shook her head. Miss Wang spoke to Mr. Yu in Chinese.

"*Hao.*" Yu scooped up Thisbe's bag.

"The car is this way," Miss Wang said. "If you would please follow me."

Following Miss Wang proved exasperating. She moved through the crowd as if dodging bodies were an Olympic sport she'd trained for since childhood. Every time Thisbe stopped to let someone pass, Miss Wang got farther ahead. Then Thisbe would look back at Yu, who nodded and gave an embarrassed smile.

Miss Wang bypassed the immigration line and approached a bored man in a green uniform outlined with red piping. Thisbe withdrew her brand-new passport from her handbag, but the official waved her through without giving it a glance. The same happened at customs. Thisbe and her party strode past the other passengers loading their bags onto conveyors that fed the X-ray machines' cavernous mouths.

Outside, the night air was hot and humid. Miss Wang led Thisbe to a beat-up station wagon. It took several tries to start the engine. Yu shifted into gear and maneuvered into traffic. His constant starts and stops made Thisbe ill. She closed her eyes and rested her head against the cool window.

After an hour-long drive they arrived. Yu punched numbers into the panel to open the iron gate. After her long flight, all Thisbe wanted was to shower and go to bed. She got her wish. Miss Wang led her up the steps of the ivy-covered brick building. They took a rickety elevator to the third floor and walked down a tiled hallway to Thisbe's room. Yu placed her suitcase inside, and he and Miss Wang left.

There was a picture on the wall of an ancient Chinese man with a long beard, who wore a cloth cap that looked like a pair of underpants. A colorful butterfly perched on the man's shoulder. Thisbe looked out the door. The nurse sitting at the end of the hall nodded and smiled. A sign over the bathroom tap said not to drink the water. Fortunately a thermos of boiled water sat on the nightstand. Thisbe poured a cup and drank. She showered, crawled between the sheets, and fell instantly to sleep.

Thisbe woke before sunrise, walked to the window, and stared at the moon. Millions of plastic sheets on its surface portrayed a cigarette logo, visible from the earth. Twenty years ago politicians had called the tobacco company's offer to fund space research "an exciting partnership between government and industry." Thisbe wondered what they called it now that the tobacco company has withdrawn its funding. Her stomach growled. No one was in the hall except for a nurse with her head down on her desk. Thisbe retrieved the *Robe of Purity* from her bag and returned to bed to read in order to take her mind off the hunger pangs. Eventually traffic sounds came from outside, as the city roused from sleep and the sky lightened, Thisbe heard voices in the hall. A half hour later a nurse entered.

"Please change." She handed Thisbe a hospital gown.

Still later a Chinese doctor in a white lab coat carried a clipboard into the room. A nurse in a white uniform trailed behind.

"Good morning, Miss …" The doctor examined his clipboard. "Anderton. I'm Dr. Lee. Would you sit up, please?" Dr. Lee produced a penlight. "Follow my finger with your eyes. Good."

During the exam Thisbe wondered if she should admit lying about her high school drug use on the questionnaire. "What's that picture about?" She pointed to the wall.

"Oh," the doctor said. "It's an old Chinese story. Once the sage Zhuangzi dreamed he was a butterfly. When he woke up, he wasn't sure if he was a man who'd dreamed he was a butterfly or a butterfly dreaming he was a man. Fitting, don't you think?" The doctor scribbled his final notes and left.

The nurse returned moments later with a wheelchair. She patted it to indicate Thisbe should sit and then wheeled Thisbe to a room with an MRI machine that resembled a giant sugar cube with a hole bored through the center. Thisbe understood that she should lie on the table. When she did, a technician placed earphones over her head and adjusted the control so the table slid inside. The opening was not much larger than Thisbe's waist. The close fit made Thisbe's skin clammy. The muscles between her shoulder blades twisted. She thought of getting trapped inside during an earthquake and wanted to claw at the walls.

"Watch the screen, please," a voice said from the earphones.

A small flat-panel display in front of her eyes turned solid blue. The solid color changed into patterns. Thisbe heard clicking while this happened. The patterns became pictures of food, animals, and people. The images paused. Thisbe wanted to scratch her knee but feared that moving would spoil the tests. A low tone alternated between her left and right ears, rising in pitch until Thisbe could no longer hear it. Her lower back began to ache. Thisbe squirmed to ease the pain.

A plastic tube extended toward her face.

"Please put the tube in your mouth."

Thisbe followed the instructions. A few drops of sugar water squirted into her mouth. Bitter, salty, and sour tastes followed. She smelled ammonia.

"You're done."

The electric motor hummed and withdrew the patient couch from the machine. Once Thisbe's head cleared the opening, she sat up and rubbed her lower back. The next patient - a black woman with a round, glowing face - waited in a wheelchair by the door.

Thisbe had had enough for the morning and looked forward to breakfast and a rest. Her stomach growled once more. Instead of returning Thisbe to her suite, the nurse rolled her to a room where a barber draped a nylon smock over her shoulders. The man walked away and returned with a buzzing set of electric clippers. Thisbe jerked away. It was all happening too fast. The barber steadied her head and mowed furrows in Thisbe's brown hair. Within a minute it lay in a pile on the floor. The barber lathered her head and shaved it smooth with a straight razor.

The nurse wheeled Thisbe into another room where a man wrapped her arm with an elastic band and injected something into her vein. When he removed the band, warmth spread through Thisbe's limbs, relaxing her muscles and easing her anxiety. She hardly worried when the man injected Novocain into her head and screwed four posts into her skull.

Soon Thisbe felt like she was flying - flying when they took her for another brain scan, flying when they stuck an IV into her vein. Thisbe flew to the operating room and seemed to hover over the table when the doctors attached her head to a metal frame. A high-pitched whining drill bored holes in her skull. Under bright lights, doctors with magnifying glasses on their spectacles inserted wires into her brain and asked what she saw, heard, and felt. Finally the anesthesiologist injected something into Thisbe's IV, and she slept.

Thisbe woke in a room full of electronic equipment. Ghostly blue traces on monitors displayed her heart and respiration rates. She sat up carefully avoiding dislodging the tubes and wires attached to her body. Her head throbbed. Her tongue was swollen with the drugs' bitter aftertaste. She longed for a gallon of water to wash away her grogginess. Thisbe ran a tentative finger over her bandaged head and stopped at the socket behind her ear. Emboldened, she pressed gently until the pain forced her to stop. She pressed the call button. A nurse arrived a few minutes later.

"Could I have some water?" Thisbe croaked.

The nurse returned with a small cup, which Thisbe downed. After making her track a penlight, the nurse abandoned her to her aches and exhaustion. Thisbe slept. Periodically the nurse woke her for the same follow-the-light test.

The next morning they moved her to a room without wires and machines. A woman rolled a cart into the room and set a breakfast tray on the nightstand.

"Good morning," Thisbe said.

The woman nodded with a bashful grin and rolled her cart to the next room. Thisbe picked at the runny, lukewarm eggs, toast, and fruit cocktail and washed them down with tea. The doctors didn't allow Thisbe to read or watch TV. Instead she watched dust motes float in the light spilling from the window as the sun swept from dawn to dusk. Traffic sounds and the hospital's rhythms distracted her from boredom, aches, and exhaustion.

On the second day after surgery, a nurse removed Thisbe's bandages. Thisbe stared at the mirror and touched the holes where the screws had been removed from her skull. Two days later Dr. Lee returned, accompanied by a technician rolling a cart of electronics.

"Time to see if everything works." Dr. Lee plugged a cable into the socket behind Thisbe's ear. "Just lie back and relax."

The technician powered up the cart. Cooling fans hummed white noise. The machinery emitted a series of beeps. The technician turned dials and typed on the keyboard. Suddenly a field of blue with a magenta corner appeared before Thisbe. The picture remained when she closed her eyes.

"What do you see?" Dr. Lee asked.

Thisbe described the scene. Speaking Chinese, the technician made adjustments until Thisbe saw solid blue. They worked through a series of colors and stopped at a test pattern. The technician sharpened the focus so Thisbe could read the letters. Once they sorted out the visuals, they adjusted sound, smell, taste, and touch virtual senses that felt eerie to Thisbe. She felt like she was there and not there at the same time.

"All right, Miss Anderton," Dr. Lee said. "Are you ready for the full effect?"

Thisbe nodded. She felt a sudden dislocation, as if her consciousness swirled down a drain. Thisbe found herself in a white room, empty except for a young Asian woman in a blue skirt, white gloves, and white blouse sitting on a wooden stool. Thisbe moved closer. Her footsteps sounded on the hardwood floor. She scratched her knee, but the itch remained.

"I'm Keiko, your Fujitsu FJ9321 cranial implant's autonomous agent." The woman bowed. "My files tell me your name is Miss Thisbe Anderson. Would you prefer to be called Thisbe or Miss Anderson?"

"It's Anderton, with a T, but please call me Thisbe."

"Very well, Thisbe. As your implant's agent, my job is to perform routine calibrations, run background diagnostics, and alert you should your implant need maintenance. Have you had any problems with your implant?"

"Well, my knee itches."

Keiko paused as if looking inside herself. "Currently wire AC92's voltage is reading out of tolerance." She paused again. "No, it's dropped back into acceptable range. Erratic readings are common immediately after surgery. Your itch should clear up once your brain adapts to the implant. I'll output a diagnostic report. Do you have any other questions?"

"I'm a little overwhelmed," Thisbe said.

"That's understandable. If you have questions or concerns about your implant, please bring them to my attention. I'll return you now to your organic reality."

Thisbe felt the spinning sensation. She opened her eyes and found herself back in the hospital room.

Thisbe flew home three days later. A few passengers eyed the gray stocking cap she wore to cover her scarred shaved head, but the flight passed uneventfully. The plane landed at noon. The shuttle took over an hour to reach home and left her drained, but she brightened when she saw Andy sitting on the couch next to Mandy.

"Mommy!" Andy turned from the television and ran to her.

Thisbe dropped her bag, swept her son into her arms, and planted a kiss on his cheek. The stocking cap aroused his suspicion. Andy stuck his tiny fingers underneath and froze when he contacted the socket.

"Mommy, no!" he wailed.

"Andy, stop it! If you're not going to act grown up, I can't get you the Deep Blue 2100 chess computer you want."

Calculation replaced the raw look of betrayal in Andy's face.

"Now, why don't you go wash your hands while I make lunch?"

Andy toddled to the bathroom.

"Your ex called a couple of times." Mandy got up from the couch and gathered her things. "I let the phone machine take it."

Thisbe sighed. She didn't have the energy to deal with Alf's manipulation at the moment.

"So how did it go?" Mandy asked.

"I'm glad it's over," Thisbe said. "Was Andy any trouble?"

"No, Maya's day care took him when I had classes."

"Thanks." Thisbe paid Mandy from her expense money, looked in the refrigerator, and began making lunch.

The next day Thisbe stopped by Maya Escorts to get a wig and went to the grocery store.

"Can I ride in the shopping cart, mom?"

"You're getting too big for that, Andy." Thisbe wheeled the grocery cart into the cereal aisle and examined the multicolored boxes to find the cocoa flying saucers Andy liked.

"Thisbe, is that you?"

Thisbe turned and found herself face-to-face with her former coworker.

"Donna, hi." Thisbe's hand drifted to her wig to make sure it covered her neural implant's jack. "You remember my son, Andy, don't you?"

"Of course. Hello, Andy."

"Hi."

"So." Donna placed a box of oatmeal in her cart. "How's the new job? What is it you're doing, anyway?"

"Oh, um," Thisbe said. "I'm a physical therapist assistant. I keep track of the charts, schedule, billing, and the like."

"You don't say." Donna placed a hand on her back. "I've been having some aches and pains lately. Do you have a business card? Maybe I'll call for an appointment."

"I don't, sorry." Thisbe looked at her watch. "Listen, I've got to get Andy to his father's. It was nice seeing you again."

"Let's get together sometime," Donna called as Thisbe wheeled her cart toward the checkout counter.

Thisbe went to the Divine Embrace temple on a night, when Alf had Andy. Pastor Nakagawa lectured on Mahamuni's *Subtle Essence of Mind*, a scripture that few in the congregation understood. The talk didn't clarify matters much. They closed by chanting Mahamuni's poem "In Praise of Self-Reliance."

When the congregation was filing out, Marjorie, a stocky woman who drove all the way from Tacoma to attend, wrapped her arms around Thisbe's waist and gave her a big smooch on the cheek. Thisbe readjusted her wig but was too late. The look in Pastor Nakagawa's eyes told her he'd seen her neural implant jack and knew what it meant.

"Good to see you!" Marjorie said.

Thisbe nodded and made her way to the car. When she got home, a message was waiting on her answering machine.

"Thisbe, it's Pastor Nakagawa. You should have told me you were in need of money. We can take up a collection. On Renunciation Day we raised over six hundred credits."

Six hundred credits! That wouldn't begin to cover the cost of her surgery, let alone rent and clothes for Andy. Thisbe pushed the erase button. It'd be weeks before she returned to the temple. When she did, she would sit in the back and leave before the service was over.

CHAPTER 4

After a month of recuperation, Thisbe was ready for her first day at work. Her hair had grown enough that she no longer needed the wig to cover her neural implant's jack. Thisbe walked down the hall at Maya Escorts and stopped in front of room eight, the intimacy room she'd been assigned. Already her smiling portrait beamed from the LCD display by the door. The picture would update when her replacement started the next shift. Thisbe entered, stepped out of her pants, and hung them in the closet. She unhooked her bra, slipped off her panties, and rubbed the indentations the elastic had made on her flesh. Maya Escorts kept its intimacy rooms warm enough to be comfortable without clothing. After inserting the antiviral suppository, she sat on the bed and hugged her knees to her chest to keep from trembling. Someone knocked.

"Come in," Thisbe squeaked.

A maid entered. "You must be Thisbe. I'm Brenda." She looked at Thisbe's posture. "First time?"

Thisbe nodded.

"You're in for a treat. I remember my first time. It was almost five years ago, and the technology wasn't nearly as good as it is now. They had this disk called *Everyday Paris*. I jacked in and suddenly there I was walking along the Seine. It was a sunny day and artists were drawing pictures on the Left Bank sidewalks in colored chalk. The disk's creators had provided me with a guidebook. I wandered all over the city, ate in cafes, and took in the Louvre and the Musée d'Orsay. I would have never been able to afford going to Paris on my own, but there I was, and I was getting paid for it." Brenda winked. "It'd be best to use the bathroom, if you haven't already."

"I did," Thisbe said.

"Just lie back, and I'll hook you up." Brenda attached the cable to Thisbe's head. "Okay?"

Thisbe nodded.

"All right, then. I'll see you when you're done."

Thisbe's awareness spun into the white room.

Keiko bowed. "Good morning, Thisbe. Your implant is working properly. You can begin your virtual reality session whenever you're ready."

Thisbe scratched her knee. "Let's start."

Night. Cicadas filled the humid air with their cries of longing. Sights, sounds, and smells were more vivid, as if Thisbe's senses were a dirty window squeegeed clean by VR. She walked behind a woman in light-colored clothing down a narrow street. They passed a restaurant with bowls of plastic noodles in its display window and a blue cloth banner hanging in the doorway. A bicycle's bell sounded behind her. Thisbe stepped onto the metal grate covering the gutter. A girl in a school uniform whizzed past, missing Thisbe and an oncoming car by inches.

They crossed a bridge and turned left. Rows of rice plants stood like tiny soldiers in a small field to their right. Something flew past and made a sharp turn. Thisbe realized it was a bat. The moon looked like it did when she was young, before they'd put that cigarette logo on it. Her guide led her to a house. They entered through a squeaky gate, passed a small garden, and knocked at the front door. A short-haired Japanese man answered the door and stepped aside to let them enter. Thisbe placed her shoes on the rack by the door. The other woman led her to the kitchen, which was barely large enough for the two of them. Pots and pans hung from hooks over the stove. Dirty dishes filled the sink.

"Oh, those men, they'll keep us so busy, we'll never get to see the ruined castle," Chikako said. How did Thisbe know her name? "Well, maybe tomorrow. Why don't you wash the dishes? I'll start the rice."

Thisbe put on an apron and pushed up her sleeves. The dishwashing liquid's label was in Japanese, but somehow Thisbe knew what it meant. She filled the sink with hot, sudsy water, scrubbed the pots and bowls clean, and set them to drain on the rack.

"Please chop the vegetables," Chikako said.

Thisbe sliced the daikon and carrots on a chopping board. She would have liked to ask where they were, but Mahamuni had cautioned against idle chatter at work in the Robe of Purity. *It was best to focus on the task at hand. They prepared a simple stew of tofu and vegetables and served it with rice and pickles. The two women carried trays of food down the hall. Chikako knocked and slid open a paper door. Thisbe bowed, entered, and set her tray on the tatami.*

There he was! He was wearing a white shirt and gray slacks, kneeling in seiza. *Surrounded by a half-dozen others was Junzo Tagaki, the industrialist who'd abandoned his corporate empire to become the sage Mahamuni. Thisbe recognized the scar left from a nationalist's failed assassination attempt and tried to fix the date, but she couldn't remember the history. She'd check the references when she got home. Mahamuni's two greatest disciples Ichiro Tanaka and*

Hiroshi Saito sat beside him. Thisbe knew Saito's tragic death had made Tanaka Mahamuni's successor, after the sage's passing.

Thisbe kept her eyes low while she set out the food lest she betray the unceremonious smile bursting from her lips.

"Ah!" Mahamuni said, "Nagano has the best pickles You!" Mahamuni touched Thisbe's wrist as she set a bowl in front of him. "You're new. What's your name?"

"Thisbe Anderton, Sage." She blushed.

"No need for titles here, Thisbe. We're all equal in God's eyes. Welcome!"

Thisbe blushed and felt warm like she had, after giving birth to Andy. The words to a hymn ran through her head.

"Is there anything else?" Mahamuni asked his advisors.

"Just one thing, Sensei." Tanaka cleared his throat. "Mr. Terada is concerned about the potluck dinner after tomorrow's sermon. It would be easy for someone to poison your food. Mr. Terada asks that you make some excuse, say a slight cold, and not attend."

"I see." Mahamuni fingered the scar on his jaw. "I have the utmost respect for Mr. Terada's loyalty and skill. Protecting me is not easy, and he could no doubt earn ten times his salary by working for a large corporation." Mahamuni paused. Neither he nor his advisors felt compelled to fill the silence. After a few minutes he resumed. "While the risks Mr. Terada warns of are not trivial, I feel I have no other choice than to attend."

"Perhaps you could go and not eat," Tanaka suggested.

"How could I refuse my followers' heartfelt gifts?"

Both advisors kept their faces impassive, but Mahamuni sensed one's reservations.

"Do you have something you need to say, Saito?"

"With all due respect Sensei, why pay this man, if you refuse to follow his advice?"

Mahamuni remained silent for a moment then responded. "Let me tell you of a dream I had. I was a giant standing with one foot on Japan and the other on North America. My head reached through the clouds, and I saw billions of stars glittering like jewels in a sky of black velvet. The stars sang the glory of God's creation, and I felt at peace knowing I was part of His plan. Then I heard the world crying and wanted to share my understanding with its suffering people. My body shattered into a billion pieces and blew like dandelion seeds all over the planet. Wherever one landed, a church grew.

"I know you speak out of love for me, Saito, but this little body is only an illusion. My greater body demands that I go, tomorrow."

Thisbe's head spun. She returned to the intimacy room at Maya Escorts, where Brenda sponged her thighs with a warm, wet cloth.

"You're back." Brenda set down the cloth and unplugged the cable from Thisbe's head. "Your last client left a half hour ago, but we let you finish the disk. I hope that was all right." Brenda covered Thisbe's naked body with a blanket. "Lie back for a few minutes. Returning from VR can be a little disorienting."

Thisbe raised herself on her elbow to look at Brenda. "So, if you liked VR so much, how come you're now...?"

"A maid?" Brenda sat on the bed and rested her hand on Thisbe's leg. "Sometimes a neural implant doesn't take. Something to do with how your brain's laid out. The doctors said a concussion I had when I was twelve might have caused it. Maya Escorts was real decent about it, though. They forgave my debt for the surgery and gave me this job. Oh well." Brenda stood. "I had a good year. Wish I'd saved more money, though. Take my advice and save yours instead of spending it. I'll be down the hall in case you need me."

The door closed. Thisbe's body felt warm and relaxed. She wondered about the client who'd found comfort in her body. Was he strong and handsome or overweight and weak? Had he cried out in ecstasy or merely climaxed quietly? And afterward did he rest his head next to her breast or simply zip up his trousers and sneak away? Since she'd never know anyway, she preferred to picture him as heartbroken after the tragic death of his young wife. Not yet able to love again, he seeks warmth and closeness the only way he can. Sometime perhaps he'll look Thisbe up and thank her for helping him through a difficult time. She stretched her arms over her head and got up to take a shower.

Located on Alaskan Way, the Strong and Beautiful gym had a view of the ferries that crossed Puget Sound. Thisbe gave her name to the attendant and pulled her old Toyota Duster into the underground garage. With an old T-shirt and pair of shorts in her gym bag, she felt almost too intimidated to give her name to the receptionist in the marble-walled lobby.

"Oh, Ms. Anderton, of course." The woman picked up the telephone. "Shelby, Ms. Anderton is here." The receptionist put down the phone. "Your personal trainer will be here in a few minutes. Would you like a wheat grass juice while you wait?"

Shelby was a spunky blonde with a ponytail, a lot of energy, and no mercy. She tortured Thisbe on the weight machines in front of a large picture window with a view of the water before exiling her to the treadmills. By the time Thisbe finished her workout and showered, she could barely make it to the elevator. Shelby was waiting for her in the lobby. She held out a violet bag.

"Your employer wanted you to have this," Shelby said. "They figure a nice outfit will encourage you to exercise more. See you on Thursday."

Thisbe opened the bag and draped the cyberskin leotards over her arm. Her body heat activated the sensors woven into the cloth and caused the hummingbirds in the pattern to hover. Thisbe broke out in a huge grin.

"Thanks. I've always wanted a pair of these. Thank you so much."

"Wow!" Andy ran ahead of his mother and entered the game store.

Thisbe followed and nodded to the bearded clerk, who looked up from a conversation with a pimple-faced teen. Andy stood transfixed in front of a display case containing civil war chess pieces and cast metal extraterrestrials.

The clerk sauntered from behind the counter. "Can I help you?"

"What do you want again, Andy?" Thisbe asked.

"A Deep Blue 2100 chess system."

"For someone his age, I'd recommend the Learn Mate 3.0." The clerk handed Thisbe a colorful box. "It has twelve levels of play and only costs forty-nine credits."

"That's for babies." Andy's face burned with indignation. "Wilson's brother has one, and I can beat it every time." He seemed ready to stomp out of the store.

"All right, I have a Deep Blue. Why don't you try it first?" The clerk retrieved a beat up backpack from behind the counter, removed a device the size of a calculator, and handed it to Andy.

"How do I start the game?" Andy asked.

The clerk gave a smug smile, touched a few buttons, and handed back the device. Andy sat on the floor with has back against the wall and bent his head over the game. His brow furrowed as he toggled the controls.

"Lots of kid want the Deep Blue," the clerk told Thisbe. "For most it's a waste of money. They never get past level three. If he doesn't like the Learn Mate, the Lasker 2C is a good choice. I recommend it for intermediate players."

Thisbe wandered around the store and looked at the boxes before returning. Frowning, Andy returned to the counter and handed back the Deep Blue.

"What's wrong, honey?" Thisbe asked.

"I stalemated."

The clerk looked at the LCD display and tapped the controls. His face registered disbelief. "But I set level eighteen by mistake. Hold on." He rustled papers under the counter until he found the one he wanted. "Here's a list of teachers in the area. Will Johnson's the best. You tell him Blake Peterson recommended the boy."

Thisbe smiled and waited.

"Is there something else?" the clerk asked.

"The Deep Blue."

"Right." He retrieved a box and rang up the sale. "With the 10 percent discount it comes to 496 credits."

Thisbe handed him her credit card. She should have used the money to make a larger payment on her surgery loan, but the rent was paid and seeing the delight on Andy's face was worth every penny.

CHAPTER 5

Thisbe swirled into the white room. After a brief chat with Keiko, Thisbe found herself in a meeting hall filled with Japanese in business dress. The men wore crisp, dark suits; the women, pastel skirts and jackets. All had neatly combed black hair. Thisbe scratched her knee through her pantyhose and crossed her legs. From her seat in the front row she had a good view of the speaker, a man whose large glasses framed his a broad tanned face. After a few minutes Mitsugi Kando (how did she know that?) finished his speech and sat down. Dressed in a gray suit, Mahamuni strode to the microphone. His face was unscarred by the assassination attempt, so Thisbe determined he was years younger than in her previous VR session.

"Thank you for attending this historic shareholders' meeting." Mahamuni beamed. A projector displayed a pie chart on the screen behind him. "Currently the world's GDP is about thirty trillion credits. This gives its ten billion inhabitants an average per capita income of three thousand credits. That would be enough to feed and house everyone were it not for the inequities in wealth distribution. Inhabitants of the industrialized world make as much as thirty thousand credits per year, while those in sub-Saharan Africa make less than a hundred."

The screen showed babies with sticklike arms and bellies swollen with hunger.

"Why should we care? If simple human compassion isn't enough, you must realize the poor won't stand for it much longer. Sooner or later they'll decide to take what they don't have. If they can't have it, they'll destroy it. Unless we act soon, the spread of weapons technology will make a nuclear attack or man-made plague more likely every day."

The screen showed shabbily dressed men with faces mottled by smallpox holding rifles beside a burning car and old photos of atmospheric nuclear tests.

"Why haven't we acted sooner? My friends, it's because we've wasted our efforts. Our economy depends on obsolescence. Each year Kin Tsuru Corporation spends 80 percent of its development effort making cosmetic changes to products so consumers will replace perfectly good home electronics with more stylish models. Walk through a shopping mall. What do you see?"

The screen showed models in a variety of fashions.

"Short skirts, long skirts, high heels, low. Narrow lapels replace wide ones. Fat ties replace skinny. Why do we need three hundred styles of shirts? What's wrong with twenty? Auto dealers sell a hundred models of cars. Isn't ten enough?

"The solution to poverty is standardization. Instead of wasting effort on pointless change, we should use economies of scale to drive down the price of quality goods and make them available to the poor. It will take years to redirect the world's economy. That's why Kin Tsuru Corporation must take the lead.

"Friends, if you reelect me as Kin Tsuru's CEO, I will consolidate our product line to the best 20 percent and work to make these goods cheaper and more reliable. This is a radical change of direction for our company. I ask for your vote of confidence,"

The audience applauded without enthusiasm. Once the votes were counted, Mitsugi Kando replaced Mahamuni as Kin Tsuru's CEO.

Thisbe's head spun, and she returned to one of Maya Escort's intimacy rooms. The sheet under her hips felt cold and damp with the day's spent lust.

The door opened and Brenda entered. "Sorry I'm late. I had a big cleanup in room five." Brenda retrieved a moist towel from the bathroom for Thisbe. "One of our customers told me you're the prettiest girl on our staff. Now let's disconnect that cable."

When she entered VR the next day, Thisbe spun into an office where a half-dozen workers sat on chairs arranged in no discernible pattern. Someone set a gray plastic box of envelopes on her desk. Thisbe attached an address label to each. She scratched her knee through her simple gray skirt. The fabric's sturdy feel comforted her. Mahamuni entered, followed by Ichiro Tanaka.

"Why are we continuing when the polls say our candidate doesn't have a chance?" the sage asked

"We can't give up, sir," Tanaka said. "The voters in Ueno and Asakusa will come through. Just wait and see."

"It'll never happen, Tanaka-san." Mahamuni flopped in his chair, lit a cigarette, and pinched it between his thumb and forefinger. "Our campaign was doomed to fail from the start because we neglected one thing."

"What's that?"

"Human nature." Mahamuni stubbed out his cigarette, stood, and began pacing. "People want to have things that make them feel better than everyone else. Why is that, Tanaka?"

"Ego."

"Ego," Mahamuni sighed. "All the religions say, 'Get rid of ego.' We've tried for thousands of years, and it hasn't worked. Maybe it's time for a new approach. Tell me, Tanaka, have you ever heard the expression 'The nail that sticks out

gets pounded down?"'

"Who hasn't?"

"Maybe if people could express differences in behavior, they wouldn't need to express them with things." Mahamuni stroked his chin. *"The world is much too complicated to understand. Of all God's miracles, human beings are the most complex. Yet this complexity frightens and confuses us. So we simplify, make models so we can feel safe and in control. When something doesn't fit our model, we try to force them to. With people, we call this social convention."*

Thisbe's head spun and her consciousness returned to the diagnostic program's white room.

"I'm sorry, Thisbe," Keiko said, "but sensor AC92 is acting up again. It's probably nothing serious, but I believe you should have it checked in the clinic."

"All right."

"Your current client isn't finished. It would be best for you to remain here. Would you like me to sing for you while you wait?"

"Please"

"Kokoro no mizu" Keiko's rich voice filled the room. She sang for five minutes before saying, "Your client is finished. I'll return you to bio reality now."

"Looks like they set the preamp's gain wrong." The man in the white coat stared at the device attached to Thisbe's skull. "Happens all the time in surgery in spite of all the automated tools." He adjusted dials and looked at the results on the readout. "There, that ought to do." The doctor disconnected the device.

Thisbe sat up on the patient table.

"Now, there's a small chance that what we're seeing is due to a post surgical infection. Have you had any loss of coordination or blurred vision?"

"No."

"Just to be on the safe side, I'm giving you a very special antibiotic." The doctor scribbled on a prescription pad, tore off the sheet, and handed it to Thisbe. "It bypasses the blood-brain barrier. Take it two times a day for a week. If you experience any more problems, be sure to let me know."

CHAPTER 6

Thisbe stepped into room eight at the start of her shift. Her fingers moved over the buttons on her blouse and paused at the one that hung by a loose thread. She'd have to mend it when she got home. After a week at Maya Escorts, Thisbe knew the routine well enough to manage without Brenda's help. She shed her clothes, inserted the prophylactic suppository, and plugged the cable into her skull. Thisbe felt the now familiar sinking in the pit of her stomach as the scene spun and transformed into the diagnostic program's white room.

"Good evening, Thisbe." Keiko bowed and smiled. "How was your day off?"

"Good I tried to take Andy to the park, but I couldn't drag him away from his new chess computer."

Keiko paused. The algorithm searching for the appropriate response seemed almost visible behind her forehead. "I think there is an interactive chess instruction disk. Perhaps you could ask for it at the control room."

"Perhaps, but right now I'd like to get back to Mahamuni," Thisbe said.

"Very well."

The white walls seemed to melt and Thisbe huddled with a half-dozen others around Mahamuni. The men had hung their suit jackets over the backs of their chairs. They wore white shirts, loosened ties, and bleary expressions.

"If we keep spending at this rate, we'll drain the bank account soon after next month's rally in Kyoto." Tanaka massaged his temples.

"What do you suggest?" asked Mahamuni, his face a mask of composure.

"Cut back on the television ads," Kenji Masuda pointed to a line on a sheet of figures. "They take up 80 percent of the budget."

"Everything depends on Kyoto." Mahamuni leaned forward and rested his elbows on his knees. "If we slack off now, all our advertising will have been wasted. Double the TV ads! Spend everything!"

"If I may, Sensei," Masuda handed Mahamuni a pie chart. "I've prepared another proposal. We can cut our TV ads and double the radio. That will still leave us enough money to pay our expenses for the next three months."

"It's a good plan," Saito said.

Tanaka grunted.

*"After all these months have you understood so little of what I've told you?"
Mahamuni asked.*

*"Even though we must simplify our needs," Kyoshi Nomura chuckled, "we
don't want to simplify ourselves out of the roofs over our heads."*

*Mahamuni looked as if he'd been stabbed. He stood. "If any of you would
follow me, do so now." He strode from the room.*

*The others stared at one another. Thisbe slung her purse over her shoulder and
hurried after the sage. A few others followed.*

"Quick! The master's leaving! Follow him!" they yelled.

*Volunteers stuck heads out of their offices to see the commotion. Some left
paperwork behind and joined the procession. The band of followers entered a
stairwell. Their feet pounded the steps until they emerged on the ground floor and
exited to the hot, humid September afternoon. Mahamuni turned right and led his
followers down Yaesu-dori toward Tokyo Station. Cars rolled past on the wide
road. Not knowing what he had in mind, his followers hustled around pedestrians
to keep up. Within minutes perspiration stuck Thisbe's blouse to her back.*

*They passed the entrances to several small alleyways crowded with karaoke
clubs and restaurants. Mahamuni turned right on Chuo-dori and headed north.
Tall buildings blocked the horizon. Mannequins gazed at the party from the
Takashimaya department store's display windows. Thisbe glanced at the
Maruzen bookstore across the street. They continued for a few blocks and stopped
at a stone bridge under a highway overpass. The memorial plaque said that this
was Nihonbashi, the start of the famous Tokaido Road. A truck rumbled
overhead. Thisbe looked up at the pale-green steel beams for reassurance before
turning her attention to Mahamuni.*

*"Less than two hundred years ago feudal lords traveled the old post roads on
foot with their entourages," Mahamuni said. "These days highways and railroad
tracks cover the Tokaido, but there is another road, one that leads into the heart
of Japan and on to Kyoto, the Nakasendo. I propose that by walking this road
we will not only explore Japan's history, but we'll explore our own hearts."*

*Thisbe looked down at the sluggish green water in the Sumida River. She
didn't have a jacket. She dug in her purse and counted thirty-five credits, not even
enough for a single night's lodging. While she was preoccupied, Mahamuni and
the others had started across the bridge.*

"Coming?" One of the followers stopped and looked over his shoulder at her.

*"Of course." Thisbe slung her purse over her shoulder and hurried to catch up
with the others.*

Mahamuni's followers numbered eight in all. There were two women (Thisbe and Chikako), Tanaka, Saito, and four other men: the retired bookkeeper Mr. Ueno, a short man with a trim moustache and graying hair; Kobayashi, an unemployed school teacher; Oda, a burly truck driver; and Yamamoto, the quiet one whose background remained a mystery. After crossing the bridge they entered a maze of concrete and traffic. Flashing lights advertised ubiquitous pachinko parlors, where gamblers with cigarettes hanging from their lips fed quarters like robots into machines that sent silver ball bearings falling through a series of obstacles. The rinky-dink of bells could be heard all the way outside on the sidewalk.

They stopped at noon for a quick bowl of soba noodles and resumed walking. After a few hours Thisbe's shoes began rubbing blisters on her heels. When they passed a drugstore across from a hospital, marked with a green cross, she thought of stopping to buy Band-Aids but didn't want to inconvenience the others.

"Hey, Kobayashi," Oda said, "how are those shoes holding up?"

"Great! The polymer design wears longer than leather and will keep my feet dry in the rain."

Oda and Yamamoto grinned.

"Laugh now." Kobayashi's face turned red. "But when you realize how much you spend on shoes in a lifetime, you'll be asking me for that shoe seller's address."

An hour later, with the pain still stabbing her feet, Thisbe wished she'd stopped at the drugstore. She began to limp. At rush hour, office buildings disgorged salarymen onto the roads and sidewalks. The crowd jostled Mahamuni's tiny band of followers, who moved against the flow like a fishing boat motoring upstream.

They stopped before sunset at a capsule hotel near the train tracks. Saito paid for the others with three crisp ten-thousand-yen bills.

"Thank you. See you in the morning." Thisbe followed Chikako to the women's side of the hotel and stopped in a locker room to change and shower.

The seven-mile walk had left Thisbe's legs as rubbery as an overcooked chawan mushi. *The Japanese seemed to love those egg custards, but Thisbe could take them or leave them. After her shower she sat on a wooden bench and examined the blood-filled blisters on her feet.*

"You need better shoes." Chikako sat beside her and began toweling her hair. She had a straight back and the tiny jewel-like breasts Thisbe imagined a man would enjoy. "We'll stop tomorrow and buy you some."

"Please don't go to too much trouble," Thisbe said.

"Nonsense! We have a long walk ahead of us. Without good shoes, you'd only slow us down."

"What were they teasing Mr. Kobayashi about earlier?" Thisbe asked.

"Oh," Chikako smiled. "He bought thirty pairs of shoes from some mail order outfit in Taiwan, and he's been trying to get everyone to buy them too. He even gave the master a pair, but Mahamuni found them too uncomfortable to wear."

Thisbe changed into a clean yukata, a thin cotton robe, and walked down the hall to her sleeping capsule. A group of giggling young women in pink nightgowns passed going the other way. Thisbe's capsule was slightly larger than a phone booth. She crawled inside, stretched out on the comfortable mattress, and closed the door behind her. Now what? Could she sleep in virtual reality?

Thisbe turned on the television and scanned the news programs, cartoons, and wacky game shows. Nothing held her interest. She turned off the TV and shut her eyes. Her legs began to throb. Thisbe scratched a tickle in her groin. Her pelvis began to rock like a boat on the waves.

Thisbe turned on the lights. Nothing was moving, though her legs began to hurt in earnest. Massaging her calves and feet brought no relief. She needed some virtual aspirin. Thisbe climbed out of her capsule and wandered the deserted halls in search of a vending machine. She found none. No one was at the front desk. When Thisbe went to the toilet, she couldn't relieve herself.

She returned to the sleeping capsule and stared at the walls. What kind of VR disk was this? She shouldn't be in pain!

"Keiko," she whispered.

No one answered.

"Keiko!" Thisbe called a little louder. There was no answer except for the throbbing ache in her legs. Sitting on a VR beach like all the other dream girls began to look pretty good. It certainly beat sitting in a coffin-sized room with nothing to think about but the pain. Thisbe hugged her knees to her chest and cried.

Thisbe emerged from VR shaken as if from a bad dream. She looked at her feet. Except for the ridge of calluses on the edges of her heels they were smooth. The blisters that had tormented her in VR were gone as was the pain in her legs. She used the bidet, showered, and dressed. She was halfway out the door when she remembered the loose button. Thisbe touched her blouse and paused. Odd, the button was now firmly attached. Brenda must have noticed it when she checked on Thisbe during VR. But why would Brenda look in the closet? Thisbe made a mental note to thank her and headed toward the parking lot.

When Thisbe returned to virtual reality the following day, she began as usual in the white diagnostic room.

Keiko bowed and smiled. "Good morning, Thisbe. How is your implant working?"

"Yesterday's session was very painful. I did a lot of walking, but I didn't expect to be in such agony. What was going on?"

Keiko scanned Thisbe's telemetry. "I detect no malfunctions. Your disk yesterday was *Mahamuni's Nakasendo Pilgrimage*, was it not?"

Thisbe nodded.

"Religious disks are exempt from the Uetrecht Standards. Sometimes they can be too intense for a viewer."

"I called for you, but you didn't come," Thisbe said.

Keiko stared.

"Well, answer me!"

"I'm sorry," Keiko said. "I'm programmed to respond only to questions and commands. Since your last statement was neither, I felt no response was needed. Would you like to rephrase the statement as a question?"

"Why didn't you come when I called you?"

"Accessing yesterday's log," Keiko said. "There's no record of any request for my assistance. Sensor AC92 was reading a little low but was statistically within tolerance. I'll send a message to tech support and ask if this could have blocked your summons. It's illegal for VR disks to disable a user's summons to her diagnostic agent. There have been only two recorded cases. In both the penalties were severe. Nevertheless, I suggest you try a different disk for today's session. What would you like?"

"You pick," Thisbe said.

The sound of rushing wind filled Thisbe's ears. She sat in a sailplane's front seat and stared at the sagging yellow nylon cord attaching the glider to the stubby tow plane ahead. As the tow plane tugged them through turns, the glider skidded through the air forcing the pilot, seated behind Thisbe, to bank the wings. The sun heated Thisbe's skin through the cockpit's glass. She watched the altimeter's white needle spin to eight thousand feet against its black background.

"Pull the brown knob," the pilot said.

Thisbe pulled, the line fell away, and they were free. The pilot banked the wings to give Thisbe a spectacular view of the granite mountains below.

"Want to take the controls?" he asked.

"Okay" Thisbe held the stick lightly and placed her feet on the pedals.

"Steer parallel to that crest and try to keep the speed at about forty-five miles per hour."

Soon the glider veered left. Thisbe pushed the stick to the right and added some rudder. The nose overshot, forcing Thisbe to bank left. The glider oscillated around the desired heading. Thisbe also had trouble keeping it level. Eventually she got the hang of it and learned to let the glider fly itself.

"Steer for those clouds over on the left," the pilot said.

They flew into a thermal and circled like a lazy hawk while the warm air lifted them thousands of feet.

"Want to do a loop?" the pilot asked.

"Sure"

The nose pitched down and they gained speed before the pilot pulled back on the stick. Thisbe saw solid blue through the windscreen and felt a moment of weightlessness. Then the glider turned right side up and gained speed once again.

"That was great!" Thisbe yelled.

They spent the afternoon soaring and turning. Despite the weightlessness and tug of g-forces, Thisbe remained calm. She trusted the atmosphere's big soft hands to keep them aloft. By the time the glider skidded to a stop on the runway, Thisbe knew she would accept whatever pain came with Mahamuni's presence. Flying was worthwhile, but it hadn't touched her heart like the sage had. Even though she could only be with him in a dream, it was better than not being with him at all. The pilot placed his hand on Thisbe's waist and helped her out of the cockpit.

"You're a natural," he said. "I'll be glad to help you get your license. Come back anytime."

He was a handsome man with brown wavy hair and a short trimmed mustache. Thisbe's eyes strayed to the burly chest exposed by an open shirt button. The world spun and she was back in her room at Maya Escorts.

CHAPTER 7

"The Mahamuni pilgrimage VR disk was encoded by the Agape Group in Helsinki," Keiko said when Thisbe returned to virtual reality the next day. "There aren't many records, but it appears they went out of business two years ago. Lester confirmed the disk's stated Gibbs rating of 4.5, which means it won't damage your neurons. Unfortunately there's no way to know how much pain or psychological stress you'll experience without more information from the manufacturer. Given that this is unavailable, I recommend avoiding this disk."

"I want to go ahead with it, anyway," Thisbe said. "A little discomfort is a small price to pay for all I have to gain."

Thisbe spun into the streets of Tokyo. Now equipped with a backpack and running shoes, she limped behind the others as they walked parallel to the train tracks heading toward Nagano. The air smelled of exhaust with the occasional whiff of sewage. Posters in office windows and four-sided billboards atop buildings displayed bold Japanese characters. The pain in Thisbe's legs wasn't as intense as the previous night, but the constant ache kept her at the back of the procession. With each step the green tea she'd bought from a vending machine sloshed in its plastic bottle. Thisbe wasn't the only one limping. Mr. Kobayashi appeared to be favoring his left foot. Eventually Thisbe fell so far behind that when she finally caught up to the others, most had already finished their snacks from a convenience store.

Chikako handed Thisbe a bag of cookies. "How are you feeling so far?"

"The new shoes help." Thisbe leaned against the wall. "My legs are still sore, but I can manage." She soon regretted that statement, when her legs began to stiffen.

Several of the others lifted their knapsacks to resume their journey. Having eavesdropped on Thisbe's discussion, Mahamuni made his way to her and squatted beside the bench.

"Thisbe, why didn't you tell me you were having trouble?"

"I talked to Chikako, and she bought me some new shoes."

"That's not good enough," Mahamuni said. "You need to tell me."

"Maybe we could take the bus today," said Saito, who with Tanaka had come to stand behind the sage.

Mahamuni looked Thisbe up and down. "No, a pilgrim must experience each step of the journey no matter how unpleasant. We'll walk."

"Perhaps," Saito suggested, "Thisbe could take a taxi and meet us at the next stop."

"Would you rob her of the chance to walk the Path, Saito?" Mahamuni asked. "We'll stick together. If Thisbe needs a day of rest, we'll wait for her."

"But, Sensei, with too many delays we won't get to Kyoto on time," Saito said.

"Should I abandon a true follower in hopes of gaining more?"

"No, Sensei." Saito looked at his shoes to hide his flushed face.

Thisbe lay face down on the massage table and looked at the tile floor through the hole the support made for her face. A brown spot the size of a ladybug on the grout captured her attention. The blind masseuse spread oil over Thisbe's legs and made her jump at the tickle on her feet. The masseuse let out a yelp of delight when she located a knot on Thisbe's calf. She bore down using her weight to concentrate pressure on her thumbs to loosen the muscles. Thisbe gritted her teeth and took a deep breath.

The woman continued. Once the masseuse smoothed the tension from Thisbe's shoulders, she had her roll over. Fingers began at Thisbe's ankles and kneaded the stiffness from her shins. Thisbe closed her eyes and relaxed into the blind masseuse's warm, healing touch. She felt as if her body had turned to wax and melted into the massage table. Hands circled her knees and stroked the long muscles of her quadriceps. When a finger brushed Thisbe's inner thigh, she felt a momentary sexual twinge and repressed a longing for more. Thisbe became drowsy, her awareness viscous like honey. The hands inched closer to Thisbe's groin and spread her legs apart.

Thisbe opened her eyes and saw a fat man thrusting his hips between her legs. She tried to resist but couldn't move. The man had a hideous, reddish-purple rash on his chest. A thick patch of black hair grew from the man's hunched shoulders. His face twisted into a pained look of concentration. Then he opened his mouth and let out a pathetic sigh. His body tensed and shuddered in climax as he squirted what seemed like a gallon of warm pus into her. Her groin itched as if a million tiny cockroaches crawled into her womb.

"Hey, wake up." The masseuse nudged Thisbe's shoulder.

Thisbe opened her eyes and squinted at the middle-aged woman, who had short curly hair and a broad, smiling face.

"You were yelling in your sleep."

"It must have been a bad dream." Thisbe tucked the towel around her torso and sat up. "How long was I asleep?"

"Half hour," the masseuse said. "Take your time. Have a shower. You're welcome to use the hot bath."

Thisbe padded to the bathroom and sat on a wooden stool while soaping her body. She rinsed off the suds with a handheld shower nozzle and washed once more before getting into the bath. The rectangular tub of tile-covered concrete was only large enough for one. Soaking in the almost scalding water, Thisbe had the schizophrenic sensation of being immaculate and dirty at the same time.

She didn't tell Keiko about her VR nightmare. She feared the autonomous agent program would forbid her to return to Mahamuni's pilgrimage. Thisbe dropped by the clinic instead, where a nurse left her waiting in an exam room. Thisbe sat on a paper-covered couch and swung her legs so her heels bounced against the support. After twenty minutes she looked at her watch and wondered whether she should have gone to the gym. Maya Escorts required their sex workers to spend at least four hours per week exercising, and Thisbe was behind schedule. She gazed at a chart of the female reproductive system on the wall. A knock came from the door. Thirty milliseconds later the doctor entered. He was blonde, wore tortoise-shell glasses, and had a pink, boyish face.

"Hello." He looked at the chart. "Thisbe, I'm Dr. Gibbs. What can I do for you, today?"

"It's about my implant," Thisbe said. "Something strange happened when I was in VR."

"Go on."

"I woke up and couldn't move," Thisbe stammered, "while a client was having sex with me."

"It says here you had a prescription for Megacillin." Dr. Gibbs looked up from the chart. "Did you finish it?"

Thisbe nodded.

"Has your diagnostic program reported any malfunctions?"

"Nothing except a stray sensor reading."

"Well, that's not unusual. I don't think you woke up from VR. The control room sends a signal that shunts sensory input away from your brain's receiving centers."

"What could it have been then?" Thisbe asked.

"The mind does strange things." Dr. Gibbs sat on the stool and wheeled closer to Thisbe. "We're still not sure how the brain controls your experience on the new active VR disks, but it has something to do with wish fulfillment. When wishes come from the unconscious, they can appear quite shocking. Most people will have a disturbing VR session from time to time. It's nothing to worry about, so treat it like a bad dream. If it persists, you might think about what your unconscious is asking for.

"When patients have recurring problems, I send them to a counselor. Those with very severe problems need to stick to the scripted VR disks, but these are a lot less realistic than the active ones." The doctor scribbled in Thisbe's chart. "We could run a diagnostic on your implant, but I don't see a reason to do so. The onboard diagnostics are pretty good these days." He stood. "I'd forget about it for now. But come back if these problems become common."

After leaving the clinic, Thisbe made her way to Maya Escort's child-care center, where a cheerful but tired woman in braids oversaw a half-dozen boys and girls running and jumping on the rubberized floor. Andy wore a Roman soldier's costume, complete with red cape, plastic helmet, and breastplate.

"Quick!" He pointed his plastic sword toward the corner. "The Remulans are about to attack. We must head them off in the K-fighters." He and a boy in a cowboy hat mounted large rubber balls, grasped the handles between their legs, and began bouncing around the room.

"Bogey at ten-o-clock." The boy, who appeared a year older than Andy, made machine-gun sounds.

"Another one at 3:47." Andy sounded an explosion, and both boys rocked on their seats to simulate the blowback.

"They're having so much fun. It's a shame to take them home," said a petite woman who'd approached from behind while Thisbe watched the boys. Like the older boy, she had dark wavy hair, brown eyes, and porcelain skin. "I'm Margot."

"Oh yeah, I've seen you at the gym." Thisbe shook Margot's proffered hand. "I'm Thisbe."

"You just started, right?" Margot hardly moved her mouth when she spoke. It was as if her jaws had been wired shut.

"About three weeks ago."

"How do you like it?" A cluster of stray hair fell into Margot's eyes. She tucked it behind her ear.

"It beats working as a reservation clerk."

"Mom!" The older boy tugged on Margot's sleeve. "Can Andy stay over at our house tonight?"

"Not this time, Tyler. It's late and you have to get up early for your doctor's appointment tomorrow."

Tyler's expectant smile deflated like a soufflé baked during an earthquake.

"Maybe Andy can come and play some other day." Margot turned to Thisbe. "When do you have a day off?"

"I'm free Wednesday and Thursday."

"Wednesday's no good. How about Thursday at noon? I'll make lunch."

"Okay."

Margot scribbled her address in a notepad, tore off the sheet, and presented it to Thisbe. "See you then."

CHAPTER 8

It took three days to escape the wall-to-wall city that was greater Tokyo. Once the pilgrims passed Omiya, the tall buildings began to thin out, and Thisbe could see to the horizon. There were large cubes of green netting that served as driving ranges. The pairs of pale-green spherical tanks that looked like giant brussels sprouts puzzled her. Mahamuni and Tanaka walked in front. Saito and the others followed. Kobayashi brought up the rear. They walked a few more hours.

"Ah!" Mahamuni stretched and took a deep breath. "It's good to return to nature."

"Yes, indeed, Sensei," Tanaka said.

Thisbe held her tongue. She wouldn't exactly call the grid of two-lane roads crisscrossing the rice fields, clusters of tile-roofed houses, and occasional grain elevators the wilderness. Still, she relaxed a bit now that they were out of the big city. The sun felt pleasantly warm on her skin. Thisbe wondered if she could get sunburned in VR.

A white bullet train raced north toward Nagano on the tracks to her left. Thisbe imagined reclining in a comfortable seat onboard. If Mahamuni had chosen that mode of travel, they could make Kyoto in four hours. Her stomach growled. Soon they arrived at a cluster of shops. Mahamuni called a halt for lunch. Tanaka went to a convenience store. Mahamuni wandered into a produce market. The rest waited by a cluster of trees.

Thisbe knelt on the tarpaulin they'd spread on the grass. In real life her feet would have gone to sleep in minutes, but she had no problem in VR. Kobayashi took off his shoes and massaged his feet.

"Aiyah! Kobayashi, get those stinking feet away from me!" Oda said. "You're ruining my appetite."

Kobayashi forced his sweaty feet back into his shoes and grimaced. Tanaka returned with food and yogurt drinks. Chikako passed Thisbe a rice cake. As Thisbe pulled the tab to remove the wrapper, she marveled how the ingenious design kept the rice from making the seaweed soggy. She devoured the rice cake and enjoyed the contrasting textures of the crisp nori, moist rice, and salted plum inside. Thisbe loved being able to feast in VR and return to her physical body without gaining weight. Perhaps she could write a diet book. Unfortunately she was always famished after completing an eight-hour shift in VR. Thisbe looked up to see Mahamuni lugging a large paper bag.

"Sensei!" Saito dropped his rice cake and rushed to Mahamuni's side. "Let

me help you!"

"Peaches!" Mahamuni pushed past him, chuckled, and spilled the bag's contents on the tarpaulin. "Don't just stare! Take some! They're perfect."

Indeed they were. Each was pink, blushed with red, and larger than a fist. Thisbe took two. Heavy with sweetness, their flesh gave with pressure from her fingers. She bit into the first. Juice dribbled down her chin and onto her blouse. The flesh was white and had a subtly wild taste. Thisbe devoured the first and started on the second. Within minutes Mahamuni's haul was reduced to a few dozen pits. Thisbe wiped her face with a moist napkin.

"Do you know how advertisers trick you into buying?" Mahamuni asked.

His followers remained silent. Mahamuni glanced at Saito.

"They sell you an image of yourself," Tanaka offered.

"Yes," Mahamuni smiled. "They sell you an image of yourself. Of course you need the product to fill your inadequacy and fulfill the image. Your body stinks, so here's some deodorant. You'll never get the girl, unless you buy this car." He looked at Thisbe. "You'll never find a husband, unless you buy these shoes.

"If we want to stop over consumption, accepting ourselves is a good place to start. Look at your body. It's pretty remarkable. You can run and jump. You have eyes to see and minds to think.

"Did you ever go to a funeral, learn something you never knew about the deceased, and think, 'Hey, he was a pretty neat guy'? All that praise comes too late to help the dead. That's why I think we should do eulogies for the living. We can start right now." Mahamuni's eyes swept the group and settled on Thisbe. "How about you?"

Thisbe blushed and looked down.

"No, no, you must listen to this." Mahamuni touched her shoulder.

With the master's touch all the tension she carried in her body fell away. It felt as if a cold stream had washed her insides clean.

"I know you as one of my most dedicated followers," Mahamuni said. "You've remained faithful in spite of great hardships. It may not seem like it, but your struggle is crucial for the future of our movement. Who else has praise for Thisbe?"

"I hear she's worked very difficult jobs," Tanaka added.

"She's scrupulously honest in spite of having little money."

The group nodded and grunted their assent.

"She's a wonderful mother."

In the midst of the praise, Thisbe noticed that Saito wasn't there. She'd been so caught up in the recognition that she'd failed to notice him sneak away. He returned a few minutes before the session concluded and the followers gave Thisbe a group hug. She felt like she could handle anything.

After Thisbe exited VR, she ran into Brenda in the hallway.

"How are the VR sessions?" Brenda put a bundle of dirty sheets into her cart. "You go to any nice beaches?"

"They've been good, although ..." Thisbe said. "Did you ever, you know, like see any customers in the act, when you were in VR?"

Brenda looked up and down the hallway. "Keep quiet about it, unless you want to lose your job," she whispered. "That's the same thing that happened to me when my implant started to malfunction."

Another dream girl came out of her intimacy room. Brenda smiled and pushed her cart down the hall. Thisbe nodded and walked on. Brenda's fears seemed a bit exaggerated. It was too late, anyway. Thisbe had already told Dr. Gibbs about her VR breakouts.

CHAPTER 9

Margot's house was on the other side of Lake Washington, Thisbe crossed the floating bridge and got on I-405 South.

"Are we there yet?" Andy asked.

"No, honey. If we were there, we wouldn't still be driving, would we?" Thisbe got off on Hemlock and turned onto Fir, following Margot's directions.

"Are we there yet?"

Thisbe reached into the backseat and tickled Andy's belly. She turned into Margot's subdivision, where cookie cutter homes lay on a grid so uniform that only Euclid suffering from obsessive-compulsive disorder could have designed it. Thisbe slowed to look at addresses. She passed several wooden skeletons of homes being built. When she found Margot's house, Thisbe parked next to the shiny SUV in the wide driveway. The dealer's price sticker was still in the window.

"Welcome," Margot said from the open front door.

When they reached the step, Margot tousled Andy's hair. The boy pulled away. He didn't like people touching his face or head.

"Come in. Lunch is almost ready."

Andy saw Tyler and darted around Margot's knees into the house.

"I got monkey bars in the back yard," Tyler said. "Wanna see 'em?"

"Yeah!" The two boys ran off.

"Don't get dirty!" Margot called toward their receding backs. "Lunch is in fifteen minutes."

Thisbe walked inside with Margot. Although new and no doubt expensive, the furniture in the living room didn't match. Margot caught Thisbe staring at the holovision pedestal.

"It's for Tyler. He loves playing along with *Commander Sampson's Asteroid Patrol*." Margot led Thisbe into the kitchen, where a professional stove squatted under a copper exhaust hood. "Hope you like sweet and sour ribs."

Margot turned on a burner. After a few clicks a blue flame burst into life and licked the bottom of a blackened wok. Margot added oil, ginger, and garlic. After a quick stir, she slid in the meat. A few more stirs, the addition of sliced bell pepper, and pouring in the sauce

51

completed the dish. She removed egg rolls that had been warming in a toaster oven and put one on each of four china plates decorated with a floral pattern. Then she ladled on the ribs.

"Lunch is ready!"

The boys ran into the kitchen.

"Can we eat in the holo room?" Tyler asked.

"Only if you take your pill first." Margot poured Tyler a glass of soda from a large plastic jug and handed him the tablet.

Tyler made a face and swallowed it. The boys carried their plates and glasses off.

"Be sure to use the trays so you don't spill anything," Margot called after them.

"What's wrong with your son?" Thisbe asked.

"Oh, he gets chronic ear infections," Margot said. "Would you like some wine?"

Thisbe shook her head. "Water's fine."

"You don't mind if I have one, do you?" Margot retrieved a wine bottle from the refrigerator and poured Thisbe's tap water almost as an afterthought.

The two women ate in the dining room. Margot had supplied plastic chopsticks, but they might as well have been Teflon as far as Thisbe was concerned. Each time she tried to pick up her food, the ribs slid back onto her plate. She gave up and used her fingers, setting the tiny bones in a neat pile after she gnawed off the meat.

"So, how's Maya working out for you?" Margot held her glass as if proposing a toast.

"Okay, I'm still paying off my surgery. Hopefully, after six months I can start taking home bigger checks."

"You didn't let them set it up. Did you?"

Thisbe nodded.

Margot pursed her lips. "You could have had it done in Tijuana for half the price Maya charges. That's what I did." She finished her wine. "Well, too late now. How about VR? Have you lived any fun disks?"

"Well, I've stuck mostly to spiritual themes."

Margot's mouth dropped open. "Why waste your time with those?"

"I went soaring," Thisbe mumbled.

"Honey, it just won't do. You're missing the best part. You could live in a mansion, drive a fancy car, and go dancing every night."

"But it wouldn't be real."

"Real, what's real? It's what you taste, touch, and smell. And why shouldn't we get a chance at the good life like those rich bastards that screw us?" Margot reached across the table and took Thisbe's hands. "I'll talk to Lester and set you up with some good disks. We can start with *Ginny's Passion* and *One Scarlet Rose.*" Margot let go of Thisbe's hands. "On second thought why don't you join me in my session tomorrow? I've been putting together my own VR disk with these guys at Triage Productions in Palo Alto."

"You mean you can make your own virtual reality?"

"It's not hard once you learn the interface," Margot said. "I've been working on it in my spare time for over a year. There are still some rough spots, but you'll get the idea. If it sells big, I'm going to quit Maya Escorts and become a full-time designer. It's the ultimate freedom, living in worlds where you make the rules."

They spent the rest of the afternoon chatting. Margot showed Thisbe the Triage Productions catalog. Thisbe had to practically drag Andy away. He pleaded to stay another hour, but she wanted to beat the traffic. She promised to bring him back another day.

When Thisbe returned to Maya Escorts the next day, a new maid was changing the sheets in her intimacy room.

"What happened to Brenda?" Thisbe asked.

"I don't know," the maid said. "I just started yesterday."

Thisbe waited for her to finish, undressed, and jacked in. A man with sun-streaked hair and bulging biceps replaced Keiko in the white diagnostic room. His open leather vest revealed a hairless, well-defined chest.

"Welcome, Thisbe. I'm Lorenzo, Margot's diagnostic program. I've checked that you implant is compatible with hers. Do you have any questions before we proceed with your mutual hookup?"

"Yes, how did Margot select your appearance?"

"It's one of the standard options with her implant. I can download the settings to yours if you want, but sometimes the image doesn't translate well between implants made by different manufacturers."

"That's okay." Thisbe straightened her shoulders. "I'm ready."

Thisbe's head spun and she found herself in a bathing suit lying beside a swimming pool. The environment lacked the real world's detail. Instead it appeared to have been drawn and colored like a cartoon. An animated Margot lay on a folding couch beside Thisbe. Her unrealistically tiny waist accentuated her wasp-like figure. She'd removed her top to eliminate tan lines.

"Thanks for joining me." As in reality Margot's mouth hardly moved when she talked. "The development interface starts out with an animation and fills in the details once you finalize the design. I kind of like it this way, though. It's more fun. I think I'll keep it."

"Excuse me, miss." A man with a jutting chin and impossibly huge shoulders interrupted. He wore skimpy shorts that molded to his buttocks. "Would you like a daiquiri?"

Thisbe took a glass from the offered tray and sipped. The powerful cocktail's alcohol brought tears to her eyes. She drank more. Indulging in VR couldn't hurt. Could it?

The male servant returned moments later and spoke to Margot. "Excuse me, madam. Chef Andre needs some supplies from the market."

"Very well. Be a dear, Brad, and bring me my purse."

The servant sauntered off and returned moments later with a dainty purse dangling from his massive forearm. Margot took it, counted a handful of bills, and handed them over.

"Thank you, madam. I'll give this to Andre. Will your friend be joining you for your customary massage before lunch?"

"Yes, why don't you get Rocko to come help?"

Brad took the money to the kitchen and returned with a man who could have been his identical twin were it not for his dark hair. Thisbe lay on her stomach while Rocko rubbed oil into her back. She felt like a stick of butter melting into a bowl of hot popcorn. Unlike her massage in Mahamuni's world, she had no disturbing flash of sex with her customers. After a half-hour she rolled over for Rocko to work on her front.

"Would you like your customary release, madam?"

Thisbe turned her head and peeked through partially closed eyes at Brad kneeling between Margot's thighs.

Margot glanced at Thisbe. "No, not today." She patted Brad on the head. "Why don't you boys check on lunch?"

The servants scampered off. A man in a white jacket rolled a silver cart to the pool. His belly was swollen to the size of a watermelon.

"Andre," Margot said, "this is my friend Thisbe."

"Pleased to meet you." Andre opened the lid and served huge plates of pasta, trout (without the bones), and chocolate mousse. "Oh!" Andre put a hand on his belly. "I felt the baby kick."

"You'd better lie down, dear." Margot patted his arm. When he'd left Margot signed, "Men!" and rolled her eyes.

Lunch was delicious, although the mousse was too sweet for Thisbe's taste. Afterward Brad and Rocko cleared the plates. Margot glanced at her watch.

"My goodness, it's nearly one! If we don't hurry, we'll miss Coco's fashion show. Brad, get the airship ready."

Thisbe followed Margot to a bedroom and threw on a lime-green shirtdress and a string of pearls. Margot tried on a half-dozen outfits and settled on a navy pantsuit. They dashed to the driveway, where Rocko held a pink blimp by its tether. Margot climbed behind the wheel, and Thisbe sat beside her.

"We'll be back before dinner." Margot waved out the window.

Rocko let go of the tether and the blimp rose into the air.

"I know they're terribly obsolete," Margot said, "but nothing beats the romance of a dirigible."

"What's the difference between a blimp and a dirigible?" Thisbe asked.

"Beats me." Margot started the engines and steered across town. "Would you look at the traffic down there?"

Thisbe looked out the window at the line of cars crawling like termites on the freeway below. Fifteen minutes later Margot set the blimp down on top of a five-story building. A wide-shouldered man in a khaki uniform grabbed the tether and tied it to a cleat.

"Good afternoon, Ms. Greatbody." He touched a gloved hand to the brim of his cap. "Ma'am." He nodded to Thisbe.

The ladies descended a carpeted staircase and rushed to a crowded room. A woman approached. She wore a black hat as large as a sombrero tilted at a thirty-seven degree angle on her head.

"Margot! You made it! Francesco will show you to your seats. Then we'll begin."

A well-preserved fifty-year-old man in a blue blazer and white shoes sat them in the front row. The lights dimmed and music started. A model in a black evening gown strutted down the catwalk.

"Good Lord!" Margot whispered. "Just look at those padded shoulders. What was Coco thinking?"

The show went on for two hours. Margot peppered Thisbe with comments like, "That girl must have an eating disorder," and, "That hat looks like an airliner crashed into her head." Thisbe smiled but didn't join in. Mahamuni had said to avoid needless criticism. When the lights came on, the models lined the catwalk to receive the audience's applause. Margot led Thisbe past a gauntlet of champagne servers and toward the stairs. The woman in the black hat approached.

"You've really outdone yourself, Coco," Margot said. "We've got to get back. You know how temperamental Andre gets if I let dinner get cold."

"Men!" Coco winked.

They took the blimp home. When they set down, Margot looked at her watch. "Looks like we're about done for the day."

"I had a wonderful time," Thisbe said. "I love what you've done with your VR world. Thanks for showing me."

"Come back any time," Margot said.

Thisbe's head spun, and she returned to her intimacy room at Maya Escorts.

CHAPTER 10

"Thanks for inviting me to speak at Single Parents United, Linda." Dr. Barry, the pudgy psychologist with bad posture and short curly hair, nodded to the woman in a pastel dress. "Tonight I'm going to talk about an issue that affects most of you, dealing with your ex-partner." He bit into a donut and showered his rumpled shirt with powdered sugar.

Thisbe squirmed in the folding chair to find a comfortable position. She'd arrived late and consequently had to take a seat in the front row.

"Issues of child support, custody, parenting, and the division of assets complicate feelings of abandonment and betrayal to make conflict almost inevitable, but there is good news." Dr. Barry sprayed those in the front row with tiny droplets of saliva as he spoke. "With work you can redefine your relationship with your ex-partner. Now, how do we do that?"

Thisbe glanced around the room. Her eyes settled on the Adonis a few chairs to her right. He had short blonde hair, a honey-colored complexion, azure-blue eyes, and the most adorable long eyelashes. He swiveled his head her way. Thisbe jerked her attention back to Dr. Barry, who plodded through the lecture. Had the handsome man seen her staring? As the psychologist outlined a method of arguing without blame, Thisbe stole glances at the man, whose golf shirt hugged his wiry frame.

"So in conclusion," Dr. Barry said, "rather than blaming realize that when your ex-partner makes you angry, he or she is only showing you a part of your own personality. Once you take responsibility for your own karma, you can transform your relationship into one that's more positive. Although you may no longer be lovers, you can become friends. Any questions?"

Thisbe's hand shot up.

"Yes."

"So you're saying that when my ex spends my child support taking some bimbo to Hawaii and I can't pay the rent, it's my fault?" A wave of second thoughts washed over her the moment she'd finished. What was wrong with her? She never spoke in front of a crowd.

"It sounds like you have some unresolved issues." Dr. Barry stroked his chin. "Why don't you come up here, and we'll try a little role-playing exercise so I can show you what I mean?"

Thisbe blushed. She stepped forward as if walking to the gallows.

"I need a volunteer to play…" Dr. Barry looked at Thisbe. "What's your name?"

"Thisbe."

"Thisbe's ex-partner." Dr. Barry's eyes settled on the hunk. "How about you?"

The man stood. His self-confidence spoke in the way he strode forward.

"And your name is?"

"Ron Murphy"

"Very good. Ron, why don't you start by telling your ex-partner, Thisbe, that you'll be late with this month's child support?"

"Thisbe," Ron began, "I'm going to be a little late with this month's check."

"Why?"

"I'm taking Bambi to Maui next week. You wouldn't believe the price of a five-star hotel, let alone the champagne, caviar, and jewelry." Ron winked at the audience.

Ron's good looks made it hard for Thisbe to throw herself into her role. She made "You selfish bastard!" sound like a compliment and went on to ask, "How am I supposed to keep a roof over your son's head? Are we supposed to eat from a dumpster while you and that floozy sit on the beach?"

"Okay, hold it right there." Dr. Barry placed his hands in a T. "Now, how do you think Ron's going to respond to that? Is he likely to change his mind?"

"I guess not."

"Let's try a different approach." Dr. Barry wagged his index finger in time with his words. "I want you to express your feelings with I-statements. Then tell your ex-partner what you need the money for."

"That makes me furious!" Thisbe said.

"Good!" Dr. Barry nodded.

"Without this month's check, I can't pay the rent. It'll be the third time, and I'm afraid the landlord will evict me."

"Excellent!" Dr. Barry turned to Ron with a patronizing nod.

"How much do you need?" Ron asked.

"Six hundred credits."

"Can I make up the rest at the end of the month?"

Thisbe nodded.

"In that case," Ron said, "I suppose we can stay at Motel 36 and drink malt liquor."

The audience applauded. Ron and Thisbe returned to their chairs while Dr. Barry wrapped things up. On the way out Ron bumped into Thisbe.

"Nice acting with you."

"I didn't think it was very realistic."

"No," Ron said. "These things never are. Dr. Barry sounds like he came from the bottom of the psych barrel. If he were any good, he'd be able to buy better clothes. So, how old is your son?"

"Andy?" Thisbe started to run a hand through her hair, felt the VR plug, and dropped her arm for fear of revealing her occupation. "Oh, he's four and a half. How many kids do you have?"

"Two daughters, April and Libby. Eight and ten."

"Do you have pictures?"

Ron patted his pockets. "Sorry, must have left my wallet in the other pair of pants."

"Joint custody?"

"No, my wife died in a car crash."

"I'm sorry." Thisbe reached a hand toward Ron, paused, and drew it back.

"Listen, I'm not very good at this dating thing, but would you like to grab a coffee sometime?"

"Okay." Thisbe blushed. She scribbled her phone number on a scrap of paper and handed it to Ron.

"Great! I'll give you a call in a couple of days."

"Talk to you then." As Thisbe walked down the hallway, her expanding balloon of happiness sprung a leak. Sooner or later she'd have to tell him about her job. Then what would he think? Maybe she shouldn't have been so impulsive. Well, he probably wouldn't call, anyway.

Mahamuni's followers paused on a narrow road on the way to Kumagaya. Two-story homes, rice fields, and greenhouses covered this section of the Kanto Plain. Thisbe lifted her hair so the sweat would evaporate from the back of her neck. Walking in September's heat and humidity had left her blouse damp.

"I was just looking in the guidebook and found this lovely picture." Mahamuni *held the book open to a photo of Mt. Fuji and asked, "What do you see?"*

"Fuji-san, Sensei," Tanaka said.

"And what is Fuji-san?"

"It's a twelve thousand foot mountain," Tanaka said. "I know because I've climbed it twice."

"Who else?" Mahamuni asked. "Saito, what do you see?"

"Four colors of ink on a page that indicate an upside-down cone the color of clouds."

Mahamuni *shook his head. "Ah, Saito, you've spent too much time talking to Zen teachers. Who else?"*

"The image of Japan," Oda said.

"The Goddess Konohannsakuyahime"

"Where Princess Kaguya hides."

"Where Godzilla fought King Kong."

A stranger, a tiny woman in a white sun hat, hovered at the edge of the gathering. Thisbe had not seen her approach and wondered where she came from.

"Those are good," Mahamuni said, "but how about something you think up yourselves?"

"A funnel," Thisbe said.

"A dragon's backbone"

"It looks like a mound of flour on my counter with a well in the center for me to crack an egg into," the new woman said.

Mahamuni *smiled. She took this as permission to join the gathering and sat between Thisbe and Chikako.*

"A flying saucer."

The followers continued until Mahamuni held up a hand for silence.

"Look at the diversity inside your brains. A human being has more neural connections than there are atoms in the universe. Which do you think is richer, the inner world or the outer?"

"The inner world, Sensei," Tanaka said.

"Then why do you chase so hard after things out there? Find a seat."

Thisbe sat on the road's edge, so her legs dangled over the embankment. The rice plants growing in the field below brushed her legs with yellow-green leaves. A small white pickup truck drove by on a parallel road. The driver gave Mahamuni's *followers a quizzical stare before moving on.*

"I want you to sit up straight, close your eyes, and breathe deeply,"

Mahamuni said. "Let the breath relax your muscles."

Thisbe followed the sage's instructions. They were similar to a practice Pastor Nakagawa had her do at the temple.

"Now in your minds picture a treasure chest. It's made of old wood with iron bands to add strength, something like you might see in a pirate movie. Can you see it?"

Thisbe nodded.

"It has no lock. You open the lid. Inside there are gold coins, a silver cup, rings, and emerald necklaces. You've never seen riches sparkle like these. Now imagine something else you love and put it inside, maybe chocolate or ice cream. Don't worry. It will never melt. And if your object is too big to fit inside, make the treasure chest larger. It can be as big as you want it to be."

Thisbe thought of Andy's chess computer and pictured it atop the gold coins.

"Now lift the chest. It's heavy due to the wealth inside, heavier than anything you've ever lifted, but you are strong. Feel the muscles in your arms strain as you raise the treasure chest face level."

Thisbe tried but couldn't feel any tenseness in her arms.

"Bring the treasure to your forehead and hold it to your third eye. Imagine that your head absorbs the treasure chest. No matter how big, your head can contain it. Once you have the treasure inside you, stop and think how wonderful it is that you and everyone else have this treasure inside that no one can take away."

Mahamuni's followers held this image for ten minutes before he told them to stop.

"I call this the treasure meditation," Mahamuni said. "Practice it twice a day to remind yourselves where your true treasure is. Some of you may say, 'But, Sensei, I don't have time.' If you think about how much time you waste chasing externals, you'll realize that practicing the treasure meditation will actually save you time. Let's take a ten-minute break and then get back on the road."

Thisbe stood and stretched.

The new woman asked Chikako, "Who are you people?"

"We're followers of Mahamuni. We're walking the Old Nakasendo Road on our way to a rally in Kyoto."

"That sounds interesting. Can I tag along?" The new woman talked with her jaw clenched.

Margot! Thisbe felt like she did the time her mother caught her with Jimmy Rogers's hand up her blouse. If only Margot had come during a Mahamuni lecture that was more immune to ridicule! Thisbe's embarrassment turned to anger. How dare Margot join her VR session without permission! She could ruin everything just when it was getting good. Thisbe balled her fists and looked away.

"What's your name?" Chikako asked the newcomer.

"Mariko"

Mahamuni gave Margot permission to join, so Thisbe could do nothing. Perhaps Mahamuni's influence would do Margot good. The followers resumed their journey and walked through a town where a stone fence separated a small Buddhist temple from the sidewalk. Worshippers had draped red cloths around a statue of Jizo to make a hat and bib. When the line of walkers had spread out enough for privacy, Margot caught up with Thisbe.

"Thisbe, it's me, Margot. I hope you don't mind me crashing your VR session like this. I was a little hurt when you didn't come back to mine and wanted to see what was so important."

"I'm sorry. I should have told you. I'm very wrapped up in this. I just wish you would have asked before joining."

"Do you want me to go?"

Thisbe wanted to scream, "Get lost!" but instead muttered, "No, just ask first next time."

With Mahamuni's teaching finished for the day, there was nothing more to do except walk. Thisbe's image of the treasure chest evaporated from her thoughts in the heat of her annoyance. She tried unsuccessfully to bring it back and blamed Margot for that failure too. Clouds gathered. Around 4:00 they dumped rain on the pilgrims. While the downpour soaked Thisbe, Tanaka and Saito opened umbrellas. Mahamuni also had an umbrella, but he gave his to Chikako. Chastened by the sage's example, Saito thrust his into Thisbe's hands. Tanaka gave his to Mariko and seemed to linger too long with his hands brushing her fingers. The umbrella shielded Thisbe's upper body, but her legs got soaked. She squished onward in her soggy shoes for another hour before they stopped in a hotel for the night.

Thisbe left VR and returned to the sheets that were damp with spent lust. As was her habit, she used the bidet and showered before taking Andy home.

CHAPTER 11

Ron called after all. On the night of their get-together, Thisbe parallel parked up the street from her rendezvous. She'd left Andy in Mandy's care. The colorful slit skirt she'd wrapped around her hips wasn't on the Divine Embrace's approved product list, but sometimes a girl had to make exceptions when dating. The church hierarchy could be a bit stodgy at times.

She paused while feeding coins into the parking meter. Should she be doing this? Maybe she should just lie about her job. It'd be breaking one of Divine Embrace's commandments, though. Oh, why did dating have to be so complicated? Why hadn't she told him she wasn't interested? She looked at the car keys in her purse and had an urge to drive away.

Thisbe took a deep breath to still her jitters, dropped another coin into the meter, and turned the knob. Two hours, that ought to be enough. She passed a record shop and an organic food store with vegetables painted on the exterior before reaching the café. From outside she saw him through the plate glass window. He sat at a table, held the coffee cup to his face, and absentmindedly stared over its lip into the distance. Thisbe's knees went weak. He was so handsome. She felt warm and gooey inside like a brownie right out of the oven. There was no way around it. She would have to tell him.

Thisbe pushed open the door and entered. Dark, rustic wood covered the walls. The cakes, apple pies, and large cookies displayed by the counter looked like they'd been made from scratch. A woman in a light-blue leotard top leaned on the counter. Her blonde hair hung in two thick braids. Thisbe made her way to Ron's table and sat across from him.

"Hi."

"Hi." Ron set down his cup. "Have any trouble finding the place?"

"No, I'll be back in a minute. I'm going to go order. Can I get you anything?"

Ron shook his head.

Thisbe ordered a soy milk latte. The carrot cake looked so good that she ordered some even though she knew she shouldn't. The woman at the counter cut a slice as thick as an unabridged dictionary. Thisbe took two forks and carried her prize back to the table.

"You got the carrot cake," Ron said.

Thisbe nodded.

"Gets 'em every time."

"You bring all your dates here?" Thisbe asked.

"There haven't been that many," Ron said. "Mostly I sit here and watch people. I've seen the carrot cake do in a lot of girls."

"I bet." Thisbe pushed Ron's fork across the table.

"So how's Dr. Barry's advice working for you?" Ron said.

"Don't ask. The less I talk to Alf the better. He saps my energy." Thisbe sipped her latte. "Your wife, what was she like?"

Ron's fork froze halfway between the carrot cake and his mouth.

"I'm sorry. I shouldn't have asked," Thisbe said. "We don't have to talk about it."

"No, it's all right. Debra was a folk singer. I met her at a local nightclub where she played. She gave up her career after Libby was born. Blonde, clear skin, she was happy. Had a wonderful voice."

"Must be hard raising two daughters without their mother."

"It's tough, but they're great kids. They're always trying to fix me up with their favorite teachers."

The conversation stalled. Thisbe grasped at topics to talk about, but the feeling she'd blown it made it hard to think. Ron asked Thisbe's advice about what to get April for her birthday. Then cake eaten and coffee cups drained they waited to see who would risk speaking first. Ron took a chance.

"Rebecca Salad, a folk singer Debra liked, is playing at the Yellow Door next Friday. I have two tickets, and I ..."

"Listen, Ron, there's something you need to know about me." Thisbe took a breath. She leaned closer and whispered, "I'm a cyber hooker."

Ron sat back. Thisbe read disapproval in his expression.

"It's the only way I can support my son." Thisbe gathered her purse. "I guess I don't blame you." It felt as if the room filled with toxic gas that scalded her self-esteem. She turned to make a break toward the exit.

"Wait." Ron sighed and ran a hand over his scalp. "I already have the tickets. Let's just go and have a good time."

Thisbe paused. "All right." She smiled. "I'll see you then."

The contraceptive Thisbe took suppressed menstruation so she could work during the weeks she would have had her period. Her upcoming date with Ron occupied her thoughts so that even in virtual reality she imagined nestling against his cheek and running a finger down his chest. It occurred to her that daydreaming in VR about the real world must be some kind of metaphysical first. Her upcoming date raised another philosophical problem – when to sleep with him. Doing so early would make her seem cheap, but given Thisbe's occupation delaying the deed seemed hypocritical.

Even though Margot hadn't returned to Thisbe's VR sessions, the character she'd introduced remained. A college student on summer break, Mariko grew so enthusiastic about Mahamuni that she decided to go all the way to Kyoto. Since she came from a wealthy family, she wasn't an economic burden. After Mariko a half-dozen others joined Mahamuni's band of followers as well.

On Friday Thisbe finished at 7:00 p.m. She had enough time to stop home for a quick bite before meeting Ron at the club. She'd left Andy with his father, cleaned her apartment, and changed the sheets. While Thisbe put on her lipstick, she went through her mental checklist: presentable underwear, antiviral suppository (courtesy of Maya Escorts), and toothbrush. She was ready for action.

Thisbe drove downtown, paid a fortune to park, and walked a block to the Yellow Door. Fifty people waited on the sidewalk to get in. An awning sheltered the club's namesake yellow entrance. Thisbe picked Ron out of the line and greeted him with a quick hug.

"You didn't park in the pay lot, did you?" Ron asked.

"Afraid so."

"Sorry, I meant to tell you the building supply store lets you park free after hours."

The line started moving. When they passed the burly man at the door, Ron handed their tickets to a busty woman in a Yellow Door T-shirt who stamped their wrists. Thisbe and Ron filed past the bar and took one of the small tables against the wall. The loud recorded music discouraged conversation, perhaps by design.

"Drink?" Ron hollered in Thisbe's ear.

"Club soda, please."

Ron muscled through the crowd to wait for a bartender's attention. Thisbe examined the yellowed band posters peeling from the walls and wondered how long the club had been in business. The seats filled up forcing late arrivals to stand around the dance floor. A woman in leather pants leaned on the wall behind Thisbe and talked on a cell phone. Thisbe marveled that the woman could hear.

Ron returned with their drinks moments before the warm-up band played the first set. They were some group from Detroit fronted by a lead singer with thick glasses and tiger stripes painted on his guitar. Over-amplified music echoed from the walls. A group of ecstatic fans rushed the dance floor to gyrate to the sonic mishmash. A blonde woman in tight red Capri pants pointed to Ron and whispered to her friend.

Ron set down his beer and leaned close to Thisbe. "Want to dance?"

"Okay."

Ron led her by the hand into the crowd of writhing bodies. In Thisbe's experience most men danced by rocking their shoulders in awkward time to the beat. If they moved their feet at all, it was as if they wore fifty-pound concrete shoes. In contrast Ron integrated his feet, arms, and hips into a fluid unit. On occasion he twirled Thisbe by the arm, caught her in an embrace, and executed a stylish pass to set her back on her feet. In spite of her disdain for the music, Thisbe began enjoying herself. Her heart rate sped with the exhilaration pulsing through her limbs. After the band finished its set, she and Ron returned winded to the table.

"Where'd you learn to dance like that?" Thisbe wiped the sweat off her forehead with the back of her hand.

"I have two older sisters. When I was a teenager, they hammered me to learn their favorite dance steps."

A half-hour later a tall woman took the stage. She sat on a stool so her long blonde hair hung over the guitar she cradled in her lap.

"How you doing tonight?" Rebecca Salad said. "This one's called 'Word Salad.'"

Rebecca began to play a tune that sounded familiar to Thisbe. Perhaps it had been on the radio. As the singer swayed the guitar to the rhythm, the spotlight's glare reflected from its polished surface. Rebecca had a good voice, but Thisbe found none of her lyrics memorable. The singer captivated Ron. When he noticed Thisbe watching him, he smiled and took her hand. His gentle fingers stroked her palm throughout Rebecca Salad's performance. Thisbe thought of leaving before the encore but didn't broach the idea since Ron so obviously enjoyed the music. With the final song completed, the last bit of applause dribbled from the audience. Ron and Thisbe joined those leaving. Like a wave the surging crowd picked them up, carried them out the door, and set them down on the sidewalk outside the club.

"I'll walk you to your car." Ron threw an arm around Thisbe's shoulders.

She slipped a hand around his waist and drew close to his body. As they walked, their hips bumped every few steps. They reached the car. Thisbe fished for her keys in her purse.

"Thanks for joining me tonight." Ron leaned forward and placed a tentative kiss on Thisbe's lips.

She pressed her body to his and clasped her hands behind his back to pull him to her. The two fell back against the car. Thisbe opened her mouth to receive Ron's tongue. She felt his erection strain against her belly.

"Seems like a shame to end a wonderful evening early," Ron whispered.

Thisbe rested her head against his shoulder. Good sense cautioned her to wait, but patience lost the argument to Ron's delicate eyelashes and the warm press of his body on hers. Didn't she have a right to be happy? Thisbe straightened and looked into Ron's face.

"Do you want to come back to my place for coffee?"

They set off in a caravan of two cars. Thisbe raced up Aurora. Only her fear of losing Ron in the rearview mirror balanced the weight of her anticipation pressing her foot on the accelerator. She got off on Forty-fifth and turned down Freemont. After parking she directed Ron to one of the visitor spaces.

Together they trudged up the stairs. Ron's insistent kisses on the nape of her neck made it hard for Thisbe to fit her key into the lock. The door sprung open. The two lovers burst into the apartment as if propelled by a sudden release of compressed air. Thisbe fumbled behind her for the light switch while Ron pinned her to the wall with open-mouthed kisses. His hot, wet mouth tasted faintly of fennel. Thisbe turned on the lights, pulled Ron's shirttail out of his pants, and caressed his hips with eager fingers. They retreated to the living room. Thisbe swept Andy's toy truck from the couch. It fell to the floor and lost a wheel. The lovers fell onto the upholstery. Ron's hands found the clasp and unhooked Thisbe's bra. She lifted her blouse over her head and let it fall to the floor near Andy's broken toy.

"Hold on a minute." Thisbe went to the bathroom, inserted the antiviral suppository, and returned naked moments later.

Ron was strangely passive when she unzipped him and peeled his pants from his legs. She pushed him back onto the couch. Then grasping his sex she mounted and guided him inside her. Ron reached for her breasts and pinched her nipples between his thumbs and forefingers. Thisbe closed her eyes and let the sensations wash over her as she rocked her hips. She started slowly at first and then increased the tempo until Ron stiffened and shuddered with climax. In an act of playful cruelty Thisbe continued to move her hips until the pain forced Ron to grasp her to a stop. Thisbe collapsed on top of him, placing her head on his chest. His heart thudded in her ear.

"God," Ron said, "that was much better than when you're comatose!"

Thisbe's feelings instantly hardened as if they were warm vapor freezing into tiny blocks of ice. "What do you mean?"

"After you told me you were a cyber hooker, I thought I'd support your business."

His revelation hit Thisbe like a punch to the gut.

"Get out!" She sprang off him and cowered by the bedroom door.

"What's your problem?"

The question was so outrageous! How could he even ask it?

"You're like some kind of rapist, you sick pervert! If you want to date me, we have sex when I say, not before. Now get out of here!"

Wearing an expression of weary annoyance Ron pulled on his clothing. On the way out he hissed, "You need to face facts. You're nothing but a high-class whore."

Thisbe slammed the door and turned the lock. When she heard Ron's car drive away, she slid down the wall and collapsed sobbing to the floor. Thisbe pulled the phone cord. It fell from the counter. She lifted the phone from its cradle and dialed. After five rings Margot answered.

"Margot," Thisbe whimpered.

"Thisbe, what's wrong?"

"This guy," Thisbe blubbered. "He was so handsome and considerate, and he turned out to be a customer."

"Didn't you know?"

"Only after." Thisbe ripped a paper towel from the dispenser and blew her nose.

"Oh, honey, I'm sorry. Do you want to come over here?"

"No, I'll be okay," Thisbe sniffled.

"Men can be such jerks. You can't change them, so why even bother?"

"What do you mean?" Thisbe asked.

"Lovers in VR never misbehave. They remember your birthday, give compliments, and don't complain when you ask for oral sex."

"Margot!"

"So why are you looking for the perfect man out there when you can find him at work?"

"I guess you're right," Thisbe said.

"You sure you don't want to come over? I've got Tyler, so I can't come over there."

"No, I'll be all right. And Margot, thanks." Thisbe cradled the phone and took a shower.

CHAPTER 12

Anne Simmons hung up the telephone and swiveled her chair to face Thisbe. "Thisbe, what can I do for you?"

"I have a problem." Thisbe took a breath while wondering how to begin. "This guy I've been dating. He's a real jerk, and I'm afraid he'll come here and hurt me while I'm in VR."

"Is he a customer?"

Thisbe nodded. "I didn't know, or else I never would have..."

"I see." Anne picked up the phone. "Melanie, would you send Kyle and Bruno in here?"

There was a knock on the door. Two burly doormen entered.

"You want us, Ms. Simmons?" the shorter one asked.

"Guys, Thisbe has an angry ex-boyfriend we need to keep out of the building."

"His name is Ron Murphy," Thisbe said.

"What's he look like?" the shorter doorman asked.

Thisbe gave a description.

"Consider it done," the taller man said. The two left.

"Anything else?" Anne asked.

"No," Thisbe said. "Thank you."

"Not at all," Anne said. "Anything to take care of our dream girls."

Moments after Thisbe and Chikako had entered their motel room after a long day of hiking, a knock came from the door. Thisbe answered.

"Thisbe, come quickly!" Saito said. "The master wants to see us." His flushed, boyish face looked almost comical in its eagerness and worry.

Thisbe followed him to another room where Mahamuni sat in his characteristic gray slacks, thin belt, and white shirt.

"Ah, Thisbe, Saito, come in."

The visitors sat across from the sage. A glass filled with water occupied the table.

"I spoke the other day about the treasure chest of the mind. Did you find it helpful?"

Both Thisbe and Saito nodded.

"Good. Some teachings are meant for the masses. Others, the esoteric ones, are reserved for those who might develop a deeper understanding. I think the two of you are ready to see the real treasure of the mind. Observe." Mahamuni took a needle from his pocket and placed it in the glass so it floated on the water's surface. *"There's nothing special here. It's due to surface tension, the same effect that lets water spiders walk on a pond's surface. Now watch the needle."*

Thisbe stared at the glass. The needle vanished. She turned to Saito, Mahamuni, and back to the glass.

"Now," Mahamuni said, *"use the treasure chest of the mind and bring it back."*

Thisbe and Saito gaped at one another. Mahamuni might as well have placed an unconscious man on the table and asked them to perform a heart transplant with a pocketknife. She didn't even know where to begin.

"Don't know how, huh?" Mahamuni chuckled. *"I'll show you. The talent can only be passed directly from teacher to student, like one candle lights another. Ladies first. Please sit quietly, Thisbe."*

Thisbe straightened and slowed her breathing. After a few minutes she felt Mahamuni's mind guiding hers like a hand moving her hand in a direction she hadn't known about. Thisbe plucked the needle from the ether and returned it to the glass. It sank to the bottom.

"A little more gently next time. Your turn, Saito."

Thisbe watched the glass. Once again the needle vanished.

"We'll practice again tomorrow. When the time is right, Saito will share this teaching with the world, and Thisbe will assist. Until then, don't speak of this to anyone."

"Not even Tanaka?" Saito tried to suppress a smile.

"Tanaka is too busy right now." Mahamuni stroked his chin. *"But you're right, Saito. We should probably have him join us once he has time."*

Saito grunted and nodded. Soon Thisbe returned to her motel room, exited VR, and found a needle on the nightstand beside her bed.

"Mom, what's this building?" Andy asked.

"It's a library. They keep lots of books here. Now, a lot of people will be reading, so you have to be quiet. If you're good, I'll get you a library card so you can borrow any book you want."

"Okay."

Thisbe took Andy's hand and led him up the granite steps. They timed their entrance into the revolving door, stepped forward as the partition passed, and exited into the library's marble interior.

"That was fun, mom," Andy said. "Can we do it again?"

Thisbe and Andy jumped back and made another revolution. A woman at the checkout desk smiled. Thisbe and Andy passed the reference section and entered a side room where students typed at computers. Thisbe took a seat next to a paunchy man with long, flyaway hair. Andy sat on her knee to watch.

Thisbe accessed a search engine and entered the phrases "Divine Embrace" and "esoteric." The search came up empty. She replaced "esoteric" with "hidden teaching" and surprisingly got only one hit. It linked to a Japanese university's comparative religion department. Thisbe accessed the site. The screen filled with squiggles. She clicked the translate icon.

After Mahamuni's passing his two lieutenants, Ichiro Tanaka and Hiroshi Saito, vied for control of the movement. Saito's followers hinted that he should lead due to his knowledge of Mahamuni's hidden teachings. His tragic death in an automobile accident solidified Tanaka's control. Divine Embrace headquarters in Iwama Prefecture denies the existence of any hidden teachings calling them "rumors spread by those trying to discredit Mahamuni's legacy."

Thisbe stared at the screen. A secret teaching! Her heart beat faster. With that knowledge she could travel the world demonstrating the truth of Mahamuni's message. Who knew what kind of progress humanity could achieve? Of course, all that travel would complicate Andy's schooling. Still, seeing the world would be good for the boy.

Andy tugged her arm. "Can we go look at books now?"

Thisbe dropped out of her reverie and looked at her son. "Okay."

Andy selected a picture book about Vikings. The librarian set him up with a card and told Thisbe the book was due in three weeks. They returned to the parking lot. After Thisbe buckled Andy into his booster seat, she drove east on Pine. Engrossed in his book Andy ceased his usual banter. Thisbe turned on the radio to fill the silence. An occasional song interrupted the barrage of commercials that blared from the speakers. Thisbe passed the convention center and maneuvered into the left lane.

When she saw the green and white freeway entrance sign, she turned on her blinker and got into the entrance lane. The color vanished from her path as if someone had brushed the scene with diluted ink. The icy enema of dread filled Thisbe's guts with its awful payload. She jerked the car into the right lane. A driver laid on her horn.

Andy looked up from his book. "What's wrong with that lady, mom?"

"Some people have bad manners when they drive, Andy."

Thisbe accelerated up a hill, took a left on Denny, and followed it back to Aurora. She turned onto the ramp and ran into a clogged river of brake lights inching north. Thisbe exhaled and tapped the steering wheel. What could she have been thinking?

"Look's like there's been a big pileup on the interstate," the radio announcer said. "Police say a big rig jackknifed and caused a chain reaction collision. Emergency crews are at the scene. Motorists are advised to take a different route."

That night after she'd put Andy to bed, Thisbe sat alone in her bedroom and watched the glass on her nightstand. It had taken several tries to float the needle from her sewing basket on the water's surface. A single candle filled the room with a comforting glow.

Thisbe rested against the chair back and breathed deeply to relax. No matter how hard she tried to reproduce the feeling of snatching the needle in VR, she couldn't affect the needle in the glass. Thisbe tried for an hour. The candle burned lower and sputtered out. When Thisbe turned on the light, the needle was still there.

CHAPTER 13

Thisbe started the following day's VR session in the dark with an alarm clock screaming. She sat up in bed and fumbled with the device to turn off the noise — 5:00 a.m. Chikako turned on the light and squinted.

"Morning so early?" Chikako stretched her arms into a Y and yawned. "Would you go wake Mariko so she can join us at the treasure meditation?"

While Chikako primped in front of the bathroom mirror, Thisbe dressed and went to wake Mariko. The hallway was deserted. Thisbe passed a groaning ice machine and stopped in front of Mariko's room. No light came from under the door. She knocked. No one answered. Thisbe knocked louder. No response. Thisbe shrugged and returned to her room.

She and Chikako hurried to the meeting room, where Mahamuni's bleary-eyed followers waited outside the locked door. With rumpled clothes and uncombed hair they yawned, stretched, or simply stared vacantly. Saito brought an attendant who removed a jangling key chain from the pocket of his overalls and unlocked the door. The employee stepped inside, switched on the light, and gave a cursory bow before hurrying off for a cup of tea.

Thisbe helped the others arrange chairs in a circle and took a seat next to Chikako. Saito placed a candle in the center and turned off the electric lights. Thisbe straightened, slowed her breathing, and began visualizing the treasure chest. She concentrated on details - a splinter, the grain of the wood, and a patch of rust - to make it seem more real. The door opened, sending a wash of light from the hall through the room. Tanaka entered and rushed to an empty seat.

Thisbe went back to the treasure chest and imagined how she'd move her body close to lift it. The door opened again. Mariko entered and sat down. Thisbe returned to the visualization. She imagined squatting to lift the chest.

"Stop fidgeting!" Tanaka bellowed. "Sit still and concentrate!"

Though not aimed at her, the outburst sent a shiver through Thisbe. Anger followed. How dare he yell like that! Mahamuni would never put up with that kind of arrogance if he were here. Thisbe let the rage cool and got back to the practice. She pictured straining with her legs to lift the chest and managed to squeeze it into her forehead. Now what? Her knee itched. The muscles in her back cramped. If she moved, Tanaka would yell again. Her eyes darted to Saito, who showed no sign of ending the practice soon.

The meditation period dragged on. Suddenly the scene melted into the intimacy room at Maya Escorts. Trapped inside her paralyzed body

74

Thisbe watched Ron Murphy pull his golf shirt over his head.

"I don't need to take you out to dinner." He unbuckled his jeans and stroked his penis hard. "I can use you any time I want."

He approached the bed and rammed his penis into her like a dagger. Automatically Thisbe's body responded to the violent thrusts of his hips as if it were an amusement park ride.

"Stop!" Saito clapped his hands.

Thisbe was back in the meeting room. At first she was too stunned to move. The others stretched. She stood and massaged her stiff back.

"Let's meet at the entrance in a half hour," Saito said. "Mahamuni wants to get an early start. We'll pick up breakfast on the way."

Thisbe headed back to her room. The greasy worm of disgust crawled down Thisbe's throat and lodged in her belly. She wanted to scream and run, but where? A maid in a pastel uniform bowed, smiled, and uttered a cheerful "Good morning." Thisbe unlocked the door, retrieved her backpack from the closet, and threw it on the bed. She removed her spare pants from the hanger and began to fold them. Halfway through she changed her mind, wadded them into a ball, and stuffed them inside. Thisbe stared at the backpack's open mouth. Should she summon Keiko and try to wake up, or was her mind playing tricks on her?

"Hey, you daydreaming?" Chikako shook Thisbe's shoulder. "Let's go. We don't want to keep the others waiting."

Thisbe couldn't eat. When Mariko handed out soy milk and rice cakes, Thisbe stuffed them in her backpack for later. As the line of Mahamuni's followers made their way down the sidewalk, her disgust turned to rage. With each step she imagined stomping Ron's smug face. Then she turned her spite to the two doormen. No matter how big they were, they wouldn't stand up to the hot pulses of hatred shooting through her body.

"Thisbe, are you all right?" Mahamuni's concerned eyes looked into hers.

"I'm sorry, Sensei. Just some unfinished business from back home."

"You can't do anything about that now, Thisbe. Attend to what's at hand."

"Yes, Sensei."

They walked until lunchtime. Thisbe noticed for the first time that mountains had appeared on the east and west horizons. As usual Mahamuni gave a lecture. Thisbe tried to concentrate, but the winds of uncertainty and betrayal scattered her thoughts. She hoped she at least looked like she was paying attention.

When Thisbe emerged from VR, she unplugged the cable, showered, and hurried into her clothes. With her blouse tucked sloppily in her pants, she stomped down the hall toward Anne's office. The maid smiled and waved from an open doorway and then piled dirty sheets into the laundry cart. Thisbe descended the stairs and rounded the corner to Anne's door. She lifted her fist to knock and paused. How could she pay back her loan if Anne fired her? Surely the doormen would have stopped Ron from entering. Maybe she'd better see the doctor before making wild accusations. Thisbe lowered her hand.

She backtracked to the clinic, spoke to the nurse, and found herself once again staring at the uterus poster in the exam room. Dr. Gibbs didn't keep her waiting long.

"What seems to be the trouble, Thisbe?"

"I had another awareness episode during VR." Thisbe's voice broke as she recounted her ugly experience.

Dr. Gibbs nodded and let her finish. She wiped her tears with her sleeve.

"Well, let's start by checking your implant." He wheeled a cart to the exam couch. Before attaching the lead to her skull, Dr. Gibbs washed his hands in the sink and dried them on a paper towel. "Lie still while I run a diagnostic."

The clean hands of science twiddling knobs and taking readings reassured Thisbe. If anything were wrong, Dr. Gibbs would find it.

"You can sit up now." Dr. Gibbs examined the printout. "I don't see anything wrong with your implant." He scribbled on a prescription pad, tore off the top sheet, and handed it to Thisbe. "This if for Ambitol. Take one capsule when you get to work. It'll keep you from having these experiences for the next ten days. As for the long-term solution I think you need to examine some emotional issues. I recommend Joan Cavendish. Let me get you her phone number." Dr. Gibbs stepped out and returned with a business card that he handed to Thisbe. "Give Joan a call. She's helped a lot of our employees. If you have any more trouble, let me know."

"Why were you so upset when you learned that Ron had had intercourse with you while you were in virtual reality?" asked Dr. Joan Cavendish, a woman whose age was hard to pin down. Her gray, kinky hair argued for more years, but her unlined face, slim body, and blue eyes that danced with childlike mirth made her seem younger.

Thisbe looked at the books cramming the office's plywood and cinderblock shelves. Why would someone with so much education ask such an obvious question? Thisbe's wounded feelings were ready to spit an answer, but finding the words proved as difficult as molding a brick out of air. Wasn't sex how she earned her living? And why should she treat Ron differently than the other customers? A cascade of guilt and justifications bounced through the pinball machine of Thisbe's mind. She turned to face Dr. Cavendish and dropped her eyes.

"It just didn't seem fair, I guess."

"Not fair in what way?"

"He could do anything he wants with me, and I don't have any control."

"No, it wasn't fair," Dr. Cavendish said. "You didn't have a chance to feel emotionally safe. For you, relationships will be a challenge. You need to establish clear ground rules from the very beginning."

"How do I do that?"

"It's tough." Dr. Cavendish sighed. "Many girls don't date while they're working. Dealing with a partner's issues proves too difficult. In those relationships that do succeed, both partners have done a lot of work on themselves. You can improve your chances by clarifying how you feel about sex. Once you feel comfortable with your body, your issues won't cloud your relationships, and you can deal with a partner more effectively."

"What if I find out I can't do the work?"

"That's a risk you'll have to take."

"All right," Thisbe said. "Let's begin."

CHAPTER 14

Thisbe took the pill before undressing and jacking in to VR. *By the time they'd reached Karuizawa, Mahumuni's followers had grown to fifteen. The unfortunate Mr. Kobayashi had begged off, citing a sprained ankle. One of the newcomers, a man in his twenties named Hideo Watanabe, wore a long-sleeved shirt that he kept buttoned to his collar. In spite of the shade provided by the trees, it was still too hot for this. Watanabe's strange habit gave rise to all sorts of speculation.*

"Do you think he has some kind of scar or hideous rash?" Thisbe asked.

"Most likely a yakuza*," Chikako said.*

"A gangster?" Mariko raised her brushstroke eyebrows and spoke without moving her jaw. "But he looks so innocent."

"Looks can be deceiving," Chikako said. "Better stay away from him. He's up to no good."

Thisbe looked at the ski lifts lining the mountains. Most of the buildings, including the factory outlet malls, resembled Swiss chalets. Groups of drunken salarymen in golf shirts roamed the sidewalks and clutched bags of merchandise. Hotels in Karuizawa were pricey, so Mahamuni's followers walked another four hours before finding a place to stay. Chikako felt like she was coming down with a cold, so Thisbe shared a room with Mariko. Saito called at 8:00. Thisbe followed him to their audience with Mahamuni. This time they sat on green tatami mats in a Japanese-style room with a brush painting of a heron on the wall. The practice was the same — the glass, the needle, and Mahamuni with his shirtsleeves rolled up.

"Saito, send the needle away."

Saito stared at the glass and squinted, until he was almost cross-eyed, but nothing happened.

"Let me help," Mahamuni said. "Reach with your mind this way." The needle vanished. "Now, Thisbe, bring it back."

Thisbe tried to reproduce the feeling from the last time, but it was like playing the piano with oven mitts.

"Like this," Mahamuni said.

Thisbe's thoughts felt numb. Mahamuni's guidance was only a dull throb.

Mahamuni shook his head. "Are you taking some kind of medicine?"

Thisbe nodded.

"Then there's no point in pushing it. You may be wondering what's happening

and why this practice is relevant," Mahamuni said. "There's a marvelous space that interpenetrates everything in this world – a gold-plated statue, a bowl of rice, even the sewage under the city streets. I'm teaching you to find this space. Right now, you're like blind beggars who've stumbled into a dark room. You feel around for something new but can't sense anything beyond the reach of your fingers. Eventually you will open your eyes and find the consciousness that inhabits this space. This consciousness loves all beings but does not interfere. I am not the first to discuss this. Others have called this consciousness God, Allah, the Buddha nature, and other names.

"So why teach this practice? To save the world. Greed is destroying the planet. The antidote to this poison is awareness of the sacredness of ordinary things. Yet it's too much to ask people merely to believe in the miracle of their everyday lives. We need to show them. That's where you come in."

When Thisbe returned to her room, Mariko was gone.

"Keep your clothes on – Party Today."

The sign greeted Thisbe at Maya Escort's employee entrance when she showed up at work the next day. She'd forgotten about the celebration of their fifteenth year in business. Thisbe pulled the door. It didn't budge. She found the appropriate key on her key chain and let herself in.

Banners and balloons decorated the walls, but the real celebrations were taking place in VR. Thisbe entered the customer lounge, an area normally forbidden to sex workers. It looked like a drawing room from a nineteenth-century novel, with dark wood paneling, a billiard table, and plush carpet. The man who normally stood behind the bar to pour drinks into crystal glasses had joined the other employees who lacked neural implants. Wearing old-style VR visors and gloves, they sat in chairs and couches.

Thisbe climbed the stairs, found an empty room, and jacked in. After exchanging pleasantries with Keiko, Thisbe found herself on a vast plain of gray rock. The earth hung like a golf ball-sized sapphire on a rich, black velvet sky. Thousands of stars glittered with the cold light of diamonds. Thisbe spotted a cluster of people fifty yards ahead and took a step toward them. Due to the reduced gravity, she traveled farther than she'd expected. It was kind of fun. Thisbe hopped and covered ten feet. She arrived at the gathering in no time. The men wore tuxedos. Women wore rich floor-length gowns that draped over their bodies like togas.

"Thisbe, glad you could make it," Anne Simmons said. "Would you care for champagne?"

Thisbe nodded.

Anne gestured to the pyramid of fluted glasses by the buffet table. "How do you like the decorations?"

"They look great." Thisbe retrieved a glass and sipped. A refreshing dryness cleansed her palate. When it's not real, you can always afford the best.

"We wanted to do something special and thought, 'Why not the moon?' Of course, the great thing about VR is we don't need those bulky space suits. You wouldn't believe the cost of the link to network in the European sites. Well, I'll let you mingle. Be sure to try golfing. It looks like a lot of fun." Anne stumbled off with the awkward gait of someone without an implant, to greet a new arrival. Her body moved more like a statue on wheels than a human being.

A robot carrying a tray of appetizers approached. "Care for an egg roll?" It asked with a mechanical voice.

Thisbe shook her head. The robot rolled off toward the other guests. Thisbe looked around for a familiar face. Three women nearby were having a hushed conversation.

"What did the police say?" a brunette with a British accent asked.

"Oh," a French woman replied. "The bastard's lawyers got to Marianne and hushed her up." She noticed Thisbe paying attention and spoke up. "So, how's your friend Jason, anyway?"

The other women looked at Thisbe and sidled away for more privacy. Thisbe spotted Margot and waved. She was wearing a red dress and talking to a tall, dark-skinned woman whose features seemed to glow as if she had a fluorescent light under her skin. The black woman wore a sequined, turquoise dress. Thisbe made her way over to them.

"Thisbe, how are you?" Margot clasped Thisbe's forearms. "This is Solange. She's originally from the Ivory Coast but now works in our Amsterdam bureau."

"How do you do?" Solange spoke with an accent. She pressed her face to each of Thisbe's cheeks and made a kissing sound.

"I meant to ask," Margot said. "How did it go with that man you broke up with?"

"Well, I spoke to Anne, and she told Kyle and Bruno not to let him into the house." Her awareness of Ron in the intimacy room felt too raw to mention. It was probably all in her head, anyway.

"I see." Both Solange and Margot avoided Thisbe's eyes as if she were a burn victim with only hours to live.

"What are we talking about men for? This is supposed to be a party," Margot said.

"What good are men, anyway? They only take your money." Solange finished her champagne and set it on top of the Apollo 11 lunar module with all the others.

"Solange, you're starting to sound like Vanessa." Margot winked.

"Or Nancy, Jan, or Leslie. You have to admit the idea has some appeal, being with someone who understands what you're going through."

"Did I hear someone call my name?" a statuesque blonde with close-cropped hair asked. Her gown's plunging neckline revealed shoulders that looked toned by years of practice with a rowing team.

"We were just wondering if Jan was going to make it," Margot said.

"No, she had to go to the dentist."

A man moved with the agility of one with an implant to the center of the gathering and raised his hand for silence. He had a solid build, ruddy skin, and hair graying at the temples.

"Thank you for coming today. I'm Wim DeVries, CEO of Maya Escorts. What started fifteen years ago as a harebrained idea has, through the work of ME's employees and dream girls, developed into a multinational enterprise. They say imitation is the highest form of flattery. ME must be doing something right since a half-dozen copycats have sprung up in the last two years.

"But claims of 'We did it first' don't guarantee success in the marketplace. To stay ahead we must innovate. I'd like to tell you about two projects that are key to our strategic vision of ME's future. The first is a wireless connection. Maartin Reinis and Daniel Short at the University of Delft are researching the use of infrared or microwave to carry VR cues. As you might expect, several problems remain. The application is years away, but when it succeeds it will free our dream girls from their tethers.

"The next project is even more far out. Consider a customer's experience. It's physically satisfying, but how can we make the experience more realistic? What if while the woman was in VR, part of her brain was available to make conversation and perform any of the customer's special requests? To him it would be virtually identical to a natural encounter, but the woman would be in VR and would have no memory of the event. Neurologists have long known that different parts of the brain can act independently. I can't say much about the current research except that we have sunk considerable resources into it and the results look promising. Even the military is interested in our research.

"Anyway that should give you a picture of where we're going. If even a fraction of our goals work out, ME's second fifteen years will be even more exciting than its first."

The attendees applauded and went back to their separate conversations. Several executives gathered around the CEO.

"Thisbe," Anne called. "Come over here. There's someone I want you to meet." Anne's image jerked its arm in an awkward imitation of a wave.

Anne stood next to a woman whose long, red hair was held in check by a barrette. An archipelago of freckles dotted her pale skin. She wore a simple silver chain around her right ankle.

"This is Stephanie. She had us buy the Divine Embrace disks you've been watching. I thought you two might have a lot in common. I'll leave you to compare notes." Anne trundled off to fawn over Dr. DeVries.

"I'm really enjoying those disks," Thisbe said. "I mean, to actually be there when Mahamuni came up with his doctrines. It's just fantastic!"

"So, which one are you watching now?" Stephanie asked.

"*Nakasendo Pilgrimage.*"

"Oh that thing." Stephanie shook her head. "I gave up on that one after a few days. The heat, the exhaustion, it just wasn't worth it."

"So, do you go to the temple?" Thisbe asked. "I'm with Pastor Nakagawa's Lynnwood parish."

"I don't get out too much anymore." Stephanie looked over at the Europeans. "Look, I'm glad you like the disks, but having your whole life revolve around them isn't healthy. Take my advice and try a Paris or Hawaii disk. I mean, we're hookers, not saints or yoginis. The only reason we're here is that it's easier to spread our legs for a group of rich guys than it is to get real jobs. The sooner you realize it, the better off you'll be. It was nice meeting you." Stephanie turned and made her way through the crowd.

Thisbe watched Stephanie's back recede toward the European dream girls. What was her problem? Thisbe spotted Vanessa by the champagne and ambled over.

"Enjoy the party so far?"

"They throw one every year," Vanessa said. "Last year it was Egypt. On the tenth anniversary they recreated an ancient Greek theater. The plays were in English, though. This is the first time it's been in outer space."

"So you've been here for at least five years?"

"Seven, I started in Amsterdam back in 35, got Jan involved a year later, and we've been dream girls ever since."

"You must have seen all the disks by now."

"Jan and I cohabit our VR space. In fact," Vanessa leaned close and lowered her voice, "we pay Lester a little something to mingle our sensory streams. That way when we make love, I feel what she feels and vice versa."

"Sounds wonderful."

"I've never been so close to someone."

"All right, everybody, it's time for a game," Anne announced in an amplified voice. She had no microphone, but of course there wasn't a need in this VR. "We're going to have a three-legged race. Dream girls, please grab a partner."

The prostitutes' long flowing gowns transformed into body-hugging leotards. Thisbe glanced at Margot, who had already latched on to Solange. Trying to hide her reluctance, Thisbe turned back to Vanessa.

"Want to try?"

"Sure."

Fifteen pairs of contestants lined up. All were dream girls except for CEO DeVries, who partnered with a Eurasian prostitute with breasts that seemed too large for her petite frame. Thisbe put her left leg into a burlap bag next to Vanessa's right. Vanessa secured the sack with several turns of duct tape before passing the roll to the next pair of contestants.

"The first team to reach the red flag will win a special prize." Anne pointed to a pennant fifty yards in the distance. "On your mark, get set, go!" She blew a whistle.

Right out of the starting block CEO DeVries and his partner

stumbled and fell face first into the lunar regolith. Laughing and spitting dust and micrometeorites, he and his buxom partner rolled around on the lunar surface. Vanessa gripped Thisbe around the waist and shifted her weight.

"Step left. Now right," Vanessa called like a rowing captain.

With Vanessa calling steps, they inched toward their goal. Thisbe hit on the idea of hopping with their free legs while suspending the bound ones. The initial progress was exhilarating. They lifted into space and floated gently to the moon's surface. Unfortunately their height mismatch sent them thirty degrees off course and forced them to zigzag like a tacking sailboat toward their goal. Margot and Solange had similar problems and fell even farther behind. The rest of the contestants mastered the hopping trick. A pair of Teutonic blondes pulled into the lead. Not to be outdone, two North American girls were right behind.

Men in tuxedos leered from the sidelines as sweat dripped down cleavage and molded fabric to shapely bodies. The Germans reached the flag and held it aloft. The North American challengers finished second. Thisbe and Vanessa came in a respectable fourth followed by Margot and Solange. DeVries and the Eurasian struggled mightily to finish last.

Anne awarded the winners a set of keys to an original Apollo lunar buggy, which they promptly drove away. Thisbe followed the others to a driving range, where they swung clubs at golf balls and tried to hit the low-flying satellites that appeared every few minutes. Periodically Vanessa and Margot shouted with joy when they sent a Dunlop crashing through one's solar panels. Due to her poor swing, Thisbe sliced to the left and only ended up littering the Sea of Tranquility with Top Flites. After an hour of frustration, she replaced her driver in the golf bag and went to thank her hosts.

"Glad to have you on our team, Thisbe." Wim DeVries flashed teeth as white as grandma's china and shook her hand.

With the gathering over, Thisbe emerged from VR, disconnected the cable, and went out into the hallway with the others. Some wanted to party on in the customers' lounge with the employees, who were struggling out of their VR helmets, but Thisbe had had enough for the day. She joined the majority, who headed for the parking lot and drove home.

CHAPTER 15

"I talked to Yamamoto-san. He told me he saw the new guy, Watanabe, coming out of the shower. His whole body is covered with tattoos from neck to ankles. Carp, waves, dragons, everything." Chikako took a sip of tea and set her cup down on the motel room table. "I knew he was trouble."

"Maybe Mahamuni's teachings have helped him repent," Thisbe offered.

"Baka! If you believe that, I have a bridge in Okayama to sell you. These criminals took money from my dad. When he didn't pay, they burned down his store. Someone needs to do something."

Saito knocked at the door and collected Thisbe for their lesson with Mahamuni. Once seated in Mahamuni's motel room, Thisbe and Saito stilled their minds with meditation and placed their hands in the complex mudras the sage showed them. Thisbe had not taken her prescription. Although a bit sluggish, her mind felt cleaner than it had the last time. This time there was no treasure chest to imagine. Only the white noise of the air conditioning blanketing the sound of traffic provided any distraction. After forty-five minutes Mahamuni spoke.

"Thisbe, your turn. This time send the needle away."

She watched the sliver of silver floating in the glass before her. Thisbe remembered plucking the needle from the void but couldn't get her mind to move the right way.

"Try, Thisbe. Step outside space and time. The answer's closer than the skin inside your nostril."

Thisbe's shoulders tensed. The comment left her even more brain-locked.

"Like this."

Thisbe felt the gentle tendrils of Mahamuni's thoughts spread over her scalp and reach inside to guide her, but her mind wouldn't move, perhaps due to the lingering effects of the prescription. Mahamuni's thoughts tightened on Thisbe's mind. She felt a pressure build inside her head until it suddenly released. The needle vanished. Exhaustion flowed through Thisbe like a drug. She sagged against the chair's back while Saito undertook the task of bringing the needle back.

Tired and bored, Thisbe looked at the dingy curtains and at the clock ticking toward 9:30. When would this be over? All she wanted was to close her eyes and feel the clean sheets around her. A blue flash and loud pop made her turn to the others. The spot on the table where the glass had been was now a charred circular hole. A mound of molten slag lay on the carpet underneath. The air smelled of ozone.

"Hmm." Mahamuni raised his eyebrows. "Maybe you shouldn't practice unless I'm around."

"The motel's going to charge extra for this," Saito said.

"Hold on a second," Mahamuni said.

A moment later Thisbe shook her head. She stared at a needle floating in a bowl of water atop an intact table. The memory of something bizarre tickled her consciousness like the whisper of a vanished dream at dawn.

"That will be all for tonight," Mahamuni said. "You may go."

On a rare clear day Thisbe relaxed in the sun's warmth. She reached for the baby oil on the cement between her and Margot and smoothed it onto her legs and shoulders until her skin glistened. Margot's backyard wasn't as decadent as her VR world, but Andy's and Tyler's presence more than made up for the lack of X-rated content. The boys sat in a wading pool with two gray, plastic battleships. Splashes accompanied their attempts to mimic the sound of the dreadnaughts' big sixteen-inch guns.

Andy wore a new blue pair of bathing trunks. A year ago he wouldn't have minded sitting in his white skivvies, but recently a modesty gene had kicked in. He'd begun demanding privacy in the bathtub.

Thisbe lifted her iced tea. A drop of condensation made a trail on the cold sweaty glass. She took a drink and smiled. Margot had made it without sugar, the way Thisbe liked.

"So what's with Stephanie, anyway?" Thisbe set the glass down.

"What do you mean?" Margot asked.

"After Anne introduced us at the party, she was really snotty."

"I wouldn't bother with her. She thinks she's too good for the rest of us. That's all."

Thisbe closed her eyes. The bright sunlight filtered through her eyelids to wash her retinas in red. Colors changed to purple and orange. She dreamed of hummingbirds hovering near a flowering agave stalk.

"Mom! Mom!"

Drops of cold water fell on her belly. Thisbe opened her eyes. Andy held an electronic device too close to her face for her to eyes to focus.

"Look what Tyler has. It's a Deep Blue 2100 chess computer

game. Can I get one too?"

"Andy, first you shouldn't touch that when you're wet. You'll ruin it. And second, I bought you one last month."

"No you didn't!"

"Andy," Thisbe lowered her voice to the tone of reason. "You borrowed one from the man at the store to try it out. Remember?"

"Uh uh!" Andy yelled.

"Andy, stop acting this way, or I'll have to take you home!"

"You never get me anything I want!" Andy started bawling.

"Okay, mister, get your clothes on! We're leaving right now!" Thisbe looked to Margot and gave an apologetic roll of the eyes.

When they got home, Thisbe sent Andy to his room and searched the living room for the chess computer. It wasn't on the table, by the TV set, or in Andy's toy box. Thisbe sank to her knees and looked under the tan couch. All she found was dust. Andy must be lying. She remembered handing the clerk her credit card like it was yesterday. The receipt!

Thisbe sprang to her feet and rushed to her bedroom, where she kept the plastic case containing her records. She removed a green hanging-file folder and dumped the disorganized credit card statements on the carpet. March, November, August, June – she ran her index finger down the list of charges. There was no mention of her purchase at the game store. Thisbe leaned against the bed and let the statements fall to the floor. What did that mean?

CHAPTER 16

The forest's shade took ten degrees off the summer heat. Thisbe sat next to Chikako on a bench in the rest area and set her sunglasses down. Mariko joined them. Others crowded in.

"No lecture today." Mahamuni arched as he inhaled the mountain air. "What could I say to do justice to this marvelous setting?" He wandered away from the others, sat with his back against a tree trunk, and closed his eyes to listen to the birds and the rush of a nearby stream.

Mariko looked at her rice cake, made a face, and set it down. Thisbe chewed hers. The high-pitched whine of a mosquito zeroed in on her ear. Thisbe swatted the air to no use. Gnats swarmed her face. To escape she moved to a patch of ground painted golden by sunlight that made it through a gap in the foliage.

No one talked. Tired from the morning walk, Mahamuni's followers napped. The warm sun and rush of food on an empty stomach made Thisbe drowsy. She closed her eyes and dreamed within a dream of how she and Alf took his old Triumph sports car down the Pacific Coast Highway. She recalled cliffs rising out of the aquamarine water and how the warm wind blew through her hair as Alf dodged motor homes in the tiny convertible. After stopping for clam chowder, they picked wild strawberries on the beach and later that night made Andy in a sagging motel bed.

Thisbe shook her head and opened her eyes. The others were collecting wrappers and shouldering their backpacks. Grogginess clouded Thisbe's head. She picked up her pack and followed the others past a stand of bamboo and down a steep trail that led to a two-lane road, which curved around a concrete restraining wall built against the hillside. Thisbe squinted. She'd left her sunglasses behind.

Thisbe reversed course, squeezing past the others until the trail was clear. She rushed into the forest and found her sunglasses where she'd left them. Twirling the glasses by the stem, she hiked up the path, turned a corner, and froze with a gasp.

Watanabe blocked the way. He wore a black shirt buttoned to the collar. His face, scarred from acne, showed no expression. Thisbe wondered what murder hid behind his sunglasses. She stepped back.

"You shouldn't wander off alone." Watanabe laughed. "It's dangerous." He stepped aside to let her pass.

Thisbe inched toward him. Her heart beat like a jackhammer trying to force its way through her sternum. Propriety squelched her instinct to scream for help. When she got within his reach, she rushed past with a slight bow. The arms that she feared would clamp her mouth and drag her to the river for rape and dismemberment stayed at Watanabe's side.

When Saito called for Thisbe that night, he motioned for Chikako to join them.

"Group meeting," he said. "Everyone must come."

Twenty followers packed into Mahamuni's motel room. Mariko sat between two men on the couch. Tanaka had snagged the chair opposite Mahamuni's. Others stood or sat on the carpet. Thisbe squeezed past them to stand against a clear bit of wall.

"We have a situation." Mahamuni gestured to the treasurer. "Mr. Ueno."

Mr. Ueno had been with Mahamuni since his days as CEO of Kin Tsuru Corporation. He rose to his feet, grinned bashfully, and adjusted his thick glasses. Thisbe strained to hear his soft voice.

"Our petty cash fund is missing. I kept it in a tan metal box in my knapsack." Ueno blushed and bowed. "I know I shouldn't have left it, but I only went down the hall for some ice to put on my sore back. When I returned, it was gone."

"Could you have misplaced it along the road?" Saito asked.

"No, I'm afraid that's impossible. You see, I used some of the money to pay for tonight's lodging."

"Perhaps," Mahamuni said, "if somebody took the money by mistake, they could return it."

All eyes turned to Watanabe, who leaned against the wall with his arms crossed over his chest.

"What are you looking at me for?" Watanabe said. "I didn't take it."

"You've been acting suspiciously." Oda leaned forward in his chair. "What's under your shirt? What are you hiding?"

"Are you queer?" Watanabe said. "Is that why you want to see me with my clothes off?"

Oda sprang from his chair and rushed Watanabe, who sidestepped the charge and sent Oda sprawling. Watanabe raised his foot to deliver a vicious kick to Oda's ribs, but Yamamoto pinned Watanabe's arms behind him and dragged him away.

"Enough!" Yamamoto said.

"Oda!" Mahamuni barked. "I'm shocked at your behavior! Sit down and we'll settle this matter peacefully." He turned to Watanabe. "We're a small movement with no room for secrets. Whatever your past we'll forgive you."

Watanabe ripped open his shirt. Buttons scattered on the carpet. Gang tattoos covered his chest.

"There! Are you happy? I made some mistakes when I was young, but I've changed. I keep covered to avoid people's prejudice. I thought you'd be different, but I see from your eyes you're just the same." Watanabe strode from the room.

"What do we do now?" Saito turned to Mahamuni.

"I still don't trust him," Tanaka said.

"If he wants to reform, it would be a crime not to help."

"He gave a fine speech, just like the scorpion to the tortoise," Chikako said. Several men grunted and nodded.

"You know, I never realized it before. But my watch went missing not long after Watanabe joined us," one of the newcomers said.

The arguments bounded back and forth until Mahamuni raised his hand for silence.

"Perhaps the money will find its way back to Mr. Ueno, and we can drop this unfortunate matter." He dismissed his followers.

By morning Watanabe was gone. The money never returned. Although Mahamuni and his lieutenants had enough to cover the missing funds, the group would never be the same.

Thisbe took Andy to the game store. It was much like she'd remembered. The bearded clerk was lost in a conversation with a pimple-faced teen. Andy examined a display case containing civil war chess pieces and cast metal extraterrestrials.

The clerk sauntered from behind the counter. "Can I help you?"

"What do you want again, Andy?" Thisbe asked.

"A Deep Blue 2100 chess system."

"For someone his age, I'd recommend the Learn Mate 3.0." The clerk handed Thisbe a colorful box. "It has twelve levels of play and only costs forty-nine credits."

"That's for babies." Andy's face burned with indignation. "Wilson's brother has one, and I can beat it every time."

"All right, I have a Deep Blue. Why don't you try it first?" The clerk retrieved a beat-up backpack from behind the counter, removed a device the size of a calculator, and handed it to Andy and showed him how to start the game. Andy sat on the floor with has back against the wall and bent his head over the device.

"Lots of kids want the Deep Blue," the clerk told Thisbe. "For most it's a waste of money. They never get past level three. If he doesn't like the Learn Mate, the Lasker 2C is a good choice. I recommend it for intermediate players."

Anticipating Andy's upcoming victory, Thisbe let him talk. Frowning Andy returned to the counter and handed back the Deep Blue.

"What's wrong, honey?" Thisbe asked.

"It beat me."

"Like I said, the Lasker 2C is a good choice." The clerk looked at the LCD display and tapped the controls to clear the game. "Would you like me to get you one?"

Thisbe nodded and handed him her credit card.

CHAPTER 17

Two needles floated in the glass the next time Thisbe and Saito visited Mahamuni for their private lesson. By now they knew the routine. They sat in chairs, straightened their postures, and began the patient work of letting the day's agitation seep from their minds. Thisbe's muscles relaxed and her thoughts calmed. A half hour into the practice one of the needles vanished. They sat for ten more minutes before Mahamuni spoke.

"Saito, send the needle away but move it a little."

Saito stared at the water. This time the needle vanished without Mahamuni's help.

"Good! But you need to move it like this," Mahamuni said.

Thisbe couldn't feel what was happening but judged it must be remarkable from the look on Saito's face.

"Sensei, the second needle? It was just this one moved in time?"

"Correct, Saito." Mahamuni smiled.

"But how can you do that?"

"Time moves in both directions, Saito. We can only see one." Mahamuni looked at his watch. "That should be long enough. Thisbe, would you please bring it back."

Thisbe reached out with her mind to find the needle. It was a little like remembering something she'd forgotten, but not exactly. She plucked the needle from the past and returned it to the glass, where it sank to the bottom.

"Well done!" Mahamuni clapped his hands.

Soon after Thisbe returned to her room, Chikako turned out the lights. Thisbe couldn't sleep. She'd always thought of the past as solid ground but now realized the present stood on a rickety three-legged table that could collapse at any moment and send history tumbling to the carpet. Thisbe rarely slept in VR. She usually returned to physical reality instead. This time was different. After hours of worry about time's fragility she fell into a dream.

Once again Thisbe was naked in one of Maya Escort's intimacy rooms. Lester, the technician who ran the VR feeds, sat on the bed and placed his glasses on the nightstand. His hands found Thisbe's breasts and kneaded them like two domes of pizza dough. Then he lowered his face to her. Thisbe tried to squirm away from the tongue that teased her nipples, but her body wouldn't obey her mind's commands. Lester's kisses traced a line to her belly. Then he buried his face in the thatch between her legs. The sensations felt dulled, as if Thisbe's nerves were swaddled in cotton batting. Nevertheless, her hips began to rock automatically. Lester unzipped his pants, inserted his three-inch penis, and climaxed on the second thrust. The expression on his face transformed from fascination to worry and disgust. Even though sickened, Thisbe had a niggling urge to reach out and comfort him. Lester pulled up his trousers, retrieved his glasses, and rushed out.

A knock on the motel door woke her. Thisbe wrapped a robe around her body and answered. A policeman and woman, both in dark-blue uniforms, stood in the hall. Each wore a cap with a visor and gold insignia.

"I'm sorry to interrupt," the woman, whose hair was pinned up for duty, said, "but there's been an accident. Would you please dress and meet in the lobby?"

"What is it?" Chikako asked having stirred from bed.

"It's the police. They say there's been an accident. We need to dress and go to the lobby." Thisbe turned to the officers. "We'll be right down." She pushed the door closed.

As they dressed, Thisbe heard the police knocking on their neighbors' doors and making the same request. She and Chikako took the elevator to the lobby and joined the bleary-eyed followers in the café. A half-dozen uniformed police had already cleared out the customers to make room for their inquiry. The belief that things turn out for the best dissolved under her feet when she saw their grim expression. A balding motel manager stared with worry and anger from the front desk. Thisbe's spirits rose a bit when Mahamuni in yukata and slippers entered.

The two officers who'd wakened Thisbe reported, "That's everyone."

"Good. Now we can begin. I'm Inspector Naguchi and I need your help with an investigation," the oldest officer said. He was a thin man. Years of smoking and suspicion had withered the skin on his face. "Do you know this woman?" He help up a photo of Mariko and arched his arm so all could see.

Thisbe gasped and put a knuckle to her teeth. Mariko's ashen face was bruised, and her eyes were closed in death. A white sheet covered her body to the neck.

"It's Mariko." Mahamuni looked at the floor. "One of my followers."

Even though Thisbe was in VR, the picture of the dead girl felt as real as a heart attack. Thisbe collapsed into a chair and wondered if the real Margot was all right while the others offered details about Mariko.

"Would anybody want to harm her?" Inspector Naguchi asked.

"That yakuza," Chikako said, "Watanabe."

"Yakuza?" A policeman raised his eyebrows.

"*Hideo Watanabe.*" Mahamuni sagged as he spoke. "*He joined us briefly. After some money went missing two days ago in Ueda, we had to ask him to leave.*"

"*And you think this Watanabe may have murdered Mariko?*"

Mahamuni shrugged. *The police asked about Watanabe for an hour. Finally the inspector said, "It's probably the gangster. Unless anyone has something else to offer, I'll let you be.*"

"*Tanaka-san,*" Thisbe blurted.

Eyes turned toward her. Tanaka hissed like a cornered snake. Inspector Naguchi raised his eyebrows.

"*They were having an affair. I saw Mariko leaving Tanaka's room at night.*"

"*Mr. Tanaka, you won't mind if we search your room,*" Inspector Naguchi said.

As the officers escorted him upstairs, Tanaka turned and glared at Thisbe. She felt the icy silence in the room was directed at her for betraying one of their own. The policewoman tried to cheer things up.

"*It's best to check these things out right away,*" she said. "*That way we can eliminate Mr. Tanaka as a suspect.*"

It only took fifteen minutes to vindicate Thisbe. The police led Tanaka through the lobby in handcuffs. He avoided everyone's eyes.

"*We found blood on the clothes in his laundry bag,*" an officer said.

"*Please provide your names and addresses,*" Inspector Naguchi said to the group, "*and stay in town for a few days in case we have more questions.*" He nodded to Thisbe.

"*I never trusted that Tanaka, anyway,*" Chikako told Thisbe, once they returned to their room. "*He has shifty eyes.*"

Thisbe's head spun and she found herself in the white diagnostic room. A blonde woman in a colorful skirt said, "Hello, Thisbe. It's time for your two-month checkup. Please make an appointment at the clinic on your way out."

"Keiko? Why do you look like that?"

"Keiko? My name is Heidi. This is the default configuration for your Norbio neural implant's diagnostic agent. I can change my appearance if it will make you more comfortable. But perhaps it would be best for you to have that checkup soon."

Thisbe woke fully clothed and reclining in a leather chair. She sat up and removed the VR feed from the jack in her skull. The small room she occupied was bare except for the chair and a window that looked into a central office packed with computers and electronics. Thisbe stood and walked through the open doorway. Ten others converged on the control station, where two people sat behind a monitor.

"Great job, people!" Margot stood and smiled. "Did you get all that, Lester?"

Lester adjusted the glasses that had slipped down his nose, tapped on the keyboard, and scanned the text dumped to the screen.

"Looks good."

"Okay, everybody." Margot rested a hand on Lester's shoulder. "We have a tight schedule. See you all first thing in the morning."

CHAPTER 18

Thisbe dashed into the bathroom and shut herself into a stall. What the hell was happening? Was this VR or some other reality? She called for Keiko, but there was no answer. That didn't mean anything. Keiko had failed to respond to her summons from VR before. Someone entered the bathroom. Thisbe flushed the toilet and made her way out.

The building had a day-care center on the ground floor just like Maya Escorts. Thisbe checked inside, but Andy wasn't there. None of the cars in the parking lot looked familiar. All had aerodynamic shapes and model names that she'd never heard of. She certainly didn't see her tan Toyota Duster. When she was about to sit on the curb and cry, she thought of the remote keyless entry. Thisbe removed the keys from her purse and pressed the unlock button on the gray plastic box attached to the key chain. Lights flashed on a sleek silver-gray BMW. She opened its gull-wing door, sank into the leather bucket seat, and looked around the car's interior. Only Andy's child booster seat was familiar. The dashboard was made of real wood, and a strange, sinuous medallion hung from the rearview mirror. Thisbe turned the key. The instrument panel came to life, but the engine made no sound. She reached for the gearshift and paused. What if she lived in a different apartment? Thisbe checked her driver's license and noted an address on Mercer Island. The license was recent, so it had a good chance of being the right place.

The LCD screen on the instrument panel had a directions icon. Thisbe entered her address and exited the parking lot. She noted the Cerebellum Studios sign and the building's address before merging into traffic. The car had good pickup and agile steering. Following the audible instructions from the onboard navigator, Thisbe got on I-90, crossed the lake, and took the Mercer Island exit. She got onto Meacher and turned into an entryway where a metal gate barred her way. A guard in an eight-pointed cap and black raincoat got out of his booth and approached her window. The cold fingers of panic gripped her heart, and she reached for her wallet. But when the guard saw her face, he merely waved, returned to his booth, and opened the remote-controlled gate.

Her home was a one-story house situated on a half-acre plot. She parked and checked the mailbox at the foot of the driveway. All the letters were addressed to her. Thisbe fumbled with her keys until she found one that unlocked the front door. A medallion similar to the one in her car hung in the entryway. She put her coat in the closet and followed the steps down to the sunken living room. The decorator had opted for a retro look. A curved floor lamp arched over a large modular couch that faced a picture window. A set of monkey bars stood in the wooded backyard. Thisbe stooped to retrieve Andy's chess computer from the hardwood floor and noticed the *Robe of Purity* under the couch. She picked up the familiar book with the intention of returning it to the shelf. As she turned it over in her hands, she read the print on the back cover:

A must for all followers of the Divine Embrace
   Most Reverend Hiroshi Saito,
   Archbishop of the Divine Embrace Order

That wasn't right. Saito was killed in a car crash not long after Mahamuni's death. And the sinuous design on her medallions was printed on the back cover too. Thisbe opened the book to the introduction. Her confusion grew with each line she read. Mahamuni didn't die. He went into seclusion. There was no mention of Tanaka. Saito had taken over and popularized the teleportation technique. This inspired Dr. Steven Bender to invent the Higgs Pump. The Higgs Pump? What was that? Thisbe closed the book and shelved it next to a hardcover mystery in a yellow dust jacket.

Thisbe carried Andy's chess computer to his room, where a bedspread designed to look like a racing car covered a bed with four mock tires for legs. She found a phone list in the kitchen filled with new burnished-chrome appliances and called Alf.

"Can I talk to Andy?"

The line went dead while Alf went to find his son.

"Hi, mom"

"Hi, Andy. What are you doing?"

"Watching Asteroid Patrol on the holovision."

"Okay, don't stay up too late."

"Mom, is something wrong?"

"No, honey. Put your father on, please."

Andy put down the phone. Thisbe opened the refrigerator while she waited for Alf to get back on the line. It was well stocked with organic yogurt, smoked salmon, and some thick slabs of lasagna from some place called Casanova's. The line went dead and a dial tone came from the speaker. Thisbe hung up. She'd deal with Alf later.

A keyboard rested on the desk in a small office. Thisbe powered up the computer. A desktop display appeared on the poster-sized LCD paper tacked to the wall. Thisbe accessed the Worldwide Information Network and searched for the Higgs Pump. She scored several thousand hits. The first few advertised products or were too technical for her to understand. Eventually she found a FAQ sheet written for the layperson:

What is a Higgs Pump?
The Higgs Pump is a clean source of cheap plentiful energy.

How does it work?
String theory tells us that we live in a 3-D surface inside a 10-D space. The unseen dimensions constitute universes parallel to ours. The Higgs Pump transfers a small amount of vacuum energy, the force that expanded the universe after the Big Bang, from one of the parallel universes to ours.

Is it safe?
Some scientists have expressed concern about the change in the psi particle's mass after the Higgs Pump's introduction. However, these particles only live for a billionth of a second, and the mass change

is less than one part in a million. Most responsible experts think there's little danger.

How was the Higgs Pump invented?

In the early twenty-first century scientists debated why we couldn't see the extra dimensions postulated by string theory. The first observations of these unseen dimensions came not from a physics lab but from the mental practices of an obscure religious movement. Through years of special training, members of the Church of the Divine Embrace are able to move small objects through these extra dimensions. After witnessing one such demonstration by Reverend Hiroshi Saito, Dr. Steven Bender realized these techniques could be applied to creating an inexhaustible source of clean power. With this proof of concept Dr. Bender was able to obtain funding to develop the Higgs Pump.

You say Rev. Saito moved objects through space-time. Does this mean he can move things backward in time?

Yes, although there's little danger of his affecting history. The amount of energy needed to move something backward in time increases exponentially with mass and delta T.

Thisbe went to the Divine Embrace web site. Saito's smiling face and the sinuous design adorned the front page. She returned to the search engine and typed "Ichiro Tanaka" and "Divine Embrace." She got no response. Then she tried the Japanese order "Tanaka Ichiro." She found one entry.

Tanaka Ichiro was a member of Divine

Embrace founder Mahamuni's inner circle. Convicted of murdering Oe Mariko in the summer of 2010, he was sentenced to life in prison. Guards found him dead in his cell in 2013. Prison officials ruled Tanaka's death a suicide.

Thisbe stared at the picture of the hollow-eyed man on the screen. This had to be some kind of horrible wrong turn in her VR session. She shut down the computer. Her stomach rumbled. Thisbe decided to make the best of the situation and made a salad of endive, heirloom tomatoes, olives, feta cheese, and smoked salmon. Although she missed her son, an evening without baby talk and cajoling Andy into bed was a rare treat. She put some soft music on, ate by candlelight, and took a long sensuous bubble bath. When the water began to get cold, she got out of the tub and dried herself with a plush towel. There was no moisturizer on the bathroom counter. She opened the medicine cabinet and found a prescription bottle with her name on it. She examined the label.

Take three times a day with meals – clozapine.

Must have been something for her implant. She replaced the prescription on the shelf and found the moisturizer under the sink.

The next morning she woke up refreshed and relaxed. After a cup of coffee and a breakfast of muesli, yogurt, and fresh raspberries, she went to her car. Despite the changes to the world, Thisbe still had a job to do. Traffic was heavier than she remembered, but Thisbe got to Cerebellum Studios on time. By 8:00 a.m. she was sitting in the leather chair and jacked into the VR feed. After a brief discussion with Heidi, Thisbe returned to the Japanese motel after Tanaka's arrest.

The door to Thisbe's and Chikako's room was propped open for cross ventilation. Chikako lay on the bed and ate wasabi-coated dried peas while watching a dreadful soap opera on TV. Thisbe looked out the window and saw a castle through a gap in the tall buildings. Chikako's crunching combined with the story about a woman in a coma got to be more than Thisbe could stand. She stepped out into the hall. Two new followers, big college-aged boys, walked side by side in front of her. She couldn't help overhearing their conversation.

"Sitting here's a drag."

"Yeah, not enough money to do anything, and I've already read the comics they sell in the convenience store. When we get out of here, let's ditch these jokers and take the train to Nagano."

"Yeah, when are the police going to let us go, anyway?"

"A few days, but you know how these things go."

"So what do you want to do now?"

"We could practice the treasure meditation."

"I'm bored with that. Let's see if there's any porno on our room's closed circuit TV."

The hotel atmosphere became oppressive. Despite the threatening clouds, Thisbe decided to take a walk. She grabbed one of the umbrellas in the stand by the door and set off. After crossing the river, she headed north toward where she thought the castle was. She ended up on streets full of auto mechanic's shops and industrial supply stores. A grandmother with a round, smiling face asked if she was lost. The old woman took Thisbe by the hand and led her to where the castle was visible.

Thisbe crossed the wooden bridge over the moat and paid six hundred yen to enter the gate in the thick walls. The castle's tower of plaster and black-painted wood rose from slanted stone walls in the middle of a grassy field. Thisbe had to remove her shoes and carry them in a plastic bag to enter. She climbed the steep stairways all the way to the top story, where she looked out at the carp swimming lazily in the moat. A sign explained how offerings to a local goddess had kept the castle safe. All the invulnerability left Thisbe feeling empty. She descended to the ground floor and used a shoehorn to put on her shoes. It had started to drizzle. She opened the umbrella and walked back to her hotel in the rain.

Thisbe didn't want to go back to her room. She sat on an uncomfortable couch in the lobby and paged through a dog-eared gossip magazine. The manager, who was no doubt wishing he'd never rented rooms to these religious idiots, glared from behind the front desk. Instead of enduring his icy disapproval, Thisbe entered the café, sat at the counter, and ordered some cold noodles. Mr. Ueno was sitting a few stools away and staring at his iced coffee.

"A real tragedy," he murmured. "But we can't blame the master for Tanaka's crime. When you're on the verge of greatness, the gods throw obstacles to test you. Now is the time to redouble our efforts to show support for our leader, Mahamuni."

Thisbe nodded. Mr. Oda, who sat at the end of the counter, kept his eyes forward and grunted. Ueno drained his coffee and left.

"That old fool," Oda said with a slurred voice. "First he loses our money, and then he says none of this is Mahamuni's fault. It's bullshit!" He took a swallow of beer. "A leader's always responsible for his followers."

"Meeting in a half hour." Saito stuck his head in the café. "Mandatory attendance." He went into the lobby. "Meeting in a half hour."

Thisbe entered the conference room and took a seat. More followers filed in. The looks on their faces said this was the last place they wanted to be. Saito entered.

"The master will be here soon," he said. "Let's welcome him by demonstrating how well we do the treasure meditation."

The two college boys stared as if Saito were crazy, but they didn't make a scene. Thisbe went through the steps of the visualization and regarded herself as a box of jewels by the time Mahamuni entered. Everybody looked up. He wore his customary gray slacks and shirt along with a tired expression. He sat and placed a glass of water by his feet.

"Friends," he said, "after the shock we've had, I know some of you are thinking of leaving. I don't blame you for feeling this way. I ask only that you hear me out first.

"I blame myself for this. I should have spotted Tanaka's weakness. I should have listened and never placed Tanaka in a position of authority. Saito warned me. He has my full confidence. From now on when Saito speaks, he speaks for me.

"Last week I told you your minds are a treasure. However much I have disappointed you, you must believe this. It's not a slogan but the literal truth. No matter how much others may ridicule me, no matter how they mock you, hold to your faith that God made your miraculous minds. Observe." Mahamuni shook a can of carbonated soda and handed it to one of the college boys. "Has this can been tampered with?"

The college boy shook his head.

"Place it on the table, please," Mahamuni said.

The boy complied. Mahamuni squinted. A second later soda jetted from the hole he created in the can with his mind. A few people gasped. Others muttered it was a trick. Saito ran to get a towel.

"To those who wish to leave, remember this and go in peace. To those who will stay, I promise to teach you to use the full power of your minds. The choice is yours."

When the police finally released them, a half-dozen followers abandoned Mahamuni, leaving him with roughly the same number of students he'd started with.

Thisbe spun into the white diagnostic room and was relieved to see Keiko sitting on a wooden stool. At least she was back in the real world instead of that other crazy place.

"Thisbe, sorry to interrupt, but I need to remind you to schedule your two-month checkup. Please be sure to make an appointment at the clinic before you leave."

"Is everything all right?" Thisbe wanted to ask about the parallel world but doubted it would turn out any better than asking about her visions of sex during VR.

"Yes, all your implant's readouts are within normal range. It's just a routine check."

"Did you ever hear of an implant maker called Norbio? One of the girls was having trouble with her implant, and I think that's the name of the manufacturer."

Keiko paused to search her database. "I'm not aware of any such manufacturer. Is there anything else I can do for you?"

"No, I'll make that appointment."

Thisbe woke lying in a cold wet spot. The skin in contact with the damp mattress itched. She cleaned up, dressed, and stopped in the clinic to make her appointment. Dr. Gibbs was standing by the front desk and talking to the receptionist.

"Thisbe, what can I do for you?" he asked.

"My diagnostic program says I need a two-month checkup."

"Oh, I must have forgotten to reset the timer when I did your last scan." He pointed to the door. "Come on back. It'll only take a minute."

Thisbe hesitated asking about the weird alternate world. Too much confusion could get her demoted like Brenda. The whole thing might have been some strange part of the VR disk, anyway. Besides, if anything were wrong, the diagnostic machine would pick it up. She followed him to an exam room where he hooked her up to a diagnostic machine and typed on the keyboard.

"There!" He pressed the enter key. "I set your next checkup for three months from now. How are things going? Are you still having those disturbing images?"

"A few."

"Well, counseling takes time." Dr. Gibbs shut down the machine. "Dr. Cavendish's the best. She'll help you get to the bottom of what's troubling you."

On the way out Thisbe realized she'd forgotten her earrings and backtracked to the intimacy room to retrieve them. A door to one of the other rooms opened and a fat man exited. Something about his hunched shoulders seemed familiar. He turned from closing the door, and Thisbe glimpsed the purple rash through his open collar. He was the same man she'd seen screwing her in VR! Cold rage hardened in her guts and turned them into steel. They'd all lied – Anne, Keiko, the doctors, everyone!

Thisbe stomped to the parking lot. Unlike the last time no sleek sports car awaited her. Instead she climbed into her rusty, eleven-year-old Toyota Duster and turned the key. The engine vibrated like a bowling ball in a washing machine's spin cycle. Thisbe maneuvered onto the street, took the freeway entrance, and came to a dead stop. Four lanes of parked cars blocked her path. The yellow check engine light winked on.

What little remained of the equanimity Thisbe had started the morning with had vanished leaving her nerves packed in broken glass. Her only outlet would be slamming her fist against the steering wheel, but what good would that do? Her anger remained bottled up just like her car was trapped in traffic. A siren's shriek cut through her. With red lights flashing, fire trucks and ambulances blasted horns to clear a path in the carpool lane. Thisbe switched on the radio.

"City engineers gave no explanation of how the structure could have collapsed. Witnesses say they felt no jolt, and the university's geology department detected no seismic activity. Unnamed sources believe the collapse was due to faulty construction. Clearly, investigators will have to do a lot of work to find the cause. This is Stacey Fong at city hall."

"For those of you just joining us, an overpass has collapsed onto I-5," a male announcer said. "No one was hurt, but state police have rerouted traffic, which as you might expect is tied up at this hour. If you can, delay your departure from work or take an alternate route home. We'll have another traffic update in twenty minutes."

It took an hour to drive a mile to the next exit. Despite the warning light, Thisbe's car didn't stall. Police cars blocked the freeway. Red flares burned and dripped slag on the concrete to mark the way to the exit. Thisbe jockeyed for position with pickup trucks and minivans before getting off the freeway. The side streets were also jammed. Sensing it was useless to fight the traffic, Thisbe stopped for dinner at a Turkish restaurant. She got home at 9:00 and immediately reached for Dr. Cavendish's appointment slip held by a magnet to her refrigerator door.

"Liar!" Thisbe hissed. She tore the slip up and tossed it in the trash.

Even with the neon lights turned off in daytime, the pink Cyber Sluts sign looked garish. Thisbe pulled into the parking lot, avoided the broken glass, and parked next to an overflowing green dumpster. She couldn't face another day at Maya Escorts, so she'd called in sick and scheduled a job interview. Thisbe got out of the car and locked the door.

"Bend over and help me get my freak on," a gravelly recorded voice sang from the bar next door.

Thisbe was glad she'd left Andy with the sitter. She circled to the front. Her high heels twisted on the cracked sidewalk. A woman with thick eye makeup lounged inside the front door. Her skirt hiked up to reveal thighs gray as overcooked kielbasa.

"I'm here to see Jerry," Thisbe said.

"Ah, a new girl. He's in there."

Thisbe entered the wood-paneled office. A poster-sized gynecological photo adorned the wall behind a man seated at a desk. He wore a tan sports jacket over an open shirt and a half-dozen gold chains. The long, graying hair he'd combed over the top of his head, did a poor job of camouflaging his bald spot.

"Mr. Klapeda, I'm Thisbe Anderton."

"Good to see you." He circled his desk and clasped Thisbe's hand in his big, hairy hands. "Have a seat."

Thisbe sat on a sagging couch. Its soft cushions swallowed her hips. Jerry returned to his leather office chair.

"So, you're thinking of jumping ship and coming to work for us?"

"That's right," Thisbe said.

"Why?"

"I don't trust them to protect me."

"Yeah, and you ain't the first either. Four of my girls got beat up over there. Only Maya's clients are rich, so they hush it up. We do things different here. Ask anybody. Jerry Klapeda takes care of his girls. How's your implant?"

Thisbe lifted her hair to show Jerry the jack.

"Okay, let's see what you got." Jerry took a soggy cigar butt from the ashtray and caressed it with his lips.

Thisbe had steeled herself for this moment before coming. Any small indignity she suffered would be better than staying with those liars at Maya Escorts. She imagined she was in the doctor's office, stood, peeled off her blouse, and stepped out of her pants. She unhooked her bra and slid the straps over her arms. It's just like the doctor's office she told herself.

"Come on, let's see the bush too."

Thisbe slid her panties down to the floor and stepped out of the leg holes.

"Turn around."

Thisbe faced the wall. Goosebumps rose on her skin.

"You got some cellulite on your thighs, so I can't pay top dollar. I'll give you six fifty a week. You pay for your own medical."

Thisbe turned to face him. "At Maya I get nine." She pulled her panties on.

"So go back to Maya then."

"Can I bring my favorite VR disk?" She put on her bra and pants.

"Hey, I don't give a fuck what you watch. Just as long as your pussy's ready for action." Jerry put the cigar down.

"Let me think about it. I'll get back to you." Buttoning her blouse Thisbe turned her back and headed for the door.

"Don't wait too long," Jerry called after her. "It could be dangerous."

Thisbe left Cyber Sluts more discouraged than when she'd arrived. With no other job prospects her confrontation with Anne looked inevitable. The prospect of returning to Splendid Resorts with a surgery bill didn't appeal to her. But would Anne believe Thisbe had actually seen Ron and Lester from VR? Would Anne make her a maid like Brenda? Thisbe took Martin Luther King to bypass the collapsed overpass and got onto the freeway. She darted into a gap in traffic, passed a slow-moving pickup truck loaded with gardening equipment, and realized she had another problem. Maya Escorts prided itself on preserving its clients' anonymity. Even if Thisbe convinced Anne that she could see clients from VR, how would Anne react to the violation of her clients' privacy? A green and white exit sign marked the Forty-Fifth Street-off ramp. Thisbe exited and stopped at a bakery in Wallingford before returning home.

"I've got cookies!" Thisbe announced when she entered. Andy sprang from the carpet and ran to the white paper bag she held.

"Don't we want to offer Mandy one first?" Thisbe asked.

Andy carried the bag to the living room and held it open for his babysitter.

"Would you like a cookie, Mandy?"

"Thank you." Mandy reached inside and plucked out a disk studded with chocolate chips.

Andy ran off with the remaining treasure.

"How did your job interview go, by the way?" Mandy asked.

"Don't ask." Thisbe removed the billfold from her purse, counted out thirty credits, and paid Mandy.

After closing the door behind the sitter, Thisbe looked at the phone and wondered what to do about her job. She called Margot and got her answering machine. Of course, she must be at work. Thisbe was about to put down the receiver when she had another idea. She dialed Vanessa, her three-legged race partner from ME's lunar party.

"Hello."

"Vanessa, hi. It's Thisbe Anderton. How are you?"

"Fine. Aren't you supposed to be at work?"

"I'm having a bit of a problem at ME. Did you ever hear of anyone waking up from VR and seeing the customers in the act?"

"No."

"Trouble is, one of the customers is an old boyfriend Anne swore she'd keep away from me. Another is our old friend Lester, and I doubt he can afford our fees."

"I wouldn't put it past that slimy weasel. Have you told anyone?"

"Just the doctor. He didn't think it was real. I didn't either until I saw one of the customers in the hall. I don't know what to do."

"You working tomorrow?"

"Well," Thisbe looked out the window at the parking lot. "I was thinking of calling in sick."

"Why don't I join your VR sessions for the next few days? We'll see if it happens again."

"All right. Thanks."

CHAPTER 19

That night Thisbe thrashed with the covers as if wakefulness would slow the alarm clock's inexorable march toward the next day's work. When she arrived at Maya Escorts, Thisbe left Andy at day care and trudged up the back stairway to her intimacy room. She peeled off the protection of her clothing and lay naked and vulnerable on the bed.

"I hope you'll be there, Vanessa," Thisbe muttered and plugged the VR feed into the jack in her skull.

Her perception morphed. She and an audience of fifty sat on folding chairs in a parking lot at night. Disposable glow sticks bathed the spectators in eerie yellowish-green light. His voice amplified by a bullhorn, Hiroshi Saito harangued the spectators from a makeshift stage, several sheets of plywood supported by cinder blocks.

"Friends, suppose a condemned man has spent the last twenty years in jail and is due to be hung tomorrow. If someone offered him a key to his cell, what should he do? Should he say, 'No thanks, I've been here so long I've gotten comfortable?'

"Friends, we are all like that convict. Our minds are imprisoned in a jail of greed – always seeking more food, more clothing, faster cars, and a bigger house. Our obsession with material objects can only end in death because like all physical things our bodies will wear out. One man offers us the key to freedom if only we'll have the courage to step out of our personal jails. Please welcome our great sage, Mahamuni!"

The followers erupted in enthusiastic applause in an attempt to supercharge the other spectators' tepid response. Dressed in a white tunic Mahamuni walked to the center of the stage and stood in the beams of several flashlights hooked up to car batteries. He poured water from a pitcher into a plastic cup, balanced the cup on his palm, and lifted it over his head. The cup vanished with a loud pop.

"Only your beliefs keep you imprisoned by dumb matter. You may be smaller than the stars and galaxies, but your mind is not small. Techniques like the one I just performed aren't limited to a chosen few. I will teach them to anyone who will follow me."

"It's a fake," someone in the audience said.

"I'll show you how real it is," Mahamuni motioned to the man. "Come up

109

here."

The heckler, a middle-aged man in a short-sleeved shirt, climbed onto the stage.

"This way, sir." Mahamuni had the man stand where he'd made the cup vanish. "Can I have another volunteer?"

A group of teenage girls chided one of their members onto the stage. Two pigtails jutted like horns from the side of her head.

"Write something only you know." Mahamuni handed her pen and paper.

The girl smiled showing crooked teeth, wrote something, and folded the paper in half.

"Is this what you wrote?" Mahamuni took a sheet of paper from his pocket and handed it to her.

"They're the same." The girl's eyes went wide when she examined the two sheets. She held them up for the heckler to see.

He stepped toward her.

"No, no," Mahamuni gestured. "Please stay in the same spot."

An empty cup materialized and fell on the heckler's head. Water splashed the stage between him and the girl. One of the sheets of paper vanished. The crowd applauded. Mahamuni led the two volunteers to the stairs.

"If you would like to learn to use your mind's full power, follow us to Kyoto," Saito said through the bullhorn. "If you can't come with us, meet us there on October 18 at the Gojo Amphitheater near Kiyomizudera."

Thisbe helped the others fold and stack chairs. Some audience members milled around the stage in hopes of talking to Mahamuni. Others wandered off. Thisbe felt a sharp pain in her heel and looked around. A tall blonde woman stood on one leg and removed a rock from her high-heeled shoe. She wore shorts and a tight turquoise top with a plunging neckline. Several foreigners had been in the audience, so no one paid any attention to her. The woman slipped on her shoe and looked around. Thisbe made her way to her.

"Vanessa, is that you?"

"Hi" She looked around some more. "Japan?"

"About thirty years ago," Thisbe said. "We're halfway from Tokyo to Kyoto on a religious pilgrimage. I felt the rock in your shoe. What's going on with that?"

"Our sensory streams are commingled. I swapped your lead with Jan's in the control room after I paid Lester his fee."

"Thanks for coming."

"So when do your VR breakthroughs happen?" Vanessa asked.

"When I'm doing the treasure meditation or lying in bed." Thisbe touched her index finger to her chin. "I guess they happen whenever I restrict my sensory input

in VR."

"*Then maybe we can make them happen,*" *Vanessa said.*

Thisbe introduced her to Saito, whose eyes welcomed her by dropping to her cleavage. He was delighted to learn that Vanessa would be joining Mahamuni's party. Mahamuni's followers placed the chairs and flashlights in a storage bin before taking the trail beside the Kiso River into town. The inn where they were staying was one of the traditional plaster and wood buildings that lined the road leading toward the bus stop. To Chikako's dismay Thisbe and Vanessa chose to share a room. The roommates left their shoes by the entrance and climbed the stairs to their lodging. The room was empty except for two cushions, a low table, and a frame to hang clothing. Tatami mats filled the air with the odor of cut grass.

"*So what am I supposed to do?*" *Thisbe asked after placing her backpack in the corner.*

"*Lie down and do nothing.*" *Vanessa moved to the light switch.*

"*You can't see through my eyes, though. How will you know if I'm back in the intimacy room?*"

In silent answer Vanessa reached into her own pants. Thisbe felt an electric throb of pleasure between her legs. Vanessa removed her hand and switched off the light.

Thisbe relaxed as if entering the treasure meditation. Rather than take the next step and imagine a chest, Thisbe let her mind drift free. With nothing but her breath to occupy her, Thisbe's insecurities bubbled to the surface. What if this didn't work? Would Vanessa abandon her? Could she read her thoughts? Soon she grew tired of these worries and began to feel groggy.

Then she flashed into the intimacy room. A bony blonde man with pink acne sprinkling his forehead gave her inner thighs a cursory caress and poked his finger inside her.

"*Oh!*" *Vanessa exclaimed.*

A shake on Thisbe's shoulder returned her to the VR motel room. Vanessa turned on the light and sat next to her.

"*Okay, I'm convinced.*"

"*Now what?*" *Thisbe sat up and leaned on her elbow.*

"*Maybe there's a way to share video feeds too.*" *Vanessa smiled. "I'll work on Lester.*"

Thisbe woke in the leather chair and rushed into the central office in time to catch Vanessa emerging from her cubicle. Vanessa opened her mouth to speak, but Thisbe held a finger

to her lips for silence. Once the others had gathered, Margot stood to address the group.

"Good news. Cerebellum Studios has been included in the Virtual Producers Guild. That means our feature will be eligible for the Taguchi Awards. So work hard and maybe you'll be nominated for best actor. See you tomorrow."

Vanessa followed Thisbe into the hall.

"What the fuck is this?"

"That's the other thing I meant to tell you about," Thisbe said. "Pinch your skin."

"What?"

Thisbe pinched her own arm. "Feel anything?"

"No." Vanessa pinched hers.

"I guess it's real then," Thisbe said. "It's some kind of parallel world where things are similar but not quite the same. Sometimes I end up here when I leave VR. Mahamuni's mental tricks opened some kind of gateway."

Vanessa accompanied Thisbe to the day care, but once again Andy was not there. The two women stepped into the parking lot.

"How do I find my car?" Vanessa looked at the strange teardrop-shaped vehicles parked in rows.

"Try the remote keyless entry," Thisbe offered, "and check your driver's license for your address."

Vanessa pressed the device attached to her key chain. Lights flashed on a lime green sedan that seemed older than the other vehicles.

"Green, that's my favorite color," Vanessa smiled and looked at her license. "Says I've got a place on Federal Way. You want to get a bite to eat before I try to find my home?"

"That sounds like a good idea." Thisbe reached into her purse for her keys and found a coupon. "This says we can get two-for-one at a place called Magic Carpet Falafel in Seeley Park. Want to try it?"

"How do we get there?"

"Follow me," Thisbe said.

Thisbe led the way out of the parking lot. Following the onboard navigator's directions, she drove north and crossed under the monorail tracks that arced over the freeway. The sun had set a half hour earlier. Lit by colorful diode lights, downtown sparkled like rhinestones in a country singer's jacket. After crossing the ship canal they hung a left and followed Eighty-Fifth Street to what in Thisbe's world was a liquefied natural gas terminal. In this world a glowing transparent dome a mile in diameter covered the remodeled landscape. Pedestrians passed through the exits like bees entering a hive.

Thisbe waited for Vanessa to lock her car. Together the two women set off toward the entrance. When they got close, warm air from under the dome blew in Thisbe's face. A pair of giggling teenagers in bikinis coming the other way almost bumped into them. After walking through the fifteen-foot corridor, she entered a different world.

"Cool!" Vanessa said.

Instead of the native cedar and hemlock, palm trees grew beside the beach, covered in sand as white as granulated sugar. The bright glow from overhead warmed Thisbe's skin like the tropical sun. Bathers lay on towels. A few swam. Others piloted paddleboats. As indicated by the map printed on the back of the coupon, Thisbe and Vanessa walked along a concrete path that ran parallel to the beach. Runners, skaters, and bicyclists passed. The two women stopped at a wooden building with an open-air kitchen. A half-dozen diners lounged at the picnic tables in front. A swarthy man in a paper hat waved from behind the grill.

"Hello Thisbe. The usual?"

"Please"

"And for your friend?"

"I'll have the same," Vanessa said.

They sat on a green wooden bench. Even the dome couldn't keep it free of white bird droppings. Two toy speed boats navigated the waters of a nearby wading pool. Their owners, two preteen boys, held controllers with silver antennae that looked like fishing poles. The cook slid two plastic plates heaped with food onto the counter and motioned to Thisbe, who handed him the coupon.

"That'll be four credits," the cook said.

"Excuse me?" Thisbe looked at two plates of sizzling lamb,

rice, and Greek salad.

"Four credits"

Thisbe handed over one of the twenty-credit notes packing her billfold. The cook made change. She left him a one-credit tip and carried the food back to the bench. Conversation halted while they ate. The tomatoes in Thisbe's Greek salad were moist and flavorful, not like the Styrofoam ones she was used to.

"This is good," Vanessa said through a mouth full of tender juicy lamb.

After finishing, Thisbe's limbs grew heavy with contentment, and all she wanted to do was relax on the bench.

"There's one thing I'm wondering," Vanessa said.

"What's that?"

"Well, while we're here, who's back in our world?"

The question troubled Thisbe. On the drive to her Mercer Island home, she wondered who was taking care of Andy back home. The last time she'd seen him, Andy seemed healthy and happy, so any alternate Thisbe must not be mistreating him. Still she could have kicked herself for not paying more attention to the date and time she was last here.

After Thisbe got to her Mercer Island house, she picked up the white news tablet from the kitchen table and displayed the front page. The date said August 4, the same as in her home world. That made things simpler. There was no reason the two dates had to be the same. Thisbe scanned the headlines. The news tablet did not mention the Eurasian Oil Consortium bribery scandal like it did in her home world. She turned to page two.

Sanderson Point Higgs Pump Ready Soon

Puget Power engineers declared last week's full-power test a success. This clears the way for the Sanderson Point Unit One to begin producing power next month. Company spokesman Laughlin Singer says consumers can expect a 5 percent drop in their power bills as soon as the unit comes on line. Prices

are expected to drop further once Puget Power recoups its investment.

Thisbe set down the news tablet and glanced at the yellow notepad on the counter. Maybe she could leave a message for the other Thisbe. She dug through a kitchen drawer and found a pen. It dug furrows in the paper but left no mark.

"Shit!" Thisbe threw it in the trash and found another. She touched the pen to the corner of her mouth. What are you supposed to write to yourself, anyway? "Thisbe," she wrote, "I'm your twin from the alternate world. Please leave a message and tell me about yourself." Shouldn't she ask something more specific? She touched the pen to paper. "Have you found yourself transported to an alternate reality like I have?"

Thisbe added the date and time, tore off the sheet, and attached it to the refrigerator door with a magnet.

CHAPTER 20

Thisbe didn't see Vanessa when she arrived at Cerebellum Studios the next morning. *When Thisbe entered VR, she was standing in front of a bathroom mirror with a toothbrush in her hand. Foam filled her mouth. Thisbe took a sip of water from the glass and spat. She was careful to remove the bathroom slippers before walking down the hall to the room that matched the number on her key. Her roommate, the tall blonde, was rolling up the futons and stowing them in the closet.*

"Morning, Vanessa. Did you find your house in Federal Way last night?"

"What are you talking about?" The woman gave Thisbe a puzzled look. "My name's Angelica, and I live in Kobe, where I teach English."

"Sorry" Thisbe shook her head. "Guess I must have remembered a conversation from last night's dream. We'd better get downstairs for the treasure meditation."

They joined the others in the lounge. After Thisbe visualized the treasure, a voice spoke in her head.

"Thisbe, it's Vanessa. I'm piggybacking on your sensory stream so I can see and hear everything you do. Sorry I'm late. It took me awhile to feel out Lester. I wasn't sure if our deal still held in this world like in the other. It does."

"Vanessa," Thisbe thought, "did you see the article about the Sanderson Point Higgs Pump?"

Vanessa didn't respond. Although she could see and hear what Thisbe did, Vanessa could not read her thoughts.

After five minutes Vanessa whispered, "Try to be real still and have a breakthrough so we can see who these clients are."

After ten minutes of meditation, Thisbe broke out of VR and returned her awareness to her intimacy room at Maya Escorts. The blonde man had returned for another visit. This time Thisbe got a better look at him. He had sticklike arms, a concave chest, and wavy hair that framed his head like a halo. Something irritated her pubic bone. She looked in the mirror and watched the reflection of his skinny buttocks working between her legs.

"Look at that!" Vanessa raged in her ear. "He didn't even bother to take off his wedding ring!"

Vanessa's distraction disrupted Thisbe's fragile concentration and returned her to the VR session, where the morning meditation ended in a few minutes. The motel included a complimentary breakfast, so Thisbe joined the others in the dining room and sat at Chikako's table.

"So how was it rooming with that big, dumb Western girl?" Chikako's tone was as bitter as her over-steeped green tea. "Look at her." She pointed to Angelica sitting at a table with three men. "On the prowl like an alley cat."

"That bitch!" Vanessa's voice hissed in Thisbe's ear. "I ought to come back to your VR session and scratch her eyes out!"

The men at Thisbe's table lowered their eyes and tried to suppress their giggles.

"She's quite sweet, really," Thisbe said to Chikako.

The waitress poured Thisbe's tea and set down a breakfast plate. Thisbe separated her chopsticks, rubbed them together, and took a mouthful of rice. She found the blandness and sticky but firm consistency comforting. Thisbe stirred mustard into the natto, or fermented soybeans, and lifted some to her mouth. Sticky, spider-web like strings stretched from the natto to her bowl.

"Please don't make us eat that!" Vanessa's voice said.

Thisbe took a bite only to be deafened by a loud internal "Yecch!" She gave up and stirred the bowl of slimy grated mountain potato.

"Don't even think about it!" Vanessa said.

Thisbe sighed and concentrated on the fish, pickles, and miso soup.

After breakfast Mahamuni's followers retraced their steps to the site of the rally and continued past a graveyard and small dam to walk the five-mile trail to Magome. Last night's performance had netted them four new converts, who marched eagerly at the head of the line. At times the trail sent the pilgrims hiking along a narrow road before veering back into the woods. Weeks of hiking had toned Thisbe's muscles, so the climb was no problem.

When the line spread out, Thisbe whispered, "Vanessa, can you hear me?"

"Yeah."

"Did you find your home last night?"

"Yeah, it's not bad. Jan had converted a bedroom into a studio. She wasn't there, though."

"Hey, would you please quiet down?" one of the followers said. "You're disturbing my mindfulness."

When the pilgrims passed the crest and started down into the town, they passed two hikers going the other way. The couple, a blonde man and woman, smiled and puffed on. Mahamuni's followers arrived in Magome around 10:30, bought rice crackers from street vendors, and continued on.

By now the merciless sun had climbed higher in the sky. With no trees for shade, the heat and humidity made Thisbe feel as if she were wading through Jell-O. Sweat stuck the back of her blouse to her knapsack. When they arrived at

Nakatsugawa, Mahamuni called a break at a convenience store. His followers crowded inside to take advantage of the air conditioning. Thisbe pulled a sports drink from the refrigerator and pressed the cold can to her forehead. Mahamuni got into a discussion with the clerk. From her vantage point Thisbe couldn't hear what they said, but from the clerk's gestures it looked like he was giving directions. Thisbe was looking forward to a two-hour lunch, but it was not to be. After walking through town and stopping for bowls of iced noodles, Mahamuni led his party on toward Ena.

When Thisbe left VR, Keiko gave her a brief status update before returning her to the intimacy room. Rather than shower off the oils left clinging to her skin from a dozen male bodies, Thisbe hurried into her clothes and dashed into the hall. She wanted to catch Vanessa before she left. The tall blonde stepped out of her room five minutes later.

"Should we talk to Anne?" Thisbe asked.

"I don't see how that's going to help." Vanessa slung her bag over her shoulder. "We need to catch Ron red-handed for her to believe us. Do you have his picture?"

"No."

"What did he say he did for a living?"

"Housing construction."

"And he can afford this place?" Vanessa raised her eyebrows. "I doubt it. We're going to need a lot more cooperation from Lester on this. To get it we'll need some leverage. I'll have Marci at the front desk check the schedule to see when you don't have any customers. That's when Lester is most likely to strike. If we can watch him from VR and relate the details of his activities, we'll scare him into helping. As for Ron, I'll see what Marci can tell me about him."

Thisbe retrieved Andy from day care and drove him home. Andy wanted spaghetti topped with chili for dinner. Since the chili came from a can, the meal was easy to make. The boy watched cartoons until 8:00, when Thisbe put him to bed. Then she checked the date on the news tablet – August 4. No time had passed in this world except for the time she'd been at work. She practiced the treasure meditation and read from the *Robe of Purity*. At 11:00 she turned on the local news.

"Still no word on what caused the Fletcher Street overpass

collapse. In other news the Adriatic crisis seems to be heating up with warships from the Magreb Confederation converging on the area."

Thisbe brushed her teeth, while an announcer read the sports scores. She rinsed her mouth and paid only cursory attention to the story in the background.

"Scientists at CERN have observed a massive burst of elusive Higgs bosons. The Higgs is thought to explain, why some particles have mass and others don't. This is the largest sighting of the Higgs boson ever detected."

When Thisbe entered VR, she was leaving a large town with Mahamuni's followers. About a mile outside, they turned onto a deserted two-lane road. The gummy, sun-heated blacktop stuck to her shoes. She stepped off the road and onto the dirt. A garbage truck passed, and a piece of paper blew out of the back and floated to the ground by her feet. They walked a half-mile up the road and came to a landfill. Mahamuni led them through a gate in the chain-link fence that surrounded the facility. A man with a crew cut came out of a small brick building near the entrance. He wore dark-blue overalls and a suspicious look. The scar under his eye resembled a toxic purple centipede crawling on his cheek. After exchanging a few words with Mahamuni, the man shrugged and went back inside.

"You sure take me to some great places," Vanessa said from inside Thisbe's head.

They followed the road to a mountain of garbage bags. Crows pecked at food containers, and the sweet smell of rot stuck to the air.

"Each day Japan produces three hundred thousand tons of garbage," Mahamuni said. "Most of what you buy ends up here. If you had a choice between feeding the hungry or feeding this dump, which would you choose?" Mahamuni pointed to one of the newcomers.

"The hungry."

"That's what everyone says, but the dumps grow fatter and the hungry grow thinner. Why?" Mahamuni looked at his followers' faces. "It's because you can't see God in all things. Your minds are weak. They turn away from what frightens and disgusts only to latch on to anything that glitters. Once you see the divinity in all things, you won't need to buy the products that feed the landfill. Then you can feed the hungry, and the world won't disturb you so much.

"Last night Mr. Oda complained he was having difficulty moving the needle with his mind. This exercise will help. I want you to spread out, find something

unpleasant, and contemplate it until you see the divinity within it. The ocean accepts all rivers. Be like the ocean and reject nothing. This will strengthen your minds, so you won't turn away from the chaos between dimensions."

Thisbe moved a few steps away and looked around to see what the others were doing. Mahamuni had plopped down beside a green dumpster. Following his example she found a bare spot in the carpet of food wrappers, crumpled paper, and broken glass. Trying to keep clean she kneeled and selected the remnants of a cheeseburger in a Styrofoam container as her object of contemplation. Maggots wriggled in the rancid meat, and mold bloomed on the bun. She told herself her problems would vanish if she could only see the divinity in it. A juicy black fly landed on her cheek. Thisbe waved it away, but it came back buzzing in her ear. Two crows, their greasy black feathers shining in the sun, cawed and fought over a bag of dried squid.

Thisbe's ankles began to ache and feel numb. She looked around. Mahamuni sat still and straight with no indication he'd call off this perverse exercise anytime soon. Thisbe slipped her butt off her heels, sat in the dirt, and massaged her ankles. She stared at a disposable diaper's blue plastic skin. Her legs and arms itched. All she wanted was to wash the stench of this place out of her pores. A truck rolled past. The driver leaned out the window and gawked.

"You know, Thisbe," Vanessa said. "Most people use VR to find someplace better than their ordinary lives."

Something wet seeped through the seat of her pants. To hell with it! In spite of Mahamuni's words, Thisbe couldn't see God in the trash, but maybe there was another way. She stood, walked past the small brick building, exited the gate, and sat on the curb outside the fence to wait for the others. Thisbe sat straight and focused her gaze on a bland patch of the road. Within minutes she broke out of her VR session and sent her awareness back to the intimacy room. A huge walrus of a man with a bushy moustache and hairy, blubbery body struggled between her thighs. It seemed he couldn't keep erect. After fifteen minutes of futility he dressed and left.

The ocean rejects no rivers. Whenever her attention wandered, Thisbe brought it back to Maya Escorts. There were nine customers in all, ranging from sweet to downright creepy. A thin, bald man greeted her with "How are you today, Lulu?" when he entered. He kept up a patter of talk about Ron and Betty while he slipped out of his clothing to reveal tufts of white hair on his chest and groin. Even though his wrinkled skin sagged with age, he'd kept his muscles well-toned. The old guy gave her one hell of a ride.

Her creepiest customers were the watchers. An older woman

brought her young stud into the room and sat primly to watch while he performed on Thisbe. Later a heavyset, bearded man pulled a chair to where he had a good view of Thisbe's vagina, and sat fondling himself while drinking a glass of scotch.

Her last customer was gorgeous – tall, fit, and tanned. He'd tied his shoulder-length black hair into a ponytail with a simple blue ribbon. Thisbe's heart raced in anticipation. For once reality was better than her VR dreams or even Margot's fantasy world. But why would such a handsome guy need Maya Escort's services?

"Oh please, let him want normal sex instead of something disgusting," Vanessa said from inside Thisbe's head.

The customer set down his briefcase, hung his suit jacket on the back of the chair, and rolled up his sleeves.

"I knew it," Vanessa said. "He's going to be a pervert."

The briefcase's catches snapped open, and the customer removed a washbasin, which he carried to the bathroom. Thisbe heard water running. When the customer returned, he placed the basin on the bed and maneuvered Thisbe's foot into the warm liquid. He worked a sliver of soap into a lather and began washing Thisbe's toes. Slippery muscular fingers tickled her sole. The cobra of desire flicked its tongue. If only the soapy hands would continue up her calves to the insides of her thighs. But the customer merely dried her foot on a clean white towel and began on the other. He finished, placed a chaste kiss on each of Thisbe's insteps, and disposed of the wash water in the bathroom sink. There had to be a way to make him stay, but with her muscle control blocked by the VR device Thisbe could only watch the handsome customer pack his basin and leave.

Thisbe let herself slip back into VR. She was lying beside the road outside the dump. The followers stood in a semicircle around her. Mahamuni, his eyes shining with joy, knelt by her side.

"Well done," he said. "Well done!"

When Thisbe emerged from VR, she was sitting on a leather couch in one of Cerebellum Studios' cubicles. She unplugged the VR feed and gathered with the others in the control room.

"Good work, everybody." Margot pointed to a man with stubble on his chin. "You might want to throttle back on the melodrama a bit, Jim. Think nuance, not over-the-top."

The man nodded.

"Okay, see you tomorrow. Oh, Thisbe, could I talk with you alone for a few minutes?"

Vanessa caught Thisbe's eye as she left with the others.

"I imagine you must be feeling pretty confused right now," Margot said. "I have something for you to watch that will help put things in perspective. Do you have that video queued up, Lester?"

"All set."

"After you watch the video, we'll talk." Margot gestured toward the conference room and turned back to the monitor.

Thisbe sat at the synwood table and faced the video-paper display tacked to the wall. The screen turned deep blue and then showed an image of Thisbe sitting in an office.

"You understand that the short-term loss of memory may cause severe emotional distress," a voice from off camera said, "and you accept the risks?"

"Yes," the image of Thisbe replied.

"Very well. Please read this statement aloud." A hand slid a paper toward her.

"I, Thisbe Anderton, freely relinquish my memories for a period to be determined by Cerebellum Studios but not to exceed sixty days. In exchange I will receive eighty thousand credits. I agree not to hold Cerebellum Studios or anyone associated with the virtual drama *The Day Before Tomorrow* responsible for any resulting emotional distress or lingering psychological difficulties I may experience as a result of this undertaking."

The video showed Thisbe signing the papers. When Thisbe looked away from the screen, Margot was standing in the doorway with her arm resting on the frame.

"We find the best way, the only way, to get decent performances from newcomers is to make them believe the virtual drama is real." Margot took a seat and folded her hands. "We could use professionals instead, but we're committed to giving the underprivileged a chance. That's how I got started in this business.

"You did some great work, but your unconscious obsession with the brothel concerns me. That's why I'm waking you up. Your major scenes are over, anyway. From now on you'll be limited to peripheral parts, but, of course, you'll still get your whole fee."

Thisbe opened her mouth to speak, but Margot silenced her with a raised hand.

"It'll all make sense once Lester restores your memories. Come out to the control room."

Thisbe followed her to a chair by some equipment, where Lester plugged a cable into the jack in her skull.

"I love those earrings. They match your eyes." He typed on the keyboard and adjusted some dials. "This will just take a minute."

A membrane dissolved in Thisbe's mind and allowed all her memories to flood back – cold nights standing of street corners, climbing into strange cars for sex in the backseat, choking on semen with her face in someone's lap, and a neon sign for the Alliance for the Less Fortunate lighting the gloom. The shame! Thisbe felt as if Margot and Lester were watching her memories too. She had to get out of there. Thisbe stood and steadied herself by leaning on the chair's armrest.

"Do me a favor. Don't mention any of this to Vanessa. She's in the same boat that you were in." Margot rested her hand on Thisbe's shoulder. "Why don't you take the morning off? We'll shoot around you."

Thisbe drove home and found the note she'd left for herself. No one had written a reply. The news tablet said the date was August 5. She checked the phone messages.

"Thisbe, this is Maria from the Alliance for the Less Fortunate. Margot informed me of your release. Your son, Andy, is eager to rejoin you. You can reach me at 249-6642."

The next morning when Thisbe was hopping around in one shoe in her rush to get out the door, the phone rang.

"Ms. Anderton, this is Maria Espada from ALF. Someone here would like to speak to you." The line went quiet as the social worker passed the phone.

"Mom, Mrs. Espada says you're all better now, and I don't have to keep secrets anymore. She says I can come live in our new home soon. Mom, I don't like it here. The kid in the next bunk farts, and Chuck Remington made me eat his boogers. Mom," Andy's voice broke, "I want to leave now. Can you come and get me?"

Memories of leaving her son in seedy motels while she walked the streets assaulted Thisbe and clogged her throat like a tumor.

"I want to bring you home soon," Thisbe stammered. "But for now you have to be brave. Can you do that for momma?"

"Okay," Andy sniffled.

"I'll call soon." Thisbe set the phone down.

She let out a moan. What had she done to Andy? Thisbe ransacked the kitchen cabinets looking for some whiskey, cooking wine, or anything that would kill the pain. There was no alcohol in the house. She was about to drive to a liquor store when she got another idea, the Divine Embrace temple in Lynnwood. She opened the phone book and turned to the section on churches. Sure enough the temple was located at the same address she remembered.

The drive took forty minutes. Instead of a simple one-story octagon, this Divine Embrace temple was an alabaster spire that seemed to reach to heaven. Thisbe went inside. A red carpet covered the floor, and a vaulted ceiling arched overhead. About a dozen people sat behind tables. A ping-pong ball floated in a bowl of water atop each one. Pastor Nakagawa looked up from helping one of the practitioners and motioned Thisbe to an empty seat.

She stared at the ping-pong ball in the bowl and tried to move it with her mind. After fifteen minutes with no results, she gave up and looked around. Evidently she wasn't the only one having no luck. Several others dressed in designer clothes fidgeted in their chairs and looked bored.

Pastor Nakagawa called it quits. "It takes practice," he said. "I had to try for six months before I made the ball disappear, so keep at it. The Divine in me embraces the Divine in you."

"The Divine in me embraces the Divine in you," the practitioners echoed.

Pastor Nakagawa hugged each of the congregants on their way out. When it was Thisbe's turn, he wrapped his arms around her and then held her shoulders at arm's length to get a good look at her.

"It's been a long time," he said. "We're all pulling for you,

Thisbe."

When she got home, Thisbe went to the medicine cabinet, got a tablet of clozapine, and washed it down with a glass of water. She slept until 9:00 a.m. and had a leisurely breakfast. The repressed memories had been difficult to deal with, but a good night's sleep put everything in perspective. Her life was on the right track now. She had a great job and a good place to live. Soon she'd get Andy back and be the kind of mother he deserved. There was nothing on holovision except a story about another big test at the Sanderson Point Power Plant. Thisbe got bored and decided to go to work.

When Thisbe arrived at Cerebellum Studios, Vanessa had already jacked in. Thisbe breathed a sigh of relief. Vanessa would be easier to avoid, and thus keep their repressed memories secret, when she wasn't sharing Thisbe's sensory stream. *Thisbe found a free couch, jacked in, and joined Mahamuni's party walking along a road that paralleled the Kiso River. Vanessa gave Thisbe a look. Thisbe nodded and silently mouthed "overslept." One of the new members, a woman whose wire-rimmed glasses could not conceal a penetrating stare, approached Thisbe.*

"I'm Eiko. Who are you?"

"Thisbe."

"Your teacher is really fantastic! Have you been following him long?"

Thisbe found the question difficult to answer due to the discontinuities in VR. "About six months," she said.

"Wow, that's so great! You must have the needle moving mastered by now. Have you ever heard of a book called The Knot of Knowing*? It's about how modern physics confirmed Hindu creation stories. Did you know that a cabal of Canadian companies has been suppressing this knowledge for years in order to protect their patents? It's really interesting. I'll loan you my copy, if you want."*

"Thanks" Thisbe found Eiko's beliefs tiring. She turned her attention to her surroundings in an attempt to let the conversation die down.

After a few hours they stopped at a convenience store and bought bento *boxes. A small park provided a good place for lunch. Thisbe found a bench. Eiko waved and joined her. After Mahamuni's blessing Thisbe opened a packet of* nori *and crumbled the dried seaweed on her rice. The simple lunch of fish, rice, and pickles tasted great after a morning of hiking. When Thisbe reached for the red pickled plum, Eiko spoke up.*

"I wouldn't eat that, if I were you."

"Why not?" Thisbe asked.

"It's a chromatic antagonist," Eiko said. "You already ate something green, so eating something red will create an imbalance in you digestive system that could lead to gastric illness."

"I see." Thisbe set the pickled plum back in the box. "But it's not really red, is it? It's more of a reddish brown."

"Well, if it were more brown, you might be able to get away with it. Personally, I wouldn't take the chance. I had a friend who thought that adding cream to her black tea would make it all right to eat with rice, but she had to have her gall bladder removed. It's really best not to mess with these things."

Thisbe excused herself to find the restroom and ran into Vanessa.

"Sorry, I couldn't enter your head today," Vanessa said. "Margot, or the alternate Margot, was all over my ass about missing some scenes when I patched into your sensory stream the last time. Maybe it's best for us to only merge our awareness when we enter VR from Maya Escorts."

Thisbe agreed, and they headed back to hear Mahamuni's lecture.

After an uneventful afternoon of VR hiking, Thisbe fully expected to emerge from VR in one of Cerebellum Studios' leather couches. Instead she woke up naked in an intimacy room. Something wet was on her face. Thisbe touched her cheek and examined the sticky semen with her fingers.

"Ugh!" Thisbe got up and dragged herself to the shower.

When she stepped into the hall, she spotted Lester coming the other way. He leaned against the wall and scanned her body up and down as she passed. Thisbe clenched her jaw and gave the technician a cool nod before descending the stairs.

She didn't feel like cooking, so she collected Andy from day care and took him to get a pizza. After she put him to bed that night, the phone rang.

"Yeah, it's Alf. I called Splendid Resorts today, and they said you haven't worked there in months. What's going on?"

Thisbe balled her fists. Her ex-husband's cocky tone irritated her like an emery board dragged across her eyeball.

"None of you business, Alf."

"It is so my business. You're holding out so you can get more welfare, oh excuse me, child support out of me. I'm calling my lawyer first thing in the morning and telling him to subpoena your employment records. Then we'll see what you're up to."

Thisbe slammed the phone so hard that she broke the receiver. That bastard! He'd probably try to take Andy away from her too. Just when she was saving a little, she'd have to spend money on a lawyer, and they didn't come cheap. Now she'd be trapped at Maya Escorts for sure.

Thisbe tried to calm herself with the treasure meditation, but it was no good. The fires of her anger torched her composure with fantasies of revenge. She got up and paced. Her life had become a nightmare. If only she could somehow wake up.

After a sleepless night Thisbe went to work. She left Andy in day care, went to her intimacy room, and jacked in. *A sense of dread hung over the town like a stubborn fog. As soon as Mahamuni's party passed the frowning stone Jizo on the dirt path and entered Shitagawa's eastern boundary, Thisbe smelled trouble. Vanessa joined Thisbe's consciousness, but Thisbe kept mostly quiet so as not to give away Margot's secret.*

The shopkeepers, who'd always smiled in other places, gave Mahamuni's followers only blank stares. A taciturn innkeeper rented rooms to the party without saying a word. They scouted the area and after much haggling found a farmer willing to rent them a fallow rice field for the night's sermon.

"I don't like the looks of this place," Saito said. "Why don't we cancel tonight's lecture and stay inside?"

"I've never run from a challenge, Saito. Even if only one person comes with an open heart, I must speak," Mahamuni replied.

The followers broke into groups of three and roamed the streets shouting their invitation.

"Come see the great master, Mahamuni, and learn the miraculous power of the mind! Seven-o-clock at Suzuki's farm."

Rather than coming out to look, the residents of Shitagawa closed their blinds. When Mahamuni's followers gathered at the rice field that night, only three spectators were present.

Saito looked at his watch. "Should we start?"

"Let's give them ten more minutes," Mahamuni said.

"I don't like the looks of this place," Vanessa said from inside Thisbe's head.

Thisbe nodded. It was the worst possible situation. Too few spectators to make any impact, but enough to force them to go through a pointless exercise. She wanted to return to the motel.

"I guess we might as well start," Mahamuni said.

Saito began with the introduction. About halfway through, two pickup trucks pulled up and a half-dozen men in olive drab nylon jackets jumped out.

"Ah, welcome friends." Saito smiled. "You're just in time for a demonstration on how to use the untapped power of your minds."

"We don't need your stinking cults in our town!" The leader, a burly thirty-year-old with a permanent frown, walked up to Saito and shoved him.

Chikako screamed. Saito stumbled and fell. Mahamuni approached with his hands open only to catch a flurry our roundhouse punches in the face. Oda pulled the assailant off and sank one of his huge fists in the man's gut, while Mahamuni bent over holding his hands over his swollen eye. The women huddled together while Mahamuni's male followers battled the local toughs. Yamamoto dropped to the ground, spun, and reaped an opponent's legs out from under him. The man crashed onto his back and did not get up. While the others struggled one-on-one, Yamamoto dispatched two more assailants with lightning-fast kicks and jabs. The toughs retreated to their pickup trucks and fled. Two policemen were waiting when the pilgrims returned to the motel.

"Thank God you're here!" Mahamuni mumbled through his swollen lips. "We were attacked at Suzuki's farm."

"Your identification," the fat cop demanded.

The followers produced ID cards.

"This woman's underage." The thin cop pointed at Eiko.

"Hmm," the fat one stroked his chin. "Kidnapping and statutory rape. I'm going to have to take you into custody."

After hours of tiring negotiations, Mahamuni's followers were allowed to pay a three hundred thousand yen fine and leave. They walked in the dark for two hours before stopping and spending a cold night huddled by the side of the trail.

Thisbe emerged from VR at Cerebellum Studios, unplugged the cable from her intercranial jack, and wandered into the control room, where Margot and Lester sat behind the monitors.

"Ah, Thisbe," Margot said, "I pulled you out a little early today because I thought you might like to go see a holovision shoot. They're taping some scenes from *Grit City Blues* down on Battery, and I can't get away. It'd be a shame to waste the ticket." She handed Thisbe a slip printed with gold lettering. "All you'd be doing in VR is shivering in the woods, anyway. You might as well go."

Thisbe drove to Battery and found a place to park. The production crew had blocked off the street to keep traffic and pedestrians out. A guard stopped her at the barricade and only allowed her to pass when he heard the "all clear" on his walkie-talkie. Thisbe had never seen a holovision shoot before. Three laser projectors bathed the run-down street in red, green, and blue. An operator wearing protective goggles sat behind a camera across from the Battery Gospel Mission, where a group of actors clustered drinking coffee out of paper cups. Among them was Jeremy Dent, whose picture Thisbe had seen on tabloid magazine covers. He wore a leather coat and had a sparse beard, as if he hadn't shaved in a few days.

A man in a headset who carried a clipboard approached Thisbe. "Excuse me, could you move? You're blocking the green reference beam."

Thisbe joined the others behind the camera. After the crew shot another scene, the man with the clipboard approached again.

"Could you come with me, please? The director would like to speak to you." The production assistant led Thisbe to a trailer a block away.

Inside three people clustered around an array of monitors and controls. A middle-aged man with graying curly hair turned to Thisbe.

"Thanks for coming. I'm Wilson Davis, the director of *Grit City Blues*. I saw you on the monitor and like your features. Have you ever done any acting?"

"Just high school theater." Thisbe's heart beat faster and she began to stammer. "I wanted to go on to college, but my father …"

"It shouldn't be hard. It's just a few lines. Dave will take you to wardrobe."

Thisbe's lines were, "Riggs, Lieutenant Margolis said Bates couldn't be the murderer. He was in Chino when Gonzalez got killed." It took four takes and three hours before the director was satisfied.

"Have I seen you in something before?" Jeremy Dent asked when the shooting was finished.

"No, it's my first time."

"You did well. I hope we work together again."

When the day's shooting was over, it seemed too early to go

home. Thisbe returned to Seeley Park and spent a few hours basking in the artificial sunlight. On her drive home she broke into a song. The moon showed through a rare gap in the clouds. It had no cigarette ad on its face.

The next morning Thisbe entered VR and joined Mahamuni's party standing around a vending machine outside a pottery shop. She noticed her shoelace flopping on the sidewalk and bent to tie it. She had a creepy feeling, as if her bottom were a deer in the crosshairs of a hunter's telescopic sight. When she straightened, Mr. Iwata, one of Mahamuni's recent converts, quickly averted his gaze.

"Do you mind if I take a look inside?" Yamamoto asked Mahamuni. "My mother loves Tajima pottery."

The others followed him in and looked at the teapots, cups, and sake bottles all finished with a distinctive white glaze. A man came out of the back room to stand at the cash register. An old woman remained behind watching soap operas on the television. She was thin, pale, and wore a knit cap over her bald head. Mahamuni approached the man at the register.

"Cancer?" Mahamuni pointed to the old woman.

The man nodded. "The doctors say it's inoperable."

"I don't know if I can cure her, but I may be able to help," Mahamuni said.

The man narrowed his eyes.

"Don't worry. I'm not looking for money," Mahamuni said. "No drugs or needles. I won't hurt her. I promise."

The man nodded. Mahamuni went in the back room, took the woman's head in his hands, and closed his eyes. He emerged ten minutes later.

After the pilgrims left the store, Saito asked, "Sensei, did you cure that old woman?"

"No," Mahmuni said. "I sent her primary tumor away, but the cancer had already spread. Her last months will be more comfortable, but eventually it will kill her."

That night some of the pilgrims went out to celebrate Mr. Oda's thirty-seventh birthday. Despite numerous pleas both Chikako and Vanessa chose to remain at the hotel. Thisbe almost stayed behind, but Mahamuni was going, and the thought of the prophet in a nightclub intrigued her, so she became the only woman in the group of revelers.

To Thisbe's dismay Mr. Iwata joined the party. Something about the man made her skin crawl. He never met her eyes, and his complexion had an oily sheen, as if he'd just ran to catch a bus. When they got to the bar, Thisbe prayed he'd sit someplace else, but he plunked down on the stool next to hers and widened his legs, so his knee rested against hers. She swiveled her stool to turn her back on the pathetic little man and face the others. Oda was waving a ten thousand yen note at the bartender.

"Whiskey!" he bellowed.

"No, no!" Saito withdrew his wallet and put a restraining hand on Oda's arm. "Let me pay."

The two argued for fifteen minutes, until Mahamuni settled the matter by paying himself. The first drinks arrived, faces reddened, and voices became boisterous. It reminded Thisbe of a T-shirt she'd seen, "Instant Asshole — Just add alcohol." She nursed a beer, while the men downed whiskey. Mr. Iwata fingered her bottle, as if it were his penis, and topped off her glass.

"You want whiskey?" he asked.

Thisbe shook her head.

"Hey, Yamamoto!" Oda said. "How come you fight so well?"

"Karate, fifth dan."

"Karate's good," Saito said, 'but judo's better. I took the city championship in high school. If it weren't for my bad knee, I'd have shown those punks in Shitagawa a thing or two."

"Next time, Saito." Oda slapped him on the back.

Yamamoto went to the men's room. When he returned, the hostess handed him a moist towel to wipe his hands.

"Sensei, how about a song?" Oda said. "Bartender, bring the song list!"

Mahamuni took the microphone and scanned the song list. "A-22."

Karaoke music began to play, and the video monitor showed a scene of a man on a bridge. Mahamuni sang the words to "My Way." Although not quite of professional quality, his rich voice stayed in tune and filled the room with the lyrics. When he finished, even those not in his party applauded.

"Thank you. Arigato!" Mahamuni passed the mike to Saito, whose voice didn't match that of his teacher.

Of all the followers the unassuming Mr. Yamamoto was the best singer. After Yamamoto finished his first song, Mahamuni asked for an encore. Oda was eager but had no talent. When Thisbe's turn came, she had a hard time selecting. The songs were so old that none were familiar. She settled on one by someone called Cat Stevens and managed to get through it without anyone dying.

"Another bistro!" Saito bellowed.

Thisbe glanced at her watch. It was almost 11:00. She felt tired, but there was no backing out. The party spilled out of the bar and wandered into the alleyways to look for another place. Two streetwalkers loitered up ahead. Thisbe wanted to turn away, but Mahamuni led his followers right toward them. Thick eye shadow turned the women's faces into caricatures. One, wearing fishnet stockings and a leather miniskirt, stood on one leg and placed her other foot against the wall, so her legs formed a letter P. Her partner, a woman in a loose top cut to bare her shoulder and bra strap, took a drag on a cigarette and flipped it into the street. The butt made a shower of red sparks on the pavement. The smoker sauntered into Saito's path and ran a fingernail down his chest. Her short hair accentuated her broad cheekbones.

"Hey," *she said.* "That little girl can't handle all you big strong men. How about letting us help?"

Saito put his hands up to wave the woman off, but Mahamuni took out his wallet and asked, "How much?"

Jaws dropped. The smoker looked to her partner, who straightened up and approached.

"One hundred thousand yen for all of you, and we'll even do the girl for free."

"No, how much just for him?" *Mahamuni pointed at Iwata, who backed away as if Mahamuni's finger were a loaded pistol.*

"No, Sensei. I ..."

"Don't think I haven't noticed the way you've been sniffing around Thisbe!" *Mahamuni handed a wad of cash to the hooker in the miniskirt.* "If you need a woman, go with them, but leave my students alone!" *Mahamuni turned his back and led his followers away.*

They ended up in a nightclub with a bartender who had a shaved head, one gold tooth, and a van Dyke. Counting Thisbe Mahamuni's party numbered six, now that Mr. Iwata had fled. Who knows, Thisbe thought, maybe he was enjoying the prostitutes' services. After snacks, drinks, and another round of karaoke Mahamuni turned to Thisbe.

"So, what do you think of the prostitutes?"

"A little harsh maybe, but I'm glad you got Mr. Iwata to leave me alone. He was starting to give me the creeps. Thanks."

"No," *Mahamuni said.* "What do you think of the prostitutes?"

"What do you mean?" *Thisbe felt as if her body were shrinking inside her clothes and tried to keep her expression neutral. Mahamuni couldn't know about her job outside VR. Could he?*

"I mean, say a whore wanted to become my follower." *Mahamuni stabbed the ice in his drink with the swizzle stick.* "Should I let her or not?"

"I think," *Thisbe spoke in a measured tone,* "that those women follow that profession, because they have no other choice. So, of course, you should let them be your followers."

"You're wrong." *Mahamuni finished his drink and set the glass on the bar.*

"You always have a choice. I think I won't let them be my student, until they find a decent way to make a living."

Thisbe didn't know what to think, when she emerged from VR. Did Mahamuni's comment mean she should stay in the alternate world, not go back to Maya Escorts, or what? How was she supposed to earn a living? She collected Andy at Maya Escort's day care, and drove home. After dinner, Andy plopped himself in front of the television to watch *Marcus Chipmunk, MD*, while Thisbe ran water for his bath. After washing the dishes Thisbe returned to the bathroom and turned off the tap. The water was barely deep enough to cover Andy's legs. Thisbe worried about him drowning now that he'd taken to bathing alone. She slid the yellow plastic duck off the tub's edge and into the water. Its head bobbed back and forth.

"Turn that off now, Andy. It's time for your bath."

"Mom, can I watch for another half hour? *Rescue Rabbit* is coming on."

"No, you need to get to bed."

"All right." Andy stood and walked to the bathroom like a prisoner on his way to the gallows.

Thisbe heard water splashing from behind the closed door as she picked up the toys on the living room floor. The lights went out. The apartment seemed to lurch onto its side and back again. Glass shattered. Tables and furniture crashed into the wall. Thisbe found herself lying stunned on the carpet. Her hip hurt. A high-pitched wail came from the phone, which had been knocked off the hook. Thisbe's eyes adjusted to the darkness. She surveyed her surroundings. Furniture legs sprouted like broken trees from the carpet. Gradually she became aware of another wail coming from the bathroom. Andy! Thisbe struggled to her feet and stumbled on the clock radio that had fallen to the floor. The couch blocked the bathroom door.

"Mom!" Andy's voice held a terror that raked at Thisbe's soul.

She yanked on the couch. Adrenalin dulled the pain of her fingernail tearing away. She yanked again and cleared the entrance.

"I'm here, honey." Oblivious to the spilt water soaking her pants she knelt on the tile and scooped her son into her arms.

"Ahh!" Andy screamed when she touched his shoulder.

"It's all right. It's all right."

She heard sirens in the distance. With her injured child in her arms Thisbe rushed down the steps and onto the street, where her stunned neighbors wandered like zombies. Dust filled the air and limited her view to ten or fifteen feet. She covered Andy's mouth with her shirt and ran toward the red lights sweeping through the gloom.

Thisbe cleared the dust cloud and stopped at a cluster of ambulances. A paramedic in a black uniform took Andy from her arms, sat him on a gurney, and covered his naked body with a thick gray blanket. Thisbe watched while he shined a penlight in Andy's eyes. For the first time since the incident, she got a good look at her son. His arm hung like a broken wing out of his shoulder socket.

"Looks like you got pretty shaken up there, partner." The paramedic probed Andy's shoulder with a gloved hand.

"Ow!"

"He's dislocated his shoulder," the paramedic told Thisbe. "Hurts a lot, but he should be fine. You should probably get a bandage on that." He pointed to Thisbe's bleeding finger. "What's the boy's name?"

"Andy."

"Tell you what, Andy." The paramedic removed a roll of tape from his kit. "I'm going to secure your arm to your body so it doesn't hurt when we take you to the doctor. Then he'll fix you right up."

Once reassured Andy was safe, Thisbe allowed herself to look around. Rescue workers held back from the dust cloud while police radios squawked in the night air. The half dozen injured who'd made it to the aid station, lay on gurneys while paramedics examined their wounds.

"Let's take a look at that hand." The paramedic, who'd treated Andy, swabbed Thisbe's finger with disinfectant and applied a bandage.

The police wouldn't let Thisbe cross the hastily erected barricade, so she and Andy waited an hour for an ambulance to take them to a hospital. They waited another hour in triage. She borrowed a cell phone from a black woman with jaundiced eyes and phoned Alf. He arrived wearing his annoyance like the form-fitting waterproof genpaaca sweater that clung to his muscular frame. Thisbe's eyes searched his body from his collar to his shoes for evidence that Alf had thought of anyone other than himself, but he'd brought no clothing for his naked son.

The nurse called her name. Thisbe escorted Andy into an exam room, where a Pakistani doctor forced the dislodged joint back into place and put the boy's arm in a sling.

"How you doing, champ?" Alf tousled Andy's hair when Thisbe brought him back to the waiting room.

Andy pressed his teary face to her leg. Alf didn't offer Thisbe a place to stay. He didn't give her any money to help out. He only said, "Since your place is a wreck, maybe Andy should stay with me for a few days."

The last image Thisbe saw of them that night was Andy riding his father's shoulders through the emergency room's exit. She borrowed the black woman's phone again and called Margot, who picked her up fifteen minutes later.

CHAPTER 21

When Thisbe returned to VR the next day, Mahamuni's followers sat in the front row of an old movie theater on the outskirts of Inuyama. Dressed in a sky-blue tunic like the others Thisbe had to tilt her head to see the prophet on the stage. He performed the stunts that had worked so well at the previous gathering and added new tricks such as guessing people's ages and addresses. To Thisbe it looked more like a magic show than a religious service. The crowd loved it.

"This guy's pretty impressive," Vanessa said after tapping into Thisbe's awareness. "Margot told me about what happened to your place. Sorry."

Thisbe turned around. All but a few of the two hundred seats were filled. The audience cheered Mahamuni's exhortation to have faith in their minds. Saito closed with his customary invitation to Kyoto and added something new. Mahamuni would provide private spiritual counseling after the show for the price of five thousand yen.

Most spectators left, but twenty people waving bills rushed the stage. Saito plucked the money from eager fingers and escorted a young woman in a pink sweater backstage. She'd dyed her beautiful Asian hair reddish brown, which seemed like a crime to Thisbe. Saito returned.

"Can I see him?" Thisbe asked.

"You'll have to wait for our guests," Saito replied.

Thisbe settled in to her seat. The other church members had already left. She had nothing to do but look at the newcomers. Most were in their twenties, no doubt still living with their parents and flush with cash from their first jobs. The first interviewee returned. Rather than speak to the others, she rushed to the exit without making eye contact. Saito ushered a young man with a wedge-shaped haircut backstage. At this rate Thisbe estimated she'd have to wait over an hour.

"You don't have any customers now," Vanessa said from inside Thisbe's head. "Let's go back and see if Lester shows up."

Thisbe adjusted her awareness until she was back in the intimacy room alone. All was quiet except for the rush of air through the vent and the distant sound of moaning from down the hall. With nothing better to do, Thisbe switched her awareness back and forth between VR and the intimacy room. Lester never showed. Eventually a customer entered, *and Thisbe returned full-time to VR, where she waited another ten minutes for the final two interviewees. Saito took her to Mahamuni.*

The sage sat in a tiny room that needed a good dusting. A draw cord for the curtain wrapped a cleat on the wall behind his head. The dark varnish had peeled from his wooden chair. Thisbe sat across from him.

"Did you see that crowd?" he asked. "I feel that my church is finally growing."

"You've got to stop this," Thisbe said. "The public isn't ready for the power of their minds. They're going to upset the delicate balance between worlds and unleash a disaster."

"Disaster," Mahamuni said. "I'm trying to prevent a disaster. Half the world is using up resources at an enormous rate, while the other half starves. We can't go on like this much longer. If saving humanity requires desperate measures, I'm prepared to do whatever it takes."

"I understand, but you're going about this the wrong way."

Mahamuni's eyes suddenly looked very old. He ran his hands over his face and sighed. "After all we've been through, I'd have never thought you'd be so selfish as to keep this knowledge to yourself."

"Selfish? I'm not the one who's turning his ministry into a sideshow. I just came from the hospital. Your antics nearly killed my son."

"What are you talking about? You were with us all day."

Thisbe searched for a way to explain, but it proved as elusive as a fugitive terrorist hiding in the mountains of Afghanistan. "You can move objects through space and time, right? Well, I can do the same with my awareness. We've changed the future. Tanaka was supposed to lead the church, not Saito. If we don't change things back, the future will be very grim."

Mahamuni clenched his jaw.

"I'll show you." Thisbe took Mahamuni's hand and shifted back to the intimacy room.

Her timing couldn't have been worse. She was immersed in a sea of flesh, her face against a giant man's chest. His cock pounded into her like a battering ram.

"Get out!" Mahamuni's scream returned them to VR. He tore his hand away as if Thisbe's touch were a twelve-amp power cable.

"Take your sick fantasies away from here! You will spend the next week in silence and seclusion. After you've completed this penance, I'll consider whether to reinstate you in my church."

Thisbe emerged from VR fully dressed and lying in one of Cerebellum Studios' leather couches. She unhooked the cable and joined the others in the control room. After Margot

dismissed the other actors, she asked to see Thisbe in private.

"You seem very agitated," Margot said. "Have you been keeping up with your meds?"

Thisbe looked Margot straight in the eye and lied. "Yes, it's just that having my memories come back takes a bit of getting used to."

"I know it's hard," Margot touched Thisbe's arm. "You can take a few days off, if you need to."

"Thanks, but I think working is best for me now."

"You know best," Margot said.

When Thisbe got home a message was waiting on her answering machine.

"Thisbe Anderson, this is Dr. Cavendish's office calling to remind you of your appointment on Thursday at 7:00 p.m.. Dr. Cavendish says she'll be forced to notify your probation officer if you miss another one. Please give us a call at 534-1234 if you need to reschedule."

What was going on? Thisbe felt as if she were being squeezed to death. She grabbed a strand of her hair and tugged. A sharp pain tore her scalp as she ripped the hair out by its roots. She paced back and forth in the living room. Which world was the real one? What could she trust now that even her memories were suspect? She got an idea. One person might be able to help. Thisbe pulled the *Robe of Purity* from the bookshelf and found the discussion of Mahamuni's seclusion in the introduction. Nagano – if Thisbe remembered correctly, the house where she'd first met Mahamuni in VR was in Nagano.

Thisbe checked her bank balance on the computer. She had a little over eighty thousand credits. Flights without an advance were expensive, but nothing she couldn't handle with her newfound wealth. Thisbe clicked the buy icon and rushed to her car. She had two hours to get to the spaceport.

Thisbe made it through traffic and check-in with twenty minutes to spare. She hadn't had time to pack but would buy toiletries and a change of clothes in Japan. The rocket plane was visible through the boarding gate's window. The Airbus SP-11 looked more like a sports car than a bus. Due to a last-minute cancellation Thisbe managed to get a window seat. Flight attendants made their customary announcements about zero g, while the plane taxied. Rather than watch the presentation Thisbe gazed at the lights reflecting off Puget Sound. The big engines roared. Inertia's omnipresent hand pushed Thisbe into her seat. Soon they were airborne.

"This is Captain McGee," a voice said over the intercom. "We'll be cruising on air-breathing engines up to ninety thousand feet. At that point we'll fire up the rockets, climb to a height of roughly ninety miles, and follow a ballistic arc over the Pacific. Tonight's flight should take two hours and twenty minutes to reach Narita International Spaceport, so sit back and enjoy the ride."

A half hour later the captain turned on the "fasten seatbelt" sign. The rocket boosters pressed Thisbe into her seat. The rumble sounded as if a freight train were passing a few feet away. Something banged in the galley. The woman seated next to Thisbe grabbed her hand so hard it hurt.

The rockets cut off, and all was silence. Thisbe felt like she was falling. Outside her window the earth curved toward Asia. Thisbe peeled the box of juice from the Velcro attaching it to the seat back in front of her, inserted a straw through the membrane, and sipped. After they drifted for twenty minutes, the outside air began to glow. Thisbe was so engrossed watching the violet and pink light show that she didn't notice her sense of weight gradually return. The atmosphere began to buffet the plane. When they reached sixty thousand feet, the pilot restarted the air-breathing engines and flew the remaining few hundred miles to the traffic pattern circling Tokyo.

After they landed a half hour later, Thisbe exited the gate into the crowded spaceport. Dark-haired Asians rushed to their destinations and spoke gibberish she couldn't understand. All the signs were in indecipherable squiggles. As she began to think the trip had been a gigantic blunder, she noticed an animated display. A text balloon filled with English words came from the mouth of a blonde girl with extra large eyes. Seconds later the black box she'd spoken into emitted a balloon filled with Japanese. Thisbe walked over and entered one of the cylindrical white plastic booths by the display.

"Hello?"

"Welcome to Japan," a voice from the speaker said. "From

your comments I understand that you speak English. Is that correct?"

"Yes"

"Excellent! The Misogi 6200 will allow you to converse in Japanese. Before we begin, I need to get a few personal details."

"Excuse me," Thisbe said. "How much does this cost?"

"The Misogi 6200 is free to all visitors to Japan. Now, I'll need your name."

After Thisbe gave her name and address, the controller played a ten-minute instruction video and dispensed a black box small enough to fit in her palm. She tried it right away.

"Excuse me." Thisbe stopped a middle-aged man in the aisle. "How do I get to Nagano?"

The man stroked his chin and listened to the box's translation before replying.

"He says practice." The box added, "It's an old joke from the Winter Olympics fifty years ago. Seriously, he suggests taking Japan Rail. But have you considered a Yottsubishi airport bus? They are a better value. For only one hundred ninety credits you can ride in air-conditioned comfort. Yottsubishi hires only professional drivers with spotless records. Buses for Nagano leave from level two every hour. Make the wise choice. Choose a Yottsubishi Airport Bus, today."

A few hours after they left, Thisbe realized the bus trip had been a mistake. It took longer than the flight across the Pacific. After a dozen stops the driver made a final announcement and pulled the lever to open the door.

"He says we've arrived at Nagano Central Bus Terminal," the Misogi 6200 reported. "Now that we're here how about relaxing at the Yottsubishi Olympic Plaza Hotel? For only two hundred ninety credits a night you can enjoy in-room cable holovision, a mini bar, and an Olympic-sized pool. Hungry? How about stopping at the Yottsubishi Grill just minutes from downtown? At the Yottsubishi Grill the finest Japanese chefs prepare delicacies from all over the world. Make it a night to remember! Try the Yottsubishi Grill!"

Thisbe looked for the "off" switch but couldn't find it, so she dialed the volume down to a low roar. Despite the Misogi 6200's protests she rented a motel room near the bus station. The long day of travel had drained her. She shut the black box in a drawer, showered, and went to bed.

The following morning she changed into the clothing she'd purchased in a hallway vending machine. The pink blouse was a bit short in the waist and sleeves, but it would do for the day. Thisbe recalled Chikako discussing a ruined castle from the first VR meeting with Mahamuni. After breakfast and a brief discussion with the proprietor, who fortunately spoke English, Thisbe summoned a cab. Much to her chagrin she needed the Misogi 6200 to tell the driver she wanted to go to Matsushiro Castle.

"Interested in sightseeing?" the box said after passing on her request. "Why not reserve a seat on a Yottsubishi tour bus? Yottsubishi operates a wide variety ..."

When they got close to the castle, Thisbe described the house she sought. After conferring with the dispatcher and a few locals, the driver pulled up to the house, Thisbe remembered from her VR session. Urban sprawl had planted homes where the rice fields had once been. A bent old woman with thinning hair answered the door. Thisbe asked for Mahamuni through the Misogi 6200.

"You won't need that thing," the old woman said. "Leave it by the door and come in."

Thisbe set the box on the step, waved goodbye to the gleaming white taxi in the driveway, and followed the old woman inside, where she removed her shoes and placed them on the rack by the door.

"We don't get many visitors anymore, certainly very few from North America." The old woman ushered Thisbe into the living room and brought her a cup of tea on a wooden saucer.

Thisbe sipped. The drink had a smoky, roasted flavor. The old woman returned pushing Mahamuni in a wheelchair. Once energetic and vital, the sage had shrunk. His flesh resembled that of a desiccated apricot. Lacking the strength to sit upright, he slumped his bony frame sideways in the wheelchair. His left eye and corner of his mouth drooped. The old woman spoke to him in Japanese. A sparkle kindled in Mahamuni's vacant eyes.

He lifted his hands from the plaid blanket covering his knees and touched his palms together in a feeble imitation of clapping.

"Thank you for seeing me." Thisbe paused for the old woman to translate. "I'm very confused, and you're the only one who can help me."

Mahamuni's only response was a drop of spittle oozing out of the corner of his mouth. The old woman wiped his face with a tissue.

"Did something happen thirty years ago on the walk to Kyoto, something that changed the world in a way it wasn't supposed to?"

The old man stared. Feeling like a fool Thisbe grasped at VR memories and flung them.

"It had to do with Tanaka and the woman who died."

The old woman's expression hardened. "Why do you want to go digging up old scandals? Can't you see he's suffered enough? I think it's time for you to leave."

Thisbe stood. Mahamuni's skeletal hand shot out and grasped her wrist.

"Abomination!" The words rattled in his chest. "This world is an abomination!"

Thisbe took the JR train back to the Narita International Spaceport. The Misogi 6200 complained the whole way. There was no return desk at the terminal, so after clearing check-in Thisbe abandoned the device in the ladies' room. The flight went smoothly. Four hours after leaving, she was back in her Mercer Island home.

CHAPTER 22

"Hey, where do you think you're going?" one of Mahamuni's recent converts yelled. "You're in seclusion. Get back in line or you're out of the church!"

Thisbe turned her back on the loudmouth and exited through the hotel's sliding glass doors. A short walk took her to the path that followed the Kiso River. Colorful flat-bottomed boats lined the banks. A picturesque railroad bridge crossed the river to Unuma. Thisbe's stomach growled. She hadn't eaten breakfast. Thisbe turned to see if any of Mahamuni's followers had come after her, but only Inuyama Castle and a dam with lookout towers that resembled parking meters lay behind her.

A man in a white shirt cooked in a food stall up ahead. Thisbe stopped and bought okonomiyaki. The cook topped the cabbage pancake with sweetened soy sauce and placed it in a container. Thisbe paid, bought an iced green tea from a vending machine, and sat down to consider her options while eating. Ever since she'd started this VR disk, the church had paid her expenses. To strike out on her own she'd need cash.

After breakfast she found a bank machine and inserted her ATM card. When prompted for her password, she instinctively spelled Andrew using the hiragana characters on the numeric keypad. A smiling, animated face welcomed her to the main menu. She checked her balance. It was over a million yen. Without knowing the currency's value Thisbe withdrew one hundred thousand yen and set off toward the train station.

Thisbe bought tickets and boarded a light-green train that stopped at every station. She transferred to an express at Mino-ota and sat next to a man holding a pair of women's high-heeled shoes in the crowded nonsmoking car. During the three-hour trip to Nagano Thisbe stared out the window at the river gorge, where power lines scaled the mountains like intrepid Sherpas. Following the cartoon images of policemen in blue uniforms, Thisbe located a koban and asked directions to the central police station. A short bus ride later she stood in front of a female officer at the front desk.

"I'm wondering if you can help me," Thisbe said. "I'm here on behalf of Mahamuni. One of his followers, Ichiro Tanaka, was involved in a murder. Although the crime shocked us all, the sage feels responsible for his former follower and asked me to check on his well-being."

"Ah, the girl who was killed in Matsumoto." The woman's face grew serious. "That would be Inspector Naguchi's case. I'll see if he's in." After a brief

telephone conversation the woman motioned Thisbe to the inspector's office.

"Welcome!" The inspector smiled and stood from behind his desk while waiting for Thisbe to sit. "Your information helped us solve this case. It's always a pleasure to have such a good citizen visit. How may I help you?"

Inspector Naguchi's desk was well organized with papers piled in neat stacks. A large thermos sat by an ashtray containing two cigarette butts. Thisbe took a seat.

"Our teacher, Mahamuni, sent me. He's concerned about Mr. Tanaka. Mahamuni is having a hard time believing that someone in his inner circle could commit such a horrible act as murder. He wonders if there's a possibility Mr. Tanaka could have been arrested by mistake."

"Yes." Inspector Naguchi lit a cigarette. Holding it between his thumb and forefinger, he leaned back in his chair and gazed upward. "This often happens with witnesses. They have second thoughts about sending acquaintances to jail and begin to question their testimony. But don't worry. We at the police department performed a thorough investigation, and in my view your Tanaka is guilty. DNA evidence confirmed he was having an affair with the victim and her blood was found on his clothing."

"But it's so hard to believe with him being a respected religious figure."

"When you've been around as long as I have, you see many cases like this." Inspector Naguchi leaned forward and stubbed out his cigarette. "The victim, Miss Oe, had previously worked as a prostitute. No doubt she was blackmailing your Mr. Tanaka and he murdered her to stop it."

"What about Hideo Watanabe? Could he have set Mr. Tanaka up?"

"The yakuza?" Inspector Naguchi waved his hand. "Now you're beginning to sound like Tanaka's lawyer, Mr. Koga. For that explanation to work, Watanabe would have had to follow your party unseen, steal Mr. Tanaka's clothing, get Miss Oe alone to kill her, and sneak the blood-soaked clothing back into Tanaka's room. Trust me, in police work, as in science, you must use Occam's razor. Pluritas non est ponenda sine necceisitate. Or the simplest explanation is the best."

"Thank you for your help." Thisbe stood. "I'm sure your explanation will set Mahamuni's mind at ease."

The phone book listed three lawyers named Koga. A few phone calls and a short bus ride later, Thisbe was sitting across the desk from Tanaka's defense attorney. Mr. Koga was in his early twenties. His big eyes seemed to carry a hurt, as if he were about to break out in tears at any minute. A blue department-store suit hung on his lanky frame. His hair gleamed from the liberal use of pomade.

"It's good that you've come to see me. I wanted to question the members of your church, but you've been a little hard to locate." The phone rang. "Hello. Can't we move the arraignment back to Friday?" Koga listened another ten minutes before hanging up. "Now, where were we?" He shuffled some papers. "Oh, yes! What can you tell me about this former yakuza, Hideo Watanabe?"

Thisbe went over what she knew.

"Well, the problem is that nobody seems to have heard of him." Koga sipped his tea. "No doubt Hideo Watanabe is an assumed name. Thinking they had an open-and-shut case, the police didn't even try to track him down. Perhaps you could meet my investigator and look through some gangsters' mug shots in hopes of identifying the elusive Mr. Watanabe."

Thisbe returned to the waiting room. A secretary pumped hot water from a thermos, added a teabag to the cup, and handed it to Thisbe. Twenty minutes later a huge man entered. His sumo-wrestler-sized belly strained against his golf shirt as if it were trying to burst through the stained polyester. He looked like the kind of guy one could hit with a tactical nuclear warhead, and it would only make him mad.

"You Thisbe?" he asked with a gravelly voice.

She nodded.

"Let's go look at some photos." He led her outside to a micro-compact car that resembled a dwarf's orange running shoe.

The investigator's body took up the whole driver's side and spilled into Thisbe's space. To her dismay she realized the investigator was taking her back to the central police station. The receptionist's formerly warm smile chilled when she saw Thisbe with the competition.

"We need to look at some mug shots," the big investigator bellowed.

The receptionist's eyes darted to the telephone. Her hand shook as she picked up the handset and dialed. Moments later Inspector Naguchi strolled into the office.

"Well, well, what are you doing here, Abe?" Naguchi turned a disdainful gaze at Thisbe before looking back at the investigator.

"Just making sure you haven't let any details slip through the cracks like in Osaka."

Inspector Naguchi's face grew red. "Officer Uegaki!" he yelled.

"Hai!" A young man rushed to Naguchi's side and stood at attention.

"Mr. Abe wants to examine our photo collection of central Japan's finest yakuza. See to it!" The inspector strode out.

"Hai!" The young officer gestured down the hall. "This way, please."

He ushered Thisbe and Mr. Abe into a small windowless room. Thisbe sat on *a metal chair across the colorless table from Mr. Abe. The young officer rolled in a cart stacked with thick binders, bowed, and left.*

"How old would you say this Watanabe is?" Mr. Abe asked.

"He was in his thirties."

"Did you see his tattoos or any distinguishing marks?"

"All over his body. The time I saw them happened so fast that I can't remember any details."

"Any regional accent?"

Thisbe shook her head.

"Well, let's start with the locals." Mr. Abe placed a binder in front of her.

Thisbe paged through the photos. At first she lingered over each, but soon the overwhelming numbers forced her to pick up the pace. She got into a rhythm, examining each hard face and pair of pitiless eyes for a second before moving on. How much misery had these men caused? Occasionally she'd stop for something incongruous such as a smile or warm look while her brain tried to sort out the contradiction. Then she moved on. She worked for three hours before stopping.

"There!" She stabbed her index finger into the page. "He's the one!"

"Toda Ishigawa of the Yamada clan." Abe made some calls. The address listed on Ishigawa's rap sheet turned out to be an abandoned warehouse. Neither the phone directory nor an Internet search turned up any sign of him. Abe returned his cell phone to his pocket and turned to Thisbe. "You've done more than enough to serve justice today. However, if you're game for a little adventure, there's one more way you can help."

"All right"

"Okay, here's what you're going to do."

They arrived in Tokyo after dark. Mr. Abe cruised the streets crowded with strip clubs and pachinko parlors in search of their destination.

"That's the place." He pointed to a garish turquoise building with the sign reading Black Mist Club over the door. Mr. Abe parked a block up the street and handed Thisbe a plastic box the size of a matchbook. "Take this with you. If there's trouble, I'll be there in less than a minute."

Thisbe slipped the device into her pocket and walked toward the entrance. With each step the clammy feeling that clung to her skin grew more intense. She stopped in front of the opaque glass door and contemplated turning back. Thisbe took a breath. What could go wrong? It was only VR? She pulled the handle and stepped inside.

A half-dozen men, some missing parts of their fingers, sat around a table covered with cash, cards, and bottles. The air laden with cigarette smoke seared her lungs. Flanked by two women in low-cut gowns, an older man sat at a booth. A bartender polished glasses while watching a sumo match on TV.

"Excuse me."

All eyes turned to Thisbe.

"I'm looking for Toda Ishigawa," she said. "He told me I could earn a little extra money by posing for some photos." Thisbe felt the old man's lizard eyes brush her breasts and thighs with a touch like a dried twig.

"Yah" One of the men from the table stood and approached. "Ishigawa's not here right now, but I can help you." He put his hand on the small of Thisbe's back. "I have a camera in the back room. We pay twenty thousand yen with a condom and forty thousand without."

"I don't think so." Thisbe squirmed out of his grasp. "You're not as handsome as Toda."

The others laughed.

"Why don't you just tell me where he is?"

"He doesn't want to be disturbed." A man at the table put down his cards and glared.

"Okay, but he'll be disappointed when he learns what he's missing." Thisbe turned toward the door.

"I have a car out front." The standing man put his arm around Thisbe's waist. "I can drive you to him."

"Enough!" The old man's voice filled the room.

The creep withdrew his arm as if Thisbe's waist were a hot iron.

"Toda Ishigawa is no longer here. He works at the Haneda Machine Works in Shinagawa." The old man drained a shot of whiskey and leveled his eyes at Thisbe. "Tell him that we had an agreement. If he wants to get back into the business, he must obey tradition and pay the penalty."

The scene swirled. Thisbe woke naked and alone in an intimacy room. After showering and dressing, she caught Vanessa on the way out.

"What did Margot say that day she kept you after work, anyway?" Vanessa held open the door to the parking lot and waited for Thisbe to pass.

Thisbe stopped. There was no point in keeping secrets any longer. "She told me that I'd agreed to have my memory erased temporarily to be in her VR movie, that the world we're in now is a product of my sick mind, and that I shouldn't tell you you've had the same thing done."

Vanessa frowned. "You don't believe her, do you?"

"I did, after she restored my missing memories," Thisbe said.

Vanessa stared.

"I was a hooker who agreed to work on Margot's project for a chance to get off the streets."

"But you don't believe her now?"

"Let's just say I discovered a few inconsistencies."

"Do you ever find yourself wanting to stay? You know, just remove the wire and never come back?" Vanessa said. "It's nicer there. People aren't so cutthroat and I don't wake up naked in a puddle of a dozen men's cum. I mean, why shouldn't we believe in the world that makes us happy?"

"Andy needs me in this world."

"Doesn't he need you in the other one too?" Vanessa asked.

Thisbe took the keys from her purse. "See you tomorrow."

Thisbe was staying at Margot's. She'd retrieved her car from the apartment's parking lot. Fortunately she'd kept a spare key in a magnetic box attached to the chassis. When she got to Margot's place, Thisbe put her bag on the kitchen counter and phoned Alf's to talk to Andy.

"He wet the bed last night," the boy's father said. "I'll get him for you."

"Hello" Andy's voice sounded weak and uncertain.

"Hi, honey. How are you?"

"Okay."

"What are you doing?"

"I dunno."

"I'm staying at Tyler's house," Thisbe said. "Maybe in a few days you could come over here. You and Tyler could share a room. Would you like that?"

"I dunno."

Thisbe fought back the urge to drill for the hurt buried in Andy's noncommittal response. "Okay, honey. You think about it. I'll talk to you tomorrow." She placed the phone in its cradle.

"So, how is he?" Margot had approached while Thisbe was occupied.

"He doesn't sound good."

"After what he's been through, it's no wonder." Margot leaned against the kitchen doorway. "But children his age are resilient. He'll be all right."

"I just know that jerk of a father isn't helping," Thisbe spouted. "He probably has Andy shooting guns, doing pushups on broken glass, or some other macho bullshit. So how was your day?"

"Good. Tyler's staying at a friend's, and I wasn't scheduled at ME, so I got to work on my VR movie."

"Can you do that at home?"

"Some of it. Want to see my workshop? It's right down the hall."

Thisbe followed Margot to a converted bedroom containing a computer with a VR feed. A ballerina doll in a pink tutu perched atop the monitor.

"So how does all this work?" Thisbe asked.

"Oh, I use the VRAnime package. Let me show you." Margot reached for the mouse. "If I do a lot of work, I plug in the VR feed and control the computer through my implant, but I don't need to do that now." She selected an icon. "This is the environment menu. It lets you design what your world looks like. You know, select the scenery, weather, and how flexible the laws of physics are. Things look artificial right now because the computer fills in the details only after everything else is done." She pulled up another screen. "These are the character pages. I use them to design their looks and motivations."

"Can you use actors?"

"Not on a home system." Margot exited the program. "Only professional studios have the equipment. But the home equipment is getting better. Computer-defined characters are more realistic than they used to be."

"Ever hear of a group called the Alliance for the Less Fortunate?" Thisbe asked.

Margot gave her a blank look.

"Just wondering," Thisbe said. "I heard something about them making VR movies in the news."

The following morning Thisbe stopped by her wrecked apartment to see what she could salvage. When she parked in front of the wooden barricade blocking the road, a fat policeman got out of his car and demanded to see her ID.

"It's in there." Thisbe pointed at the wrecked two-story building.

The cantilevered portion that was her bedroom had collapsed over the carport and crushed her neighbor's Honda Ladybug like a giant fly swatter. Thisbe was glad she couldn't afford the extra one hundred credits a month for covered parking.

"I can't let you go in there," the policeman said. "The structure's unsafe. Take my advice. Write it all off, and let your insurance company pay."

Thisbe shrugged. She couldn't afford insurance. At least the cop didn't cite her for driving without a license. She got in her car and headed to work.

Mr. Abe pulled into the underground parking lot at the Kyo Shimbun building. Thisbe had just entered VR and was unaware of how much time had passed since her visit to the yakuza club. Mr. Abe maneuvered his tiny car into a gap next to a concrete pillar, removed a gift from behind the seat, and pushed his bulk against the door to get out. Seemingly without concern for Thisbe, he strode toward the elevator. She hurried to catch up. Abe held the doors open for her. He pushed the button for the newspaper building's seventh floor. The doors slid open on a scene of chaos, as if a giant had scattered desks in random orientations in the office.

"Abe-san," a voice from the corner bellowed.

The big man's face lit up. He hurried toward the newspaperman in thick glasses, who was waving them toward his corner desk. Abe made a slight bow.

"Sensei, I brought you a little gift." Mr. Abe presented the box.

The newspaperman held the box up to admire its wrapping before opening it. "Ah, whiskey!" He set the bottle down and motioned the others toward the chairs.

Thisbe sat down and noticed the cane leaning against the desk. The newspaperman's name plate read, "Kimura."

"So, what can I do for my old student today?" Kimura asked.

"I need to know about the Haneda Machine Works in Shinagawa."

"Haneda" Kimura stroked his chin. "I believe they supply components to one of the big corporations. Mr. Fukuda!"

A subordinate came to the desk.

"Get me the files on the Haneda Machine Works." Kimura turned back to Mr. Abe. "So Abe-san, how are Hatsu and the boy?"

"Good, although my son is a bit willful. He neglects his school work."

"Like his father."

Mr. Abe hung his head and blushed. In his moment of vulnerability the big man resembled the stuffed lion Thisbe had kept on her bed when she was little. Of course, she wasn't about to snuggle up and kiss him on the forehead. The assistant handed Mr. Kimura some papers.

"Ah, Haneda Machine Works," Kimura read. "90 percent of their business comes from the Kin Tsuru Corporation."

"Kin Tsuru?" Abe said.

"Yes, Haneda supplies chassis for consumer electronic goods."

"Who heads that division at Kin Tsuru?" Abe asked

"Sasaeburo Inoue"

Abe pursed his lips. "How about before?"

"That would have been Mr. Hiroshi Saito." Kimura sat back in his chair. "He was one of Junzo Tagaki's rising stars until they all got voted out in that disastrous shareholders' meeting. Whittling down Kin Tsuru's product line by 80 percent, really!" Kimura shook his head.

Thisbe turned to Abe, whose face registered no surprise.

"Any yakuza *connection?" Abe asked.*

"What company the size of Kin Tsuru doesn't have one? Shakedowns, call girls for visiting executives. It's almost impossible to trace."

"How about Toda Ishigawa? Ever heard of him?"

Kimura shook his head.

"Thank you, sensei. We've troubled you too much."

Kimura waved the formality away.

On the way to the elevator, Thisbe asked, "So he was your teacher?"

"Ju jutsu." Abe pushed the down button. "Until he was shot in the knee."

The doors slid open. Two salarymen and an office girl made room for the enormous Mr. Abe and his friend. They rode to the garage in silence. Once they got in Abe's car, Thisbe resumed her questioning.

"Why would Saito hire Ishigawa to frame Tanaka?"

"We don't know that yet." Abe turned the key and started the engine.

"You don't believe it's a coincidence, do you?"

"No, but let's make sure."

Vanessa joined Thisbe's VR session on the drive to the next stop. Mr. Abe had just paid a uniformed woman in a tollbooth and accelerated onto the highway when she spoke from inside Thisbe's head.

"Thisbe, it's Vanessa. You have a free period now. Pop back and see if Lester shows up."

Thisbe shifted her awareness to the intimacy room, where she lay trapped in a naked unresponsive body. No one was there. Out of boredom she tried to wiggle her finger. It seemed that the memory of how to move had deserted her. She worked at trying to remember and thought she might have moved the finger a millimeter when Lester arrived.

He closed the door behind him and rushed to the bed, where he began kissing Thisbe's knees. Soon his lips ascended to the delicate skin on her inner thighs. Using one of her legs as a pillow, he lay on his side, tongued her vagina, and unzipped his fly to fondle himself.

"Ugh!" Vanessa said. "You must be full of juice from three or four guys by now."

Lester stiffened and made a childlike whimper.

"That should give me the leverage I need to get Lester's cooperation," Vanessa said. "I'm out of here. Talk to you later."

Thisbe watched Lester wipe semen from his belly with a towel, pull up his pants, and slink out the door. Pitiful! *She shifted her consciousness back to VR. Mr. Abe peered into her eyes.*

"Where were you just now?" he asked.

Hot scarlet embarrassment flowed to her face. She looked out the parked car's window so Abe wouldn't see.

"It's 6:00. You ready?" Without waiting for her reply he got out of the car.

Thisbe followed him into a bar up the street.

"Irassahimase!" the bartender and hostess said in unison.

The hostess's thick makeup hid her wrinkles like the dim light hid the carpet's tears. The air carried the bitter smells of beer, stale tobacco, and failure. Mr. Abe took a seat at the bar, where he ordered a biru for himself and one for Thisbe. She sat beside him, nibbled the pickles the bartender set out, and waited to see what would transpire. Soon four men in gray overalls with Haneda Machine Works stenciled over their chest pockets entered and sat at a table.

"Bartender, four beers!" the oldest bellowed. Years of drinking and disappointment had shriveled his features, but here in the company of three men, twenty years his junior, he enjoyed a fleeting modicum of the respect.

Abe whispered to the bartender, who poured the drinks for the hostess to carry to the table. The senior man nodded and raised his glass to Abe. Voices grew boisterous and gathered a singsong tone from almost the first sips. Words like asshole, wanker, and faggot peppered the conversation. Thisbe imagined the terms were much more colorful in the original Japanese. When the workers finished the first round, Abe sent another.

After an hour the three youngest left to search for more thrills than an old man's tired stories and self-pity. With no one else to brag to, the eldest worker staggered to the stool next to Abe. Thisbe could smell the fumes on the worker's breath all the way from the other side of Abe.

"Hey, why'd you buy us all the drinks? You need my help pleasing your woman?"

Thisbe gritted her teeth. The private detective placed a finger on her forearm to restrain her rage.

"I used to work for a second-tier supplier like yours," Abe said. "I promised myself to remember where I came from if I ever got a lucky break. Sake?"

The old man nodded. The bartender brought a warmed porcelain bottle, which Abe used to fill the worker's cup.

"So how did you get a decent break?" The old man drained his sake and set the cup down.

"Marriage," Abe said. "My wife's uncle works for Yottsubishi Corporation's human resources department."

"Isn't that always the way?" The old man turned his bleary, bloodshot eyes to Thisbe. "Your wife's very beautiful."

"How would you know?" Abe asked. "I haven't showed you her picture."

The men giggled.

"The worst part," Abe poured the old man another drink, "was the favoritism. They'd promote some new guy to be my supervisor, even though I had fifteen years experience. But I suppose that never happened to you."

"Ishigawa!" The worker drained his cup and rested his forearms on the bar, where his sleeves soaked up the spilled liquor. "Vice President Sasaki made that greenhorn my supervisor. A former yakuza! *I'll never forgive that bastard."*

CHAPTER 23

The scene swirled to the cubicle at Cerebellum Studios. Vanessa was absent from Margot's customary pep talk. Thisbe wondered why. Perhaps Vanessa hadn't made it to this world, because she'd abandoned Thisbe's VR session early. When Thisbe got home she called, but Vanessa didn't answer.

The doorbell rang. A deliveryman in a purple uniform stood on the step. He handed her a tablet and stylus and exchanged them for a cardboard box once she signed. Thisbe set the box on the kitchen table and rummaged through coupons, pencils, and papers in a drawer until she found a rusty pair of scissors. She slit the box's packing tape, sunk her hands into the Styrofoam peanuts, and removed a familiar black box.

"Hello, Thisbe. I'm your Misogi 6200. I'm sorry we were separated in Japan. Say, I bet you're hungry. The Circle Bar Corporation, one of Yottsubishi's alliance partners, has just opened a new restaurant in your area."

Thisbe let the device prattle on while she filled the kitchen sink. She turned off the tap, carried the Misogi 6200 gently to the sink, plunged it into the water, and held the hated black box under as if she had her hands wrapped around a boa constrictor's throat. Then to be sure, she retrieved a hammer from the battered toolbox in the closet, carried the now silent Misogi 6200 to the patio, and bashed it into twenty thousand pieces.

When Thisbe entered VR from the Cerebellum Studios facility, she found herself topless in a motel room with a strange man fondling her breasts. She jerked her hand away from the erection, straining against the fabric of his boxer shorts like a tent pole, and jumped off the waterbed. The man's eyes widened in astonishment. Her sudden motion set up a standing pattern of waves sloshing against the frame. Someone knocked at the door. Thisbe scooped her blouse from the carpet, covered her breasts, and answered. Abe rushed into the room.

"Mr. Sasaki," Abe held out a video camera and approached the man cowering on the bed. "I have some pictures your wife and father-in-law would find very upsetting."

"What do you want?" Sasaki squeaked.

Thisbe turned her back long enough to slip on her bra and button her blouse.

"Just a little information." Abe pulled a chair next to the bed and sat.

Thisbe glanced at the scene reflected from the mirrored ceiling and wondered where Abe had hidden the camera.

"Tell me why you hired Toda Ishigawa, a known yakuza *with no experience."*

"Can't we offer a sincere penitent an honest chance to reform?" Sasaki seemed bolder once he'd pulled up his trousers.

Abe's cold stare told Haneda's vice president he wasn't convinced.

"Mr. Saito said it would be a good way to ensure Kin Tsuru Corporation's continued goodwill. When your biggest customer tells you to put someone on the payroll, you do it."

"And what do Mr. Ishigawa's duties entail?"

"He isn't in the office much," Sasaki said.

"Where did he go?"

"He never said, and I never asked."

"Write it all down." Abe moved to the desk, removed stationery and a pen from the drawer, and slapped them on its surface.

"But!" Sasaki's eyes widened in panic. "I could lose my job."

"You could lose your job if I send this video to your father-in-law." Mr. Abe moved closer until his face was inches from Sasaki's. "Which way do you prefer?"

Sasaki scribbled his statement and handed it over. Mr. Abe examined the paper before folding it and tucking it in his pocket.

"We'll need copies of Mr. Ishigawa's employment records and travel receipts too," the big man said. "Once we get those, I'll hand over the video."

Thisbe met Vanessa in Maya Escorts' parking lot after work. The two women drove to a diner and took a booth near the restrooms.

"How did it go?" Thisbe asked.

"Very well." Vanessa picked up the sugar dispenser and fiddled with the metal flap that covered the spout. "As you might imagine, Lester became very cooperative after I described his extracurricular activities in detail and threatened to report him to Anne."

"Couldn't he deny everything?"

The waitress coming to take their orders delayed Vanessa's response. Thisbe ordered a Greek salad. Vanessa had a chicken sandwich and fried cheese sticks. Once the coast was clear, Vanessa continued.

"I had the maid collect your towels and told Lester we could prove his guilt with DNA."

"So what happens now?" Thisbe asked.

"Lester will rig up a sensor on your door. In VR you'll hear a bell when anyone enters. Pop back and see if it's Ron. If it is, scream your bloody head off. Lester will also disable the brain-stem block that prevents you from moving." Vanessa poured a pile of sugar on the table. "Jan and I will sit in on your sessions. When you leave VR, we'll be able to do the same and come help."

"Thanks."

"Don't mention it." Vanessa used the dispenser to draw swirls in the spilled sugar. "That Japanese crime caper of yours is getting kind of interesting. I want to see how it turns out."

Thisbe returned to Margot's, tossed her keys in the dish by the door, and entered the living room, where Margot and Tyler sat engrossed with a holovision news story. A 2-D amateur video image showed a giraffe galloping down Forty-Ninth Street while stunned motorists gaped from car windows.

"Another earthquake struck today at 3:00. This time the epicenter was the Woodland Park Zoo," the announcer said. "Animal control officials are struggling to cope with the escapees. They cornered Millie the orangutan on Sixty-Fifth Street."

A man in khaki broke open an air rifle, loaded a tranquilizer dart, and aimed at the orangutan sitting in a hemlock tree. The dart lodged in Millie's flank. After a few seconds she lost her grip and fell into a net.

"Millie was returned to the zoo unharmed."

The scene changed to monkeys scampering into trees. Tyler smiled, pointed, and bounced up and down. The next images changed the mood. Wolves ran through the park. A woman watched in horror from her front door while a lion bit into the back of her dog's neck. Margot placed her hand over Tyler's eyes and pulled him to her.

"Why do they let them show pictures like that?" Margot asked.

Before Thisbe could disagree, the announcer added, "Inside the zoo workers euthanized injured animals."

"That's enough!" Margot lifted Tyler off the floor and carried him to his room.

The holovision showed men in white suits moving among the

prostrate animals and firing pistols into their heads. An elephant nudged a dead companion with its trunk. The lower half of the dead elephant's body had disintegrated into a pool of gore and stringy intestines. Thisbe turned off the holovision and took a shower.

Thisbe went to work and entered VR the next day. She found herself sitting beside Mr. Abe in a library. Microfiche readers perched on the desks in front of them.

"As you can see from his credit card receipts," Abe pointed to the papers, "Mr. Ishigawa made several trips to Sendai and Tsukuba."

"What's the significance of that?" Thisbe asked.

"Perhaps because Kin Tsuru's advanced research group is located in Sendai, and because of the research groups in Tsukuba. But that's what we're here to find out." He handed her a sheet filled with dates. *"Check out the Sendai Times around these dates for anything of interest."*

Thisbe went to the front desk and got microfiches of the newspaper for the first date and the following three days. Mr. Abe had already dimmed the room lights, by the time she returned. Thisbe threaded the film over the spools, switched on the display lamp, and adjusted the focus knob on her machine. The headlines contained the usual: the local LDP member of the Diet's trade mission to China, delays on the tunnel to Hokkaido, the winner of a sumo match, and the city council's dealings. The inside of the paper proved even less interesting.

"This is pretty dull," Vanessa said from inside Thisbe's head.

"Yeah, does anyone know any jokes?" Jan asked. This was the first time Thisbe had heard her voice. "Hi, Thisbe. I'm Jan," she added.

"You've heard all my jokes already," Vanessa said.

Having computerized records would speed up Thisbe's search, if only she knew what she was looking for. She became groggy. An electric beep shook her out of her stupor. Thisbe looked around before realizing the beep was indicating that someone had entered her room back at Maya Escorts. Thisbe shifted her awareness back to the flesh world in time to see the man with the rash step out of his pants.

"Ugh! What a creep!" Jan's voice said.

Thisbe hurried back to VR. Scanning boring articles was preferable. The next time Thisbe shifted back, she felt the bristle of moustache hairs as a customer kissed her nipples. The beeps came at irregular intervals. Either ME staggered her customers, or time didn't flow at a constant rate in VR. Thisbe worked through the morning. Mr. Abe brought in sandwiches so he and Thisbe could man the consoles through lunch. Around 2:00 Thisbe found what she was looking for.

Local Executive Dead of Apparent Suicide
Responding to neighbors' complaints,
police found the body of Dr. Takeshi Ogino
in a home in the Shimabashi District. Police
spokesmen refused to rule out foul play
until the coroner makes an official
determination.

The tone sounded in Thisbe's head. She ignored it to keep reading.

Dr. Ogino supervised the DNA computing
team at Kin Tsuru Corporation's Research
Park. Once a leader in high technology, Kin
Tsuru has seen its market share decline
recently due to competition from Korea and
Singapore. To make up for the loss, CEO
Junzo Takagi announced the Bootstrap
Initiative to focus on breakthrough
technologies. Business analysts cite
numerous delays in the release of the Amber
DNA chip. Industry experts believe the
project was seriously over budget. Dr. Ogino
is survived by his wife Yoyoi and his son
Taro.

Thisbe shifted her awareness to the intimacy room for a quick
check. The current customer wasn't Ron, but due to her delay she
arrived in the middle of the sex act. The customary numbness that
came with her loss of body control had vanished due to Lester's
adjustments. Thisbe felt the man's weight on her chest and the
hydraulic plunge of his penis into her. With her awareness the
automatic rocking of Thisbe's hips ceased.

"Maybe you can tell him you're just not in the mood," Jan's voice
said.

When the customer paused and looked at her face, *Thisbe shifted*
quickly back to VR. She sat in the dark room and took a deep breath to
compose herself. A strange fascination, like a finger stroking her inner thigh,

tempted her back to the workings of the flesh. She wanted to grasp that hand and pull it to her, but Thisbe couldn't admit she was that kind of woman. She turned and spoke to Mr. Abe instead.

"One of the executives on the DNA computing project committed suicide the day after Ishigawa's visit."

"Blackmail?" Mr. Abe raised his eyebrows. To Thisbe his expression looked like that of one of the monkeys who sit in the hot springs in winter.

Mr. Abe had correlated a few plant accidents with Ishigawa's visits. Only two men could reveal the cause of the animosity between Saito and Tanaka. One almost certainly wouldn't talk. That left Tanaka. Mr. Abe phoned lawyer Koga to clear the visit. After a three-hour drive on Route 17 he and Thisbe arrived at the Hattori Correctional Facility, where authorities held Tanaka pending trial. Abe parked in the lot. He and Thisbe entered the solid one-story building for official visitors.

"We're here to interview Ichiro Tanaka, serial number SAR5531," Abe announced.

The officer at the desk located their names on the computer, bowed, and motioned Thisbe and Abe through the metal detector. A female guard ran gloved hands down Thisbe's sides and up her thighs to check for contraband.

"She's kind of cute," Vanessa whispered from inside Thisbe's head. "Have her come back. She missed a spot."

Thisbe ignored the comments. After a quick search of Thisbe's purse, the woman allowed her to pass. A guard in a gray uniform and peaked cap escorted the visitors to a reinforced glass door. The lock buzzed. The guard opened the door and led them through the passage that cut through the parallel chain link fences that circled the prison's perimeter. A group of prisoners in the exercise yard tilted their bodies and outstretched their arms while the leader counted in Japanese. "Ichi, ni, san, shi."

Thisbe and Abe entered a large, colorless building and passed through corridors of concrete and steel as hard as the eyes of the men they confined. The guard ushered them into an interview room. Thisbe and Mr. Abe sat on one side of the steel table to await the prisoner. Moments later a guard led Tanaka in. Hair shorn to a half-inch, the former executive wore a bright-blue jumpsuit. The guard glared from behind as Tanaka sat and rested his manacled hands on the table. Abe nodded to the guard, who then removed Tanaka's handcuffs and left.

"Mr. Tanaka, I'm Shintaro Abe. I perform investigative work for your attorney, Mr. Koga."

"What's she doing here?" Tanaka's flinty gaze fell on Thisbe.

"Actually, she's been very helpful." Abe sat back. "She came to us with

second thoughts about your guilt and helped us identify the yakuza *you know as Hideo Watanabe. His real name is Toda Ishigawa."*

Tanaka grunted.

"Have you ever heard of him?"

Tanaka shook his head.

"It seems," Abe said, "that Hiroshi Saito pulled some strings to get Mr. Ishigawa his current job. Whenever Mr. Ishigawa visited your company's facilities in Sendai or Tsukuba, some kind of accident followed. We believe Mr. Saito was paying Ishigawa to sabotage your projects. In order to use this information to help your case, we need to know why Saito has it in for you."

"Hiroshi Saito," Tanaka took a tired breath and sighed, "is a man of limited abilities. To be fair he has come far for someone with his upbringing, but he lacks the vision and will to lead." Tanaka looked from Thisbe to Mr. Abe. "Saito lobbied for the DNA computing project to be added to the Bootstrap Initiative. Mahamuni recognized the project's worth, but being a good judge of character, he chose me to lead the effort. Saito always resented that."

"I hope you enjoy your new surroundings." Mr. Abe walked to the door and called, "Guard!"

"What do you mean?" Despite Tanaka's deadpan expression, panic showed in his eyes.

"If you expect a judge to believe Saito framed you for murder due to petty jealousy, you'll be spending the rest of your life here."

The guard unlocked the door. Abe looked at Tanaka, who slumped his shoulders in defeat and nodded.

"Would you bring Ms. Anderton a glass of water, please?" Mr. Abe asked the guard.

The guard left, and Mr. Abe returned to his seat.

"Saito and I were involved in a scheme to manipulate Kin Tsuru's stock prices. From my position as manager, I derailed the project's progress from the inside. Saito affected things from the outside. I assume Mr. Ishigawa was employed in that capacity."

"So what happened?" Abe asked.

"Saito got greedy," Tanaka said. "To overcome any qualms on his part, I told him we'd lower Kin Tsuru's stock price until our investors bought shares. Then we'd allow the project to proceed, the prices would rise, and the investors would turn a tidy profit. Saito liked the idea so much that he found his own investors too."

The guard bringing Thisbe's cup of water interrupted Tanaka's story. When he left, Tanaka continued.

"Letting the stock price go back up was never part of the plan. Kin Tsuru's competitors paid me to sabotage the Bootstrap Initiative, period. Mahamuni lost his position as CEO, and Saito was left holding the bag for some very upset investors, the kind of people you don't want mad at you. He had to liquidate most of his assets to pay them back."

"And the girl's death?" Abe asked.

"Revenge."

"That's a good story," Abe said, "but why would Ishigawa jeopardize his contract with Saito by doing something so stupid as stealing the church's money?"

Tanaka looked at the table. "I stole the money," he said. "I wasn't sure who Ishigawa was, but I viewed him as a threat. Stealing the money was the easiest way to get rid of him."

Mr. Abe finished scribbling his notes, set the pen on the legal pad, and looked Tanaka in the eyes. "There's one thing I don't understand. If you have all this money from selling out Kin Tsuru Corporation, why hire Koga? Surely you can afford someone better."

"Gambling!" Tanaka looked at the table. "The same reason I got into this scheme in the first place. I lost the proceeds at the casino."

Mr. Abe stood to leave.

"Why did you follow Mahamuni into religion?" Thisbe asked.

"Where else would I go?" Tanaka lifted his head. "With Mahamuni gone my career at Kin Tsuru would have been mediocre at best. Better to follow my leader into exile and be seen as loyal when Mahamuni returns to the boardroom."

Thisbe spun out of VR and into the alternate world, where she unplugged the feed, got off the leather couch, and joined the other actors in Cerebellum Studio's control room.

"We got some great scenes, today, people," Margot said. "Tomorrow, we begin shooting the confrontation between Mahamuni and Saito. If we keep to the schedule, we can finish by the middle of next week. That means a hefty bonus for all of you. Could Alex, Toby, and Thisbe stay behind for a few minutes? I'll see the rest of you tomorrow."

The others laughed and joked on the way out. Vanessa gave Thisbe a wave goodbye. Alex, a dark man in a black muscle shirt, struck a pose against the wall. Toby, a slender man with long blonde hair, stood with his hands in his pockets and shifted his weight back and forth.

"Don't worry," Margot said. "It's nothing bad. Mr.

Brentwood was impressed with your work and would like to meet you. He's waiting upstairs in the conference room."

Margot led them up the wood-paneled staircase. Both men's eyes homed like heat-seeking missiles on the thong revealed by her short skirt. She walked down the hallway and entered the first door on the left.

"Mr. Brentwood, here are the actors you asked to meet."

"Excellent!" The man rose from his seat at the conference table. He was in his late forties and wore an open white dress shirt and tinted glasses. "I'll take it from here, Margot."

Margot nodded and left.

"Charles Brentwood!" The man extended his hand.

"Thisbe Anderton"

After the introductions everyone sat.

"Thanks for coming." Mr. Brentwood snapped open his briefcase and arranged the cover as if to shield him from the others. He handed out business cards. "I represent Ube Media Group, the producers of your VR drama. With electromagnetic brain stim about to replace neural implants, we feel VR dramas will grow from a pursuit of the privileged few to mass entertainment. We want to be on the leading edge of this trend. That's why we're investing in all facets of VR entertainment: directors, technology, and most importantly stars.

"I've seen your work and I'd like you to act in a new big-budget VR drama. I can't tell you the director's name, but you'd be familiar with his work. The lead, and this information can't leave this room, is Jeremy Dent, star of *Grit City Blues.*" Mr. Brentwood passed out some folders. "This is our standard employment package. I think you'll find the terms generous."

Thisbe opened the folder and gulped when she saw the salary of seven hundred thousand credits. The contract called for Thisbe to cease work on Margot's production and fly to Hollywood immediately.

"I'm in." Toby scribbled his signature and slid the notebook back to Mr. Brentwood.

"The rest of you take your agreements home and read them." Mr. Brentwood put Toby's contract in his briefcase and snapped it shut. "As you can imagine, I can't keep an opportunity like this open for long. I'll need your answers first thing in the morning."

Thisbe had barely enough time to make it to her psychiatrist's appointment. She'd considered ignoring it, but Dr. Cavendish's threat to notify her parole officer gave her pause. Parole officer? Even with her restored memories Thisbe had no recollection of a parole officer. After a half hour drive she turned into the parking lot and walked into Dr. Cavendish's office. Thisbe sighed. As if she didn't have enough to deal with already with saving the world and all!

Thisbe sat down in the waiting room and leafed through an old fashion magazine. A woman, wearing leather hot pants, stepped out of Dr. Cavendish's office. She snapped her bubble gum, licked her painted lips, and left. Dr. Cavendish stuck her head out the door.

"Come in, Thisbe."

No sooner than Thisbe taken her seat in the office, did Dr. Cavendish start in on her.

"You broke your promise to me." Dr. Cavendish paced in front of Thisbe.

"Excuse me?"

"Even though I was skeptical about someone with schizophrenia working in virtual reality, I agreed, provided you let me supervise." Dr. Cavendish stopped pacing and stood in front of Thisbe. "You've broken three appointments. I have half a mind to bounce you out of that program."

"I'm sorry." Thisbe searched for some excuse for offences she didn't remember. "I think it messed me up, when they took my memories away."

"You got them back?" Dr. Cavendish sat down.

"Yes"

"And how was that?"

Thisbe weighed her words carefully. Too little and Dr. Cavendish would suspect a cover up. Too much and she might not let Thisbe return to VR.

"It was upsetting at first, but I think I've got a handle on it. You know, the guilt about abandoning Andy ..." Thisbe's voice broke. "I just want to get him back, so I can make it up to him."

"I suppose you should keep the job." Dr. Cavendish sighed.

"It's a risk, but so too is poverty." She opened Thisbe's file. "You been keeping up with your meds?"

Thisbe nodded.

"Have the delusions come back?"

Thisbe shook her head.

"Delusions are very seductive." Dr. Cavendish touched her pen to the corner of her mouth for a moment. "Often they relieve guilt, give the patient permission to indulge an urge, or boost her ego. You know, something like being the only person, who can save the world. Often the patient won't confide these thoughts to her therapist. That's what makes them so dangerous.

"With your medical history, you need to be on the lookout for delusional thinking and tell me right away. They could be the first sign of a psychotic break. And once that happens, it will be almost impossible to get you back.

"I'm on your side, Thisbe. But I can't help you, unless you work with me."

Dr. Cavendish's words sowed a new crop of confusion in Thisbe's garden. What if the Mahamuni she'd seen in this world was only a crazy old man? What if the apartment collapse that injured Andy was only a projection of her guilty mind? If only someone could help her sort things out. Thisbe looked at Dr. Cavendish sitting in her cardigan but held back.

"I'll let you know, if I have any problems," Thisbe said.

Thisbe spent the evening second-guessing her plan. What if this were reality and she was throwing away a once-in-a-lifetime opportunity? Guilty memories of her abandoning her son for hypodermic needles and "gentleman callers" vied with the image of him hurt in the demolished apartment. Thisbe tried unsuccessfully to shift her consciousness back to Maya Escort's intimacy room to prove this world was an illusion. She slept little. In the morning she flipped Mr. Brentwood's card into the trash and drove to work.

CHAPTER 24

Mr. Abe's female assistant taped the transmitter to Thisbe's belly and ran the microphone and antenna lead through her bra.

"This should have a range of a mile," the young woman said. "Try to stay in the center of the room. Metal beams in the walls can interfere with the signal."

Thisbe put on a loose blouse and thanked the woman.

"Good morning," Vanessa said from inside Thisbe's head.

"Yeah," Jan's voice said. "This other world's pretty weird."

Thisbe went out into the hall, where Mr. Abe waited.

"You don't have to do this, you know," Abe said.

"Even though Tanaka's a sleaze, he's not a murderer. I couldn't live with myself if I let him go to jail for Mariko's death."

"Try to get Ishigawa talking about the girl's murder. I'll be close by. If you get into trouble, say 'kite' and I'll be there in a minute." Abe handed Thisbe a knapsack full of cash. "Good luck."

Thisbe had heard that the Japanese drive on the left side of the road, but in VR they drove on the right. She had no trouble driving Mr. Abe's tiny car to the rendezvous. It took only ten minutes. Thisbe entered the store and walked past porn disks, inflatable dolls, and foot-long rubber phalluses. The cashier, a woman wearing a short skirt, too much makeup, and pouting lips, looked up from filing her nails at the sound of the door chime. Thisbe nodded to her and took the stairway to the second floor. The walls had been painted a glossy green that gave the interior a vague institutional feel.

Thisbe entered the second door on the left.

"I don't like the looks of this place," Vanessa's voice said.

Ishigawa sat on a leather couch. A cigarette in the ashtray balanced on the couch's arm and sent a stream of noxious smoke flowing upward. The TV monitor played a Japanese porn video. The resolution around the actors' genitals had been degraded to the point that their anatomy was reduced to flesh-colored squares. Ishigawa made no move to stand. The tone rang in Thisbe's head. She ignored it and sat in a faded lounge chair. Its sagging cushions sucked her behind like quicksand.

"So, Thisbe Anderton, what brings you away from the world of religion?" Ishigawa took a drag on his cigarette. He didn't resemble a man so much as a cobra in a business suit.

"Sometimes the worlds of the spirit and matter intersect," Thisbe said. "You

know as well as I do, Mr. Ishigawa, of the necessity to make hard choices for the good of a religious movement."

Ishigawa nodded.

"Saito was very pleased with your last job." Thisbe opened the knapsack to show Ishigawa the cash inside. "So pleased that he'd like to offer you another."

"What does he have in mind?" Ishigawa reached for the bag.

Thisbe snatched it away. "Saito believes Mahamuni's movement needs a martyr to capture the public's interest. Naturally, this martyr's removal should leave Saito in control."

"And why would Saito want to care for all those followers' souls?" Ishigawa giggled.

"Mahamuni's message has the power to change the world and comfort millions. Of course, those millions of followers will be expected to tithe to the church, tax free." Thisbe smiled. "Mahamuni's death mustn't be traceable to Saito. Perhaps it could be an accident or be blamed on someone else. But of course you've done that before. What kind of patsy would be best, a crazy follower or someone with an axe to grind regarding Mahamuni's teaching?"

"I'm just a workman," Ishigawa said, "not a writer of legends. What did Saito have in mind?"

Thisbe glanced at the TV screen. The man withdrew from the woman and ejaculated on her face. Unlike the actors' genitals, the dripping semen and the woman's hurt look were shown in full resolution.

"Oh, come now, Mr. Ishigawa. Your setup of Tanaka was brilliant. Surely an artist like yourself has some ideas. Saito is interested in your suggestions."

"It's better to choose someone with a motive. And if there is no motive, manufacture one."

"Like what you did with Mariko?"

"What makes you so curious about her?" Ishigawa narrowed his eyes. "You ask too many questions for a delivery girl."

"I'm Saito's partner," Thisbe said. "Haven't you noticed how much time he and I spend with Mahamuni?"

Ishigawa struck with the speed of a serpent. Thisbe saw a blur as he crossed the room and slapped her hard enough to spin her head.

"Saito takes no partners! Especially not a woman!" He snatched the bag from her grasp and dumped its contents on the floor.

"You'll regret that when Saito sends up the kites." Thisbe's throbbing, swollen mouth made her slur the words. Her ears rang. She heard the tone advising her of another Maya Escort client in her room.

Ishigawa unwrapped a stack of bills and discovered it was merely paper sandwiched between ten thousand yen notes. A butterfly knife sprung into his hand, flapped its steel wings, and lighted on Thisbe's throat. Ishigawa tore open her blouse, sent its buttons flying, and discovered the hidden transmitter. The sound of Mr. Abe's footsteps charged up the stairs.

A line of steel severed Thisbe's throat. Her lungs struggled for breath but only created a gurgle of suffocation. Thisbe looked down at the bright red arterial blood slicking her chest.

"Fuck!" Vanessa cried from inside Thisbe's head. "You can't die in VR. Can you?"

"Maybe in a level three adventure game," Jan's voice responded, "but I've never heard of it in a reality sim."

A jackhammer of pain shattered Thisbe's temples. She grew dizzy and soon viewed the scene from above. The door burst into splinters. Mr. Abe crashed into the room and took three slugs in the chest from Ishigawa's pistol. The big man's momentum carried him into the gangster, bowling Ishigawa off his feet and onto the carpet. The yakuza squirmed out from under the mountain of dead flesh and limped out the door.

The scene grew bright and forced Thisbe to close her eyes as if blinded by the sun. She felt the rays warm her skin and heard a seagull's cry in the distance. Thisbe turned away and opened her eyes to find herself on a beach next to Andy, now a young man with shaggy hair hanging over his eyebrows.

"Thanks for all you've done for me, mom."

Thisbe opened her mouth to speak, but the molecules of her body flew apart like grains of sand in the wind. Eyes, nose, tongue, and mind dissolved into the void. Only the tone remained to call her to the flesh. Thisbe followed that tone back to her body and the press of men's hips against hers. Sweat (she wasn't sure if it was hers or theirs) slicked skin against skin. Kisses greedy as piranha teeth nibbled her flesh. Copulation went on for hours with each new customer writhing atop her body until he stiffened and spurted his pitiful cargo of DNA into her womb.

Then Thisbe stood in a darkness filled with thousands of tiny lights. At first she thought they were stars, but she soon realized they were lamps carried by the crowd of spectators. Thisbe turned to face a stage. Mahamuni stepped into the spotlight and rested his elbows on the podium. The crowd erupted in cheers.

"Great Sage! Great Sage!"

Mahamuni raised a hand to still the chant, with no effect. Eventually the crowd quieted.

"My followers and I have come to you on foot." Mahamuni's amplified voice

echoed from the auditorium walls. "We traveled along the road that leads through the heart of Japanese history. Four hundred years ago warlords traveled this road to pay homage to the dictator in Edo. Today we reverse the direction, returning power and responsibility to you."

Thisbe's eyes had adjusted to the dark. She looked around at the others standing in the aisle next to her.

"Nothing worthwhile is easy," Mahamuni said. "Hunger, fatigue, and even the murders of two followers tested our resolve. Ichiro Tanaka spent two weeks falsely imprisoned. I see now that all those hardships were necessary. God was trying to teach me something, but I was too full of opinions to learn. He had to wear me down before I would listen. You see, despite what I'd been preaching, I secretly believed I had to develop extraordinary powers to be worthy of God's love. While my experiments with ESP and psychokinesis proved fascinating, they were in fact dead ends.

"Friends, the real spiritual struggle isn't in some mental universe, it's right under your noses. All you have to do is realize that God made you just the way He wanted you to be. He loves you just like you are. No matter where you go or what you do, you will never be away from His embrace. If you don't see this, you'll spend a lifetime enslaved by corporate ad departments and political spin machines. In fact, all humanity's troubles stem from trying to fix what God made. Just believe in your inherent goodness and the world will be a better place, but you must believe in your bones not just your heads. Turn to the person next to you and recite after me, 'The Divine in me embraces the Divine in you.'"

After a moment of reluctance, followers hugged one another. No one touched Thisbe. It was as if she were invisible.

"I'd like to say a few words about Hiroshi Saito, who was savagely murdered by reactionary militarists two nights ago." Mahamuni continued. "I first met Mr. Saito …"

"So, there you are." A soft voice came from behind Thisbe. She turned to see Tanaka with his hands in his pockets.

"It's good to see him back on message, don't you think?" Tanaka leaned against the wall. "I suppose I should thank you for getting me released. After they found your bodies, the police recovered Ishigawa's taped confession along with Abe's notes and freed me. The yakuza died a few days later in a shoot-out."

"What happened to Saito?" Thisbe asked.

"Perhaps his creditors made him an example." Tanaka's stony face yielded no clue as to the truth of his statement.

Thisbe glanced at the stage. Mahamuni removed a brocade cover from a lacquer box and poured Saito's ashes onto a tray. The sage placed a bit of bone on his tongue, chewed, and swallowed.

"Now Saito will be with me always." Mahamuni handed the tray down to the followers lined up in front of the stage.

"It was kind of you to stop by," Tanaka told Thisbe, "but the movement must concentrate on the physical world, not on spirits. It would be best for you to go and not return."

Once again the tone sounded in Thisbe's head. She took a last look at Mahamuni and shifted back to her body in the intimacy room. Ron had just entered.

"Time for a little fun, bitch." He unbuckled his trousers. The heavy belt buckle dragged them to the floor.

Without even removing his shirt, Ron approached the bed. Thisbe spied a green bottle of Scotch left on the nightstand by a previous customer. When Ron got within reach, she swung it with all her strength into his face. Glass shattered into a thousand shards. Ron howled. His hands covered the bloody skin around his eyes.

"You son of a bitch! I told you to stay away from me!" Thisbe yanked out the VR feed and sprang to her feet.

The door flew open. Still naked from servicing their last clients, Jan and Vanessa burst into the room.

CHAPTER 25

The thick-necked vice president's close-cropped hair was the color of a bullet. His expression wasn't much friendlier.

"Do you know what you've done?" He glared at Thisbe. His skin turned so red that Thisbe expected steam to erupt from his ears like in one of Andy's cartoons. "By attacking Senator Murphy's son, you've enraged our most powerful supporter in Congress and put the entire North American operation at risk. The corporation could lose billions. As of now you're officially terminated." He slid an envelope across the table. "Here's your last check. I wouldn't use us as a job reference. By the way, you still owe us fourteen thousand credits for your surgery. We expect to be paid in full by the end of the month, or we'll begin legal proceedings. Now get out of my sight!"

Thisbe didn't look back when she left Maya Escorts for the last time. She half expected a bullet to strike her in the back on the way to her car, but she made it. The weather matched her mood. At least there had been no more unexplained disasters. Traffic stalled on the I-90. Her windshield wipers swatted fat raindrops from her view. It took over an hour to drive to Margot's.

"How did it go?" Margot asked, when Thisbe entered.

"Not good." Thisbe shook out her umbrella, propped it against the wall, and closed the door. "They want me to repay my loan by the end of the month."

"Can they make you do that?"

Thisbe shrugged and walked into the living room. Andy looked up from the carpet and smiled. He and Tyler squatted next to a toy castle and an army of plastic knights.

The gossip columns saved her. Thisbe first got wind of the growing scandal on a late night run to the convenience store. When she carried her basket loaded with chocolate bars, Cheesecake Spongees, and ice cream to the check stand, she saw Ron's bruised face on a tabloid cover under the headline, "Nebraska Senator's Son Discovers M in S&M." The wags at the *National Inquisitor* had also included an old photo of Ron and his father at a campaign rally along with a photo of a leather-clad woman holding a whip. Suddenly feeling less need for high calorie consolation, Thisbe put the ice cream back and bought the tabloid instead.

The journalistic snowball continued rolling. When she got back to Margot's, Thisbe switched on *Celebrity Tattle Tales* and noted with glee that the story had made it to holovision. The gossip show played stock footage of Ron, his pregnant wife, and his high-powered parents sitting in a church pew, while the announcer speculated on how Ron had gotten his injuries. Officially, he'd fallen in the shower, but the announcer repeatedly mentioned his adventurous lifestyle, a euphemism for what the tabloid paper called deranged sexual perversion. A spokesman for Harborview Medical Center stated that Ron had been released after treatment but refused to comment on the nature of his injuries.

"There must be some way to make money out of this," Margot said. Thisbe had been too engrossed in the holovision to notice her entrance. "I'm sure the tabloids would pay for your story. There might even be a book deal in it for you."

Thisbe nodded. She didn't want her name splashed all over the headlines with the word prostitute, although she supposed she could use an alias.

Next morning Thisbe received a request to meet Senator Murphy's lawyer. She drove to a downtown law firm that afternoon and met the man in an empty conference room. His suit hung like a sack over his large frame. The bags under his eyes testified to a lifetime of observing other people's suffering.

"Ms. Anderton, I'm Chester Dunlap. Thanks for coming in." He scanned a report. "I see you're a parent. I assume you understand the urge to protect your child regardless of what he's done. Senator Murphy regrets the hurt Ron may have caused you. To make up for it, he'd like to offer you a payment of one hundred thousand credits. All you have to do in return is keep this matter private." The lawyer slid an agreement across the table.

"That's very generous of him, but I'm wondering what the tabloids will offer for my story," Thisbe said.

"One hundred fifty thousand," the lawyer offered.

"Do you have a pen?"

Thisbe entered the last of the environmental settings into the VRAnime program. Too tired to test the jumps to the alternate world she saved her work and shut down the computer. The one hundred fifty thousand credits had paid off her loan and allowed her to invest in Margot's VR drama. She estimated the money would give them six months to complete the project. Margot had a good sense of style, but her characters and plot lacked depth. That's where Thisbe came in. So far Triage Productions had shown some interest, but they hadn't committed yet. Thisbe would give it her best. If it worked, maybe they could bring Vanessa and Jan on board. The lesbian couple had managed to stay on at Maya Escorts. Lester had said he'd released everyone from VR when he'd heard Thisbe's scream, so the management never suspected Vanessa and Jan. If the VR drama didn't sell, there was always Cyber Sluts.

Thisbe stretched and rubbed the kinks out of her back. She stuck her head in the boys' room and observed Andy's nose peeking out from under the covers. Thisbe smiled, crossed the room, and kissed her son on the forehead.

ABOUT THE AUTHOR

Jon Wesick is the author of *Hunger for Annihilation, Yellow Lines*, and the poetry collection *Words of Power, Dances of Freedom*. He hosts San Diego's Gelato Poetry Series and is an editor of the *San Diego Poetry Annual*. Jon Wesick has published hundreds of poems and short stories in journals such as *The Atlanta Review, The Berkeley Fiction Review, Pearl, Slipstream,* and *Tales of the Talisman*.

51888018R00108

Made in the USA
Charleston, SC
05 February 2016